HELPING LIZA

Jacob helped Liza out of the cellar. She exited and held his fingers, meeting his gaze.

He hugged her and kissed her softly on the lips. "I was so worried about all of you." His cheeks pinked and he let her go. "I know I shouldn't have kissed you. I reacted without hesitation." He released her.

Liza touched her warm cheeks. His lips on hers, and his strong arms holding her tight moments ago, had her heart racing. She had longed to stay in his arms and never move. His shirt damp, she didn't mind. She had to gather her thoughts and hide her emotions. Ellie trusted her. They could be fleeting. She had to stay firm on her plan. Ellie's disapproval of Jacob and her having more than a friendship took precedence.

She stepped farther back from him. "Let me get you a towel." Her mind in a fog and her voice weak, she pulled a towel off a shelf. "Here you go."

"I was helpless to get to you and the girls. The weather was too bad to travel here."

This man was in agony. It showed in his worried eyes and inability to stay still. To ease his unwarranted guilt, she said, "We're all in one piece, and we had what we needed. I'm glad you didn't kumme. I would have been sick thinking of you out in this mess. I don't know what I'd do if anything happened to you." She cupped her mouth. She'd let her guard down. Closing her eyes for a moment, she opened them and avoided eye contact.

He brushed her cheek with the back of his fingers. "I'm going to wait for as long as it takes for you to realize we are meant for each other . . ."

Books by Molly Jebber

The Keepsake Pocket Quilt series
CHANGE OF HEART

GRACE'S FORGIVENESS

TWO SUITORS FOR ANNA

The Amish Charm Bakery series
LIZA'S SECOND CHANCE

Collections
THE AMISH CHRISTMAS SLEIGH
(with Kelly Long and Amy Lillard)

AMISH BRIDES
(with Jennifer Beckstrand and Amy Lillard)

Published by Kensington Publishing Corporation

Liza's Second Chance

MOLLY JEBBER

ZEBRA BOOKS
KENSINGTON PUBLISHING CORP.
http://www.kensingtonbooks.com

First Printing: February 2018
ISBN-13: 978-1-4201-4483-3
ISBN-10: 1-4201-4483-9

eISBN-13: 978-1-4201-4484-0
eISBN-10: 1-4201-4484-7

10 9 8 7 6 5 4 3 2 1

Printed in the United States of America

ACKNOWLEDGMENTS

Thank you to:

My husband and soul mate, Ed, who is my best supporter and encourager.

Misty, my beautiful, talented, and smart daughter who lights up my life and helps me in so many ways.

Mitch Morris, the best brother, friend, encourager, and someone I admire.

Sue Morris, my mother. A beautiful, elegant, and amazing woman.

To Debbie Bugezia, Lee Granza, Mary Byrnes, Connie Melaik, Elaine Saltsgaver, Kelly Hildreth, Ginny Gilmore, Donna Snyder, Melanie Fogel, Linda Schultz, Sigrid Davies, my Southbridge, Quilt, Church, and many other friends. You know who you are and how much you mean to me.

Aunt Sharon Sanders and Aunt Sheila Walter for their encouragement, love, and memories.

Patricia Campbell, DJ Welker, and Southwest Florida Romance Writers' group for your advice, love, and friendship.

To Marilyn Ridgway: You've lifted me up more times than I can count! You're such a blessing!

To Sandra Barela: Thank you for your friendship, advice, and encouragement!

To my readers: I couldn't do this without your support and prayers. Thank you so much.

Chapter One

Charm, Ohio, 1912

Liza Schrock clenched her teeth and dug her fingers in the fresh dough in her Amish bakery. The forced smiles, nods to her friends' compliments, and suppressing the truth about her husband had been difficult, but she'd managed to keep her miserable marriage a secret. She kneaded the dough harder. Yesterday at the after-church meal, Mrs. Hilty couldn't stop prattling on about how much she missed Paul. She'd moved away from the woman, giving her a polite smile, but Mrs. Hilty had followed her to get her point across. The woman set her teeth on edge. Mr. Hilty interrupted his fraa and insisted it was time for them to leave. She'd hurried to Esther before Mrs. Hilty had time to turn back around. Friends wouldn't stop mentioning Paul to her. The pretending didn't get any easier.

Esther lifted her rag off the white table in the corner. "The counter, stools, tables, and chairs are clean until customers dirty them again." Hand on her ample hip, she went to Liza behind the glass counter lined with desserts and fresh loaves of bread. "Sweet schweschder, you are quieter than usual. I overheard Mrs. Hilty talk on and on to you about Paul yesterday. Today's April eighth. It's been a year since he passed. Is the date of his funeral the reason?" Esther stood next to her.

"Jah, I'd prefer if townsfolk didn't mention him, but I understand they mean no harm." Liza sighed.

"They miss him. He was a good husband to buy this bakery and name it after you. You've made it quite a success with your talent for creating new recipes."

The bakery had become her peaceful place away from Paul before his passing, and she enjoyed kumming to work. Located next to the post office, she had the best spot on the street. She gazed out the window, giving her a full view of the busiest part of town, the general store, the apothecary, and the livery across the way. She had two wood-burning cook stoves and a big dry sink. A large, oblong, waist-high wooden counter held a bowl filled with flour. Her quiet hideaway to escape and experiment with new dessert recipes to sell to customers on the rare occasions when Esther and Hannah were absent. Cabinets and shelves provided easy access to her ingredients. Simple, plain, organized, and functional. "My favorite part is working with you and Hannah."

"Paul was a good man. If it wasn't for him, we wouldn't be working together doing what we love." Esther clicked her tongue. "He was generous to hire Abe as the manager of your large property and hired hands. Abe and I are very grateful to you and him."

Liza bit her tongue. *No, he wasn't a good man. He provided a good living for them, but it didn't kumme without a price.* Paul's big smile, generous donations to her family and other people in need, and supposed obedience to following the scriptures in the Bible had been to disguise his real nature. His shiny, thick dark hair, big brown eyes, broad shoulders, and strong arms had been attractive at first. Certain they'd fall in love given time, she'd been wrong.

These same features changed to ugliness in her eyes as he criticized the way she cooked his meals, cleaned their haus, did their laundry, and the list went on. He'd sent her to her room as if she were a child. She'd coveted the quiet. He yelled and screamed and banged his fist on the table if she didn't have meals ready at his designated times. She'd forced smiles and kept secret his mistreatment of her from her family and friends.

Resentment riveted through her as she jerked her eyes from Esther back to the window. A young woman shared a laugh with the man beside her. She had golden hair cascading halfway down her back. Her pale yellow fitted dress showcased her perfect frame and matched the stylish straw hat with white ribbon and rose flowers. He smiled back at her with his perfect teeth. The man was handsome in every way. The spark between them showed in his gaze of admiration at her and his playful nudge and wink, as if she were the only woman for him. He opened the door for her before taking his seat in a no-frills Ford motorcar.

Her marriage to Paul hadn't mimicked this couple in the slightest. It had been the most miserable ten years of her life. She'd expected a happy future with a soul mate, someone she could love and respect. She dropped her gaze from the couple. Not telling her schweschder about Paul had been the hardest part.

"I'm grateful our needs have been met." She bent and set a fresh apple pie in the glass case to avoid Esther's questioning gaze. A forced smile would be difficult to muster at the moment.

"Several Amish men have sat next to you on Sundays

at after-service meals and you've hastened to excuse yourself and move to another seat to avoid having conversations with them. Why? You're young. You should consider them." Esther wiped off the top of the glass dome over the plate on top of the counter showcasing a shoofly pie.

Esther scrutinized Liza. "Don't you want to remarry someday? You cared for our sick parents and declined men's offers to marry you until Paul came along. I was worried you were never going to become a fraa." Esther gave her a lopsided grin. "You're not getting any younger."

Her schweschder was pushing her hard for answers. More persistent than ever. Should she tell Esther the truth about Paul? It would be selfish on her part. No good would kumme from it. The only reason to tell her would be to keep Esther from prodding her to consider the available Amish men in town for marriage. Her schweschder enjoyed matching couples, and she had instigated a couple of men to speak to Liza at social gatherings. The interested men had told her this, hoping Esther's approval would enhance their chances with her. Liza swallowed the sour taste in her mouth. She'd never trust another man. Once was enough.

The door opened. She wilkomed the interruption. A tall and lanky Amish man with kind, deep brown eyes stepped into the bakery with a young woman. The petite girl had pale, flawless skin and perfect, high cheekbones. She was strikingly beautiful.

Her heart leaped at the sight of this gentleman. Liza didn't understand. Why this man? She grinned at them through the open doorway leading to the front room. "Wilkom. I'll be with you in a minute." She dipped her hands in a bowl of clean water on a side table, grabbed a towel, and dried them, then followed behind Esther to greet them. She met his deep brown gaze and blushed. He was of average height with square shoulders and long arms. "I'm Liza Schrock and this is my schweschder, Esther Lapp. How may we help you?"

He removed his faded straw hat and unveiled a head of attractive, thick brown hair. "I'm Jacob Graber and this is my dochder, Ellie. We're new in town. Moved to Charm from Nappanee, Indiana. We walked past the bakery and the enticing aroma of fresh bread and cinnamon sugar lured us in. We had to stop in and have a gander." He ogled the pies, tarts, cookies, and bread in the glass cabinet. "I can't go home without a dozen butter cookies and a sugar cream pie."

Esther passed Jacob and Ellie each an oatmeal cookie. "Nibble on these while you shop for more delicious treats. I'll leave you with Liza. Sit on a stool at the counter or a chair at one of the tables and make yourselves comfortable." She patted Liza on the shoulder. "I'll bake the bread you were working on." She raised her eyebrows and gave Liza an impish grin.

Her schweschder didn't miss an opportunity to play matchmaker whenever it arose. She ignored Esther's obvious approval of Jacob. Esther would hound her about the man if she hinted she found him eye-catching. She studied him. He had been the first man to capture her attention since her husband's funeral. Jacob's cheerfulness and kind demeanor added to his appeal. She cleared her throat.

"Danki for the treat and nice meeting you, Mrs. Lapp."

"No formalities needed. Call me Esther, and my schweschder, Liza."

"Only if you both call me Jacob."

"I'd be glad to." Esther grinned and padded to the kitchen.

Liza bit her tongue for a moment. Her schweschder

had wasted no time putting her on a first-name basis with Jacob. She pushed Esther's well-meaning intentions out of her mind. She darted her eyes toward the young woman. Ellie's age must be around Hannah's at seventeen. Sandy blond curls escaped the pinned bun under her kapp and her light blue eyes resembled a cloudless sky. The scowl on the young woman's face did nothing to diminish her beauty.

Ellie brushed crumbs from her lips. She lifted her shoulder in a discourteous shrug. "Danki for the cookie." She opened the door. "Daed, I'm going to the general store to buy lemon drops."

"Don't take too long. I'll meet you at the wagon."

Ellie rolled her eyes. "Don't be in such a hurry, Daed."

Jacob gave her a hard stare. "Watch your tone, young lady."

Ellie ignored Liza and left.

Jacob raked a hand through his thick brown hair and put his hat back on. "I'm sorry for Ellie's rude behavior. She's been short-tempered and a handful since her mamm passed three years ago. Maybe our move to Charm, a new haus, and new friends will change her attitude for the better."

His sincere, sad eyes and honest confession warmed her heart. "I have a niece, Hannah. She's Esther's dochder. She'll be arriving any minute. Ellie and she should meet. Do you have time to wait?"

He shook his head. "I wish we did, but I've spent too long in town already. I have a tight schedule for chores at home. Do you mind if I bring her to the bakery another day?"

Liza snapped her fingers. "I have an idea. I'm having a social in the bakery for Hannah and some of her friends on April seventeenth at three. I'd love for Ellie to join them. I created a recipe for cookies they're going to bake. They'll chat and have fun."

His eyes sparkled. "I'll bring her. Danki for the invitation." He accepted and paid for his cookies and pie. "I'm glad we met. I'll be back with Ellie a week from Wednesday. It's been a pleasure to meet you, Liza." He lingered a moment and smiled wide. "Have a good day." He shut the door behind him.

A few minutes later, Hannah arrived, snatched her apron off the hook, pulled the first band over her head to rest on her neck, and tied the strings at the waist in a tight bow. "How has the morning been?"

Liza hugged her. "We had our usual morning rush, but business has slowed at present. Esther and I met Jacob Graber and his dochder, Ellie. They're new to Charm. She's about your age and I invited her to your social. I hope you don't mind."

She shook her head. "I'm happy to meet her. Where are they from?"

"Nappanee, Indiana. Her mamm passed three years ago, and her daed said she hasn't adjusted well without her. Ellie had bad manners. She spouted off to him in front of me. My heart goes out to her. It can't be easy for her without a mamm to guide her through these years when she's choosing to join or not join the church, thinking of her future, and many other things."

Hannah frowned. "I couldn't imagine life without Mamm or you. Daed and I are close, but he doesn't understand about certain things like Mamm and you. I'll be patient with her."

Esther joined them. "There's my beautiful dochder. You missed Mr. Handsome and his dochder, Ellie. He couldn't take his eyes off Liza."

"Did you notice, Liza?" Hannah gave her an impish grin.

Liza's stomach churned. She didn't need her niece to jump on the matchmaking wagon with Esther. "Both of you stop this instant. I'm happy with my life the way it is."

Esther nudged her. "Jacob came in and interrupted our conversation about marriage, and you didn't answer my question. Why are you against the idea?"

Liza's hands shook and tears trailed down her cheeks. She'd lost the battle of holding in her emotions. She took a clean cloth and dabbed the tears threatening to dampen her face.

Esther rushed to her side. "What is upsetting you?"

"Paul hid his true self from everyone but me. He mistreated me. He yelled and screamed at the way I cooked, cleaned haus, did the laundry, and stitched his shirts. He sent me to my room for punishment as if I were a child. He portrayed himself one way to you and others, but to me, he was an angry man. He hit the wall and table several times showing his temper."

Esther gasped and covered her mouth. "What? I'm shocked! Why have you kept this a secret from us for such a long time? When did his mistreatment start? Did he lay a hand on you?"

Pale, Hannah placed a hand on her mamm's arm. "Mamm, please slow down. You're peppering Liza with questions." She nodded to Liza. "Allow her to answer one at a time."

Pausing, Esther shifted her gaze to Hannah. "You're like your daed. You remain calm in the midst of a storm. I should be more like you." She squeezed Liza's hand. "I'm sorry. Tell us about him."

"I'll start from the beginning. Since Paul arranged our marriage with Daed, we didn't have much time to get acquainted before our wedding day. I had doubts because he was ten years older than me, but I married him anyway. According to him, his mamm adhered to his demanding schedule and he expected no less from me. He was an only child who inherited this large, profitable property, and he expected me to manage the bakery to add to our wealth. He hid his greediness, arrogance, and boorish temperament from everyone but me."

"I'm flabbergasted he put you through that. We had no idea." Esther bowed her head and spoke just above a whisper. "You are rich with beauty, talent, and a kind heart. You could've waited to fall in love with an Amish man. Why didn't you?" She froze. "You married him to provide financial freedom for us, didn't you?"

She didn't want them ridden with guilt for why she'd married Paul. "It was my decision and you are not to blame yourself. I chose to marry him for you, Hannah, Abe, me, and our parents. I had no reason to believe he wouldn't be an ideal husband, despite our age difference. I've had a wonderful daed, and Abe is a stellar bruder-in-law and close friend. I assumed Paul would be like them. His behavior was devastating. I believe he would've taken the bakery away from me had he discovered it had become my refuge."

"Uncle Paul never once raised his voice around me. I'm astounded he could put on such a cheerful front for as long as he did. I would've had to tell you or Mamm and seek comfort if I'd been in your position. You were strong to keep this hush-hush from us."

"I agreed to an arranged marriage for financial reasons. I promise you won't be in the same predicament. Our crops, the bakery, and the inheritance I received from Paul's estate provides us with more money than we need."

Liza didn't want Hannah to worry. Hannah was soft-hearted and compassionate toward others. The right man would appreciate those qualities in her. "You're pretty, with your fire-red hair, deep green eyes, and kind heart. Amish men will be knocking your door down before long to get your attention. You can take your time and fall in love with a man of your choosing." Liza wanted Hannah to find the right man, learn all she could about him, and then marry him.

"Your safety and happiness is worth more to me than fretting about people judging us for your divorce or having to survive on a lot less money. I can't imagine leaving the Amish life, but I would've for you." Esther dabbed a tear with her sleeve. "I'm angry with you, Liza. You shouldn't hide things from me. Even if you chose to stay with him after telling me, I'd have listened to you."

Hannah came alongside her mamm. "Don't be cross with Liza. She kept her secret to protect you, Daed, and me. This information would've robbed you of enjoying your life. You'd have fretted about Liza night and day had you known about the real Paul. You couldn't have done anything. She made the right decision."

Esther circled her arm around Liza. "Hannah's right, but I should've realized you were in pain."

"I didn't want you to." She cupped her schweschder's cheek in her hand. "You couldn't have fixed this problem. You have nothing to regret. I'm responsible for my own actions." She threw back her shoulders and brushed her palms. "Paul's gone, and we no longer have to concern ourselves with him." She didn't want to discuss him anymore. Enough had been said. Had she been wrong to tell Esther the truth about him? She didn't want her family to dwell on her revelation.

"Do you have to tell Abe?"

Esther stilled. "Jah. We don't keep secrets from each other. He'll be all right once he has a chance to let it settle in. Abe will be upset when I tell him about Paul. He loves you like a schweschder rather than a schweschder-in-law. I won't tell a soul except him, and he won't tell anyone."

Hannah put a finger to her lips. "Your secret is safe with me. Are you able to forgive Paul?"

"I'm learning to let go of my bitterness and anger toward him through reading the scriptures and prayer." She would change the subject and change the mood. Forcing a smile, she waggled her finger at her schweschder. "Your approval of Jacob didn't get past me with your impish grin. Stop playing matchmaker for me. I have no intention of marrying again. After what I've been through, it's not worth the risk."

Esther harrumphed. "I won't agree not to play matchmaker, but I'll let up on you until Jacob shows at the bakery again. You're thirty. I want you to consider good, eligible men for a potential husband. Remember, I'm your wiser and older schweschder. You should listen to me."

Liza harrumphed in turn. "Only five years older, and I don't have to listen to you."

Esther tapped her on the nose. "But you do, because you know I love you. And look at Abe and me. He's ten years older than me and we're enjoying a wonderful and full life together. I want you to find a partner and be as happy as we are."

"I must agree. You have a match made in Heaven." She dipped her chin and gave Esther a stern look. "But you should respect my wishes and quit sending men in my direction."

"I must end this conversation. I have pies, cookies, and pastries to bake. I'd better get busy." Esther hugged Liza and bustled to the back room.

Hannah kissed Liza's cheek. "Mamm is a hopeless romantic. She won't stop talking to hassling you about this until you are married. You may as well give up." She kissed her aunt's cheek and strolled to join her mamm.

Liza rested her hands on the countertop. She was thankful for many things. Her loving and close family, the bakery, and her spacious white haus, sturdy barn, and vast fields of hay. Their crops and herds of sheep, cows, and horses would bring in revenue for the winter. The many rows of vegetables were planted and sprouted green leaves next to the haus. She could picture the lovely scene as if she were standing in front of it.

The plain haus had six bedrooms, a generous kitchen with oak cabinets and a built-in hutch, and front and sewing rooms. If Paul had been a loving husband, they could've had a wonderful life there together. Jacob came to mind. What kind of husband had he been to his fraa? The moment she'd laid eyes on him, her heart had raced and she'd felt giddy. She couldn't erase his tanned, chiseled face from her mind.

Jacob glanced at Ellie. She plopped another lemon drop in her mouth as she sat quietly, scanning the countryside. He'd have to address Ellie's ill manners at the bakery earlier, but he didn't want to spoil his cheerful mood. The sunshine, thoughts of lovely Liza, and taking in the sights on the way home brought a smile to his lips. Charm was a smart choice for starting over. The quaint town was simple, but it suited him. He focused on an Amish man plowing his field with a fine, muscular pair of horses. An Amish woman and two kinner planted vegetables in the garden. A man in a wagon passed and waved, and he waved back.

Liza had been a wilkom surprise. She was beautiful, with her honey-blond hair pulled back in a bun under her thin white kapp. Her steel blue eyes captivated him. She had a cheerful voice, and her movements were far from clumsy or abrupt. The bakery case was filled with goodies, and the tables and chairs and the stools at the counter were arranged in perfect order. She had an eye for making the most of her space. The woman had occupied his mind since he'd left town. He couldn't explain why he was so drawn to her.

Ada Fisher in Nappanee had been a good woman he'd considered marrying a year ago. They'd taken canoe rides, fished, and shared meals together. She was a year older than him and had big green eyes and dimples in her full cheeks, but otherwise there was nothing remarkable about her appearance. Kind, a good cook, smart, and merry, he'd enjoyed her company.

Ellie's temper, constant refusal to uphold Amish law, and disrespect toward him and Ada had ruined their chance of having a calm and happy relationship. The woman had attempted to befriend Ellie, offering to teach her to sew, quilt, and bake. No matter how much Ada catered to Ellie, his dochder wanted nothing to do with her.

He shook his head. He'd surmised Ellie was in mourning for her mamm. But there was no excuse for her being rude. He'd scolded her, taken away privileges, and tried to reason with her, to no avail. The shoofly pie incident had been the final blow. Ellie had suggested she and Ada use her mamm's recipe. Ada had taken a stand with her and insisted on using her own. Ellie said it was the worst pie she'd ever put in her mouth. He'd insisted Ellie apologize. Ellie had, but the woman had pulled him aside later in the evening during their final meal together and told him she was no longer interested in pursuing a future with him. She'd had enough of his dochder's belligerent behavior. He'd ceased seeking a woman he'd like to befriend and consider for a potential fraa until he'd met Liza.

Did Liza have a husband or kinner? He hoped not. He'd like to pursue her for friendship first and maybe something more serious later, depending on how they got along. He glanced at Ellie. "I expect you to treat people with kindness. You were rude to Liza Schrock."

She harrumphed and slumped her shoulders. "I'm sorry, Daed."

"Follow your mamm's example. Be cordial and pleasant. She'd be ashamed of your ill-mannered behavior."

She remained sullen and quiet.

"Why do you try my patience, Ellie? I'm tired of having this same conversation with you over and over again."

She stared at her hands in her lap and shrugged.

Silence again. What more could he say to get through to her? Maybe the social gathering would interest her. "Liza invited you to meet Hannah, her niece, and her friends next Wednesday at three for a social at her bakery. I told her I'd bring you. The get-together will provide a good opportunity for you to make friends."

"I'm not interested."

"You're going to the social and I expect you to behave and participate with a charitable heart. Do you understand?"

She rolled her eyes.

Their disagreements had been frequent since her mamm had died. She'd been happy, cheerful, a delight before then.

"I mean it, Ellie. Treat Liza, her family, and the guests with respect."

She ignored him and pointed. "We have a visitor."

He halted the wagon, jumped down, and tied the horse to the hitching post. "Good morning. I'm Jacob Graber."

"I came to introduce myself. I'm your neighbor next door, Ezra Yoder. My fraa, Annabelle, is at home cooking. You'll meet her another time. Wilkom to Charm." He shook Jacob's hand.

Ellie joined them.

Jacob gestured to her. "This is my dochder, Ellie."

"Call me Ezra, Ellie."

"A pleasure to meet you, Mr. Yoder. I mean, Ezra." She

pointed to the wagon. "I'll take care of unharnessing and putting the horse in the barn."

"Danki." Jacob was pleased at her small attempt to soften the tension between them. At least it was something. He'd had to order her to do chores lately. Doing work on her own had been a rare occasion. A glimmer of hope sparked within him. "Ezra, may I offer you a glass of lemonade?"

He shook his head. "I'm not going to stay but a few minutes. Just wanted to get acquainted. Have you met many people in Charm yet?"

"I met Liza Schrock at the bakery." He held up his box. "I couldn't pass up a sugar cream pie and cookies. Are you sure you don't want a piece of pie or a cookie?"

"No, my fraa will snatch me baldheaded if I do." He removed his hat and put it back on. "I can't afford to lose much more. She was cooking chicken and dumplings when I left, but she's not a baker like Liza. Liza's been a widow for a year and has managed to keep the bakery profitable in the midst of her tragedy. Her husband, Paul, couldn't have been a better man. Generous, kind, and a good businessman, my friends and I admired and respected him. Any Amish man would be blessed to have Liza for a fraa. Are you married?"

"I'm a widower. My fraa passed three years ago. We moved here from Nappanee, Indiana. I'm hoping the change of scenery will cheer my dochder. She's having a hard time without her mamm."

"I'm sorry about your fraa." Ezra shifted his gaze to his horse and wagon. "I don't want to take you away from your chores. It's been a pleasure talking with you. I should head home." He shook Jacob's hand.

Pleased to find out Liza was available, Jacob decided he would visit the bakery often. "You're wilkom here anytime, Ezra. Danki for kumming by." He watched Ezra guide his horse to their dirt lane to head to the main country road. The man's warm wilkom had made him feel as if they'd been friends for a long time even though they'd just met. His new friend's news about Liza gave him hope. Paul Schrock, Liza's husband, had been generous to provide jobs for her and her entire family, although he was taken aback that Paul would want his fraa to work outside the home if it wasn't necessary.

Ellie hurried past him. "I'm going inside, Daed."

He followed her. "Danki for taking care of the horse and wagon. I do expect you to mend the holes in my socks and cook dinner."

She scowled. "What do you want me to fix?"

"I'll be satisfied with eggs and bacon again. We can have sandwiches for supper this evening."

She grabbed the sewing box and the worn socks and then stomped off.

Needing distance from her, he strolled to the barn, passing two cats chasing each other. A family in a buggy passed by and waved. He waved back. He, his fraa, and Ellie had been happy taking rides to town together. They'd had few problems and were close knit. He overturned a bucket, sat, and held his head in his hands. His dochder had worn him down. The struggle weighed on his shoulders. He couldn't give up on her. He loved her. He'd be patient and continue to ask for God's guidance.

Standing up, he eyed a loose wall board. He lifted his toolbox from the wooden shelf overhead and repaired it. He sneezed in the musty barn. A breath of fresh air would be good. The place was starting to take shape the way he wanted it. He stepped outside and studied the medium-size tree he'd sawed down the day before and cut it into smaller sections. The tree leaned at an angle and was too close to the haus.

A smile crossed his lips as he stacked it. To cut, repair,

or build with wood was satisfying work. The tension rolled out of his body. Wiping the sweat from his forehead with his shirt sleeve, he swallowed to wet his dry throat. Time to take a break. He stowed his tools, closed the barn door, and went inside the haus. He found Ellie in the kitchen. The scent of sizzling bacon filled the air. One place setting decorated the oak table. "Aren't you joining me?" He poured water into a glass from a white porcelain pitcher and drank it.

"I already ate mine. I cooked yours when I checked outside and you were stacking the last of the wood." She served his dinner and poured his coffee but didn't make eye contact.

"Young lady, you will sit with me at this table. Mealtime is the best time to discuss our matters. I'm weary from one argument after another with you. Your mamm's passing wasn't easy for me either, but I don't disrespect or take out my frustration on you. Please stop fighting me on everything."

"I'm still angry you and Ada got all cozy. I noticed your silly smile and the sparkle in your eyes when you met Liza today. No woman can take Mamm's place."

"Ada didn't try to take your mamm's place. She wanted to befriend you, but you wouldn't give her a chance."

"We're doing fine on our own."

"No, we aren't. You are angry, rebellious, and ill-mannered to me and others. I understand you miss your mamm. So do I, but you shouldn't take out your frustration on me and everyone else. Have you even considered I may need and want a fraa? If I choose to marry again, it doesn't mean I don't still love or would ever forget your mamm. I'm only thirty-six and I'd like to marry again while I'm fairly young if I find the right person."

She bowed her head. "I can't imagine having another

woman washing our clothes, cooking our meals, and being a part of our lives like Mamm. I'm sorry I haven't done my part around here. I'll do her chores."

"I wilkom your help, but I may meet and want to pursue a friendship with a woman hoping it turns into something more."

She stood and kicked the chair back with her foot. "I'll wash the dishes."

Again, as had happened often, she'd shut him out. It was up to him to take a stand as her daed. She couldn't dictate what happened in his life. This was something she had to accept. He got up and poured himself a cup of coffee and sat back down. He longed for a decent conversation with her. To share a laugh or small joke. They'd done this often as a family. Her mamm had had such a good sense of humor.

He sipped his coffee, then came alongside her at the sink. "I miss her too, sweetheart."

She softened. "Mamm was my rock. She and I did everything together. I could talk to her about anything. She didn't act shocked if I broached a forbidden subject like some of my friends' mamms did. She listened and answered my questions without skirting around the truth."

"You can talk to me."

She sighed. "You're a man. You wouldn't understand."

"I'll do my best."

"It's not the same." She stared at the dishwater.

His heart ached for his confused and unhappy dochder. "At the social you may make a new friend and, in time, maybe you can talk to her. Keep in mind, she has to want to befriend you too."

"I'm not going to hold back if I have a difference of opinion on something. I want people to accept me for who I am, not who you and the Amish community think I should be."

He and his fraa had raised Ellie to pray, read her Bible, and adhere to the Amish laws. For years, she'd had no problem with any of those things, until her mamm passed. Maybe these girls would be a good influence on her. "You're disrespectful to bring up the outside world to the Amish we meet in Charm. You'll stir up trouble and I won't have that."

Before she could answer, he headed outside to finish his chores. Determined to impress upon her the importance of following God and the Amish life, he wouldn't let her arrogant attitude defeat him.

Hours later, he went inside. They had supper in silence. He chewed and swallowed his last bite. He didn't want to end their evening with dissention between them. He had hoped supper would go better than their earlier dinner. "I'm going to read my Bible in the front room. Would you like to join me?"

"No, you go ahead. I'll clean up and then go to my room to read scriptures before bedtime."

He nodded and went to sit in his favorite high-backed chair. He flipped the pages to the Book of Isaiah in the King James Bible, Chapter 41:10: *Fear thou not; for I am with thee: be not dismayed; for I am thy God: I will strengthen thee; yea, I will help thee; yea, I will uphold thee with the right hand of my righteousness.*

He bowed his head. "Forgive me of my shortcomings, Heavenly Father. Equip me with the wisdom to guide Ellie off this path of rebellion. Change the desire of her heart to obey You and me. Prick her heart to long for the Amish way of life and scriptures. I pray one of the young women will befriend her and be a good influence on her life. I praise You, Heavenly Father, for Your love and power. Amen."

He raised his head and Ellie dashed past him without a word. He was puzzled. He'd thought they'd ended supper on a good note. He got up and knocked on her closed door. "Ellie, is everything all right? Are you saying your prayers before bed?"

"I'm doing fine. I'm going to bed early. And jah, I'll say my prayers."

"Sleep well. Good night."

She opened the door, stepped over the threshold, embraced him, then stepped back in her room and shut the door.

His heart soared. He'd take whatever glimmer of hope he could get. Returning to his chair, he blew out a breath and the tension from his conversation with Ellie eased out of him. He leaned back and rested his head on the smooth wood of the chair. Liza flashed in his mind. Ezra had given him good news. Not delighting in the loss of her husband but in his timing in moving to Charm and finding her available. Ellie wasn't the only one who needed friends. He could use a few too.

His cornfields, large garden, and livestock would provide a better-than-average living for a family, but not to the extent of what Paul had left Liza. Their financial difference didn't intimidate him, but Paul's reputation as a pillar of the community, according to Ezra, did a little.

Knock knock.

Ezra stood on the porch with a covered plate in his hands. "I'm sorry to bother you. You're probably getting ready to go to bed soon, but the missus insisted I bring this warm cinnamon bread over to you. Annabelle thought you might enjoy it for a snack this evening. I hope you don't mind."

"Tell her I'm going to enjoy a piece right away. Danki." He opened the door wider. "Kumme in and share a piece with me."

"No. I've got a long day tomorrow."

"Please tell your fraa I'm grateful to her for thinking of

us." He hoped this was the beginning of a good friendship with Ezra and his fraa.

"Will do. Have a nice evening."

He waited until his new friend was in his wagon before shutting the door.

Ellie rubbed her eyes and padded into the front room. "Who was at the door?"

"Our neighbor, Ezra. His fraa sent him over with some dessert." He unwrapped the warm, fluffy bread and waved it under her nose. "Want to join me for a slice?"

"It's my favorite. I'm going to enjoy having Ezra and his fraa living next door."

His heart warmed as he followed her to the table.

Ellie grabbed two plates, poured them water, and handed him a fork. She took a bite. "Delicious! I wish I could bake like this."

He grinned. "In our short time here, I've been quite pleased with the people in Charm."

"Me too."

Her childlike glow as she took bite after bite of the bread and her happy countenance was a wonderful change. She needed to shed herself of the anger and hurt she held inside and enjoy more happy moments.

Thunder clapped and lightning lit the dark sky. Hard rain pelted the roof. The weather reminded him that trouble could be lurking around the corner when he least expected it. Ellie had taught him this through her struggle to obey him and Amish law. He'd savor the moment with his beautiful but discontented dochder.

Chapter Two

Liza had glanced at the front door of the bakery each time it opened for the last week and a half. No sign of Jacob. She hugged herself. *Wednesday has finally arrived.* The day Jacob would bring Ellie to the social. Her heart fluttered. He had a strong stature but a gentle way about him. It had been easy to politely say no to other men showing interest in her. Fear reared its ugly head. *Don't trust any man.* She tightened her fists. One minute she'd told herself to get better acquainted with the charming man and the next she warned herself to avoid him. She was driving herself mad.

Dr. Harrison and Sheriff Williams entered the bakery and sat on their usual oak stools. Right on time. They had made visiting the bakery their ritual since the day she opened and she enjoyed having them. She could use the distraction. She poured and served them coffee. "Greetings, Dr. Harrison and Sheriff Williams."

"Good morning. Do you have any nut bread?" Dr. Harrison peered over his spectacles, his silver-gray hair perfectly in place and his crisp white shirt and pants pressed. Mrs. Harrison did a fine job on pressing his clothes. Liza's heavy, sad iron wasn't her favorite thing to use. She'd rather bake desserts than iron her dresses.

She guessed the age of the two men at around fifty-five. They'd known each other all their lives and were close friends. The sheriff was the doctor's opposite. He might not own a comb, and his rumpled clothes hadn't been touched with an iron. He'd been married for thirty years when his fraa had passed from consumption five years ago. He'd never remarried. They were extraordinary men with their big hearts, doing a good job serving the townsfolk of Charm.

"I'd like brown sugar and cinnamon bread if you have it." The sheriff unfolded his paper and handed his friend half of the pages. "Paper's got another article on the sinking of the *Titanic*. The last one was about the vessel's construction and exquisite design inside and out. It was the largest and most luxurious ship ever built. I had hoped to read passenger accounts of their voyage after they returned." He took a sip of coffee.

Dr. Harrison lifted his cup. "April fifteenth will be a day that goes down in history."

"What a frightening thing to experience!" The families whose loved ones met their tragic death in the icy waters of the Atlantic must be devastated. The pictures the sheriff and Dr. Harrison had showed her in the newspaper before the ship sailed came to mind. To imagine it disappearing into the vast, dark water brought chills. She prayed a quick, silent prayer for them, then served the men.

"Remember the stunning photographs in the paper? The chandeliers, staterooms, grand ballroom, and more. The *Titanic* had both comfortable and elaborate accommodations. The menus made my mouth water." Dr. Harrison spread butter on his bread.

The sheriff darted his eyes from the newspaper article to his friend. "The passengers must've been shocked to find out the boat had only twenty lifeboats. The water was freezing, and the ones who had only life vests must've known they wouldn't survive long."

Dr. Harrison shook his paper to straighten it. "The anguish the travelers and crew must have felt." He pulled the paper closer. "The *Titanic* hit the iceberg, then sank four hundred miles off the coast of Newfoundland. All those lives lost. What a shame."

Liza wiped the counter and stopped. "How many souls were lost?"

The sheriff brought down his reading material and peered at her. "Somewhere around one-thousand, five hundred and seventeen passengers and crew."

She held a hand to her open mouth. "How terrible!" Families would never be the same. Memories of this tragedy would haunt the survivors for the rest of their lives. The last words spoken to loved ones, the tears, the longing to hold on to them. Her eyes pooled with tears. She couldn't bear to dwell on it. Dabbing her eyes, she swallowed hard. She listened to the men chat as they finished their bread and coffee.

Dr. Harrison stood and patted his middle. "Delicious, as usual, Liza."

Sheriff Williams tucked his paper under his arm. "My buttons are about to burst! I shouldn't have eaten the whole thing." He shrugged. "I won't complain. It was worth it! Enjoy the rest of your day, Liza."

"Good day, gentlemen." She smiled as they left and four women entered. She served a steady flow of regular customers all day and met some new ones. She shifted her gaze to the small oak clock on the shelf behind her. Three o'clock. Where had the time gone? Her guests would arrive any minute for the social. A smile crossed her lips. Jacob would be here soon.

Hannah peeked around the door. "I've arranged the

ingredients we need to make your peach cookie recipe."
She held up two jars. "I brought extra canned peaches
from home in case we need them."

"You're a sweetheart. Danki. How's your mamm doing
in the back room? I haven't had a chance to check on her
or you."

"Wiping sweat off her brow as we speak. Loaves of nut,
white, and cinnamon sugar bread are cooling on the
counter. Dozens of assorted cookies are stowed and ready
for tomorrow's crowd. We've had a successful baking day."

Walking to the back with Hannah, she grinned at
Esther. "Sweet schweschder of mine, you are a whirlwind.
The rows and rows of bread on this table are astounding.
Hannah said you made cookies too."

Swiping the flour from her apron, Esther laughed.
"Hannah and I baked one thing after another. We didn't
even stop for dinner. She checked the shelves and told me
how empty they were earlier. We didn't want to stay late,
so we worked together to have extra for tomorrow. You
sold out of almost everything today."

"Sales were good," she said, then told them about the
Titanic.

Esther and Hannah paled and froze.

Hannah hugged herself. "A happy occasion switched
to a life-altering one in a split second. Life can be scary."

Esther said, "I'm relieved the rescuers found survivors."

Voices caught Liza's attention. She raised her head,
along with Hannah and Esther, from praying. She greeted
Leah Mast and Eva Fehr.

Hannah ran to her friends. "I'm glad you came. Ellie
Graber is going to join us."

Leah wrinkled her freckled nose. "Who is she?"

"She's new in town. Nappanee, Indiana, is where she
and her daed lived before moving to Charm. Mrs. Graber
died three years ago. According to Mr. Graber, Ellie's

having a difficult time adjusting to life without her mamm. Liza invited her to bake with us today to help her make new friends. Let's do our best to wilkom her." Hannah backed up and leaned on the counter.

"Mamm and I are close. She's the one I tell everything to. Speaking to my daed about my worries and concerns wouldn't be the same. I love him, but he doesn't listen with interest like mamm does." Eva straightened a loose straight pin in her white bonnet and pushed it tighter into her thick black bun.

Liza gazed at them. "Be patient with her. It would mean a lot to Jacob if she could have friends to support her through this sad time in her life."

Quiet until then, Esther came alongside Liza. "Maybe God sent her to Charm to meet you girls and heal."

Jacob and Ellie entered the bakery and let the door shut behind them.

"Good afternoon to all of you." Jacob tipped his hat.

Liza went around the counter to meet them. "Jacob, kumme in and have a seat. Ellie, I'm glad you're joining us."

Ellie wore the same scowl she had the first time they met. Would she be cordial to the girls? Hannah had the gift of patience and could make conversation with anyone. Leah and Eva were more timid. This social would be interesting to say the least.

Ellie shuffled her feet and whispered, "Danki."

Hannah introduced Ellie and Jacob Graber to Eva and Leah.

Esther untied her soiled apron from her waist and hung it on a hook. "Girls, head to the back room and get started. I'm going to Albert's Apothecary for some liniment. I'm out and I like to keep it on hand. Liza will be here if you have any questions."

"Take your time, Esther. Enjoy the spring air." Liza watched Esther go and then spun on her heel to Jacob as

Hannah took Ellie and her friends to the back. She and Jacob were alone. Her heart skipped a beat. His warm brown eyes stared back at her and she held his gaze for a moment. The connection between them was undeniable. Did he feel it too? She had to stifle her urge to learn more about him. Marriage had proven a mistake for her. Handsome and genuine wasn't enough to tempt her to consider him for more than a friend. She'd be hospitable.

"Would you like coffee and something from the display case? I have ginger cookies, nut bread, and apple tarts."

"Will you join me? If so, I'll take a ginger cookie, please, and a cup of coffee." He pointed to the one closest to them.

Should she? No harm in keeping him company for a few minutes. "I'd be glad to, but I'll have to wait on customers if they kumme in. It could get annoying."

"I don't mind. I'll take whatever time you can spare."

Her shoulders tensed. His statement made clear his interest in her. Part of her was flattered, but the other part wanted to run. No doubt she was drawn to his kind manner, sweet nature, and openness. Curious, unnerving questions swirled in her mind. Why not find out more about him? She might not like what he had to say and her curiosity about him would dissipate. Did he have siblings? A mamm and daed? Did he have a temper? Was he the gentleman and good daed she had observed so far? Did she dare risk finding out? His answers might entice her to consider a deeper friendship with him. She couldn't stop the struggle going on inside her. Her heart said sit down and enjoy her time with Jacob. Her mind told her to guard her heart. She prided herself on being decisive. Her decisions about him were another story.

Lifting out a cookie, she silently commanded her hand to stop shaking. Much good that did. It was like trying to bring a train to an abrupt stop. Her nerves were getting the best of her. She served it to him with a cup of coffee. She poured a cup for herself and sat across from him. A shiver of excitement surprised her. *Quit thinking and acting like a silly schoolgirl.* "How is Ellie adjusting to Charm?"

He traced the rim of his cup with his forefinger. "She's a challenge for me, Liza. If I say one thing, she will argue the opposite just for the sake of irritating me. I'm praying to God for guidance. I follow the scriptures, but I'm at a loss most of the time as to what to say to her. I can't win. If I'm lenient or if I'm strict, it makes no difference. She's rebellious and not happy. I wilkom any advice."

Raising a dochder couldn't be easy, let alone one who wouldn't listen. "Bringing her to the social today might help. The girls will talk to her. Hannah will do her best to get her to relax. Having girls her age to confide in and share what's in her heart may lighten your load and lift her mood."

Cupping a hand to his ear, he leaned in a little. "So far, no sound of her causing a ruckus. Maybe you're right." He tilted his head and grinned. "Was owning the bakery a dream of yours?"

Jacob didn't waste any time. He asked direct, personal questions. Clearly, he wasn't going to ease into getting better acquainted. She should at least be amiable. "I love to bake and the shop has been a dream kumme true. I never thought I'd manage a bakery. The customers are an added pleasure."

"What do you like to do in what little spare time you have?"

"I knit, take walks, fish, and create new recipes." She grinned. "Enough about me. What do *you* like to do?" *Don't ask too many questions that will give him the wrong idea.* Or did she really want to learn more about this man?

There it was again. The struggle in her brain about

him. Pushing her back against the chair and crossing her legs, she swallowed. His deep brown eyes captivated her.

"Long walks and fishing are two of my favorite things to do. I also like to build furniture when I have the time. I haven't made anything for the last couple of years. My daed and I used to build pieces together. He and my mamm died within a year of each other. My daed got kicked in the head hard by a stallion he'd tried to tame. He was killed instantly. I believe my mamm died of a broken heart. They were older when they had me and I was an only child."

"My parents are both in Heaven too. I miss them."

"My late fraa's parents died in a wagon accident. She didn't have any siblings. Ellie is the only family I have left." Sadness shone in his eyes.

"I'm sorry you've experienced such tragedy in your life. I think you'll find Charm a wonderful place to settle down. The people are friendly for the most part, and the Amish are close here."

He glanced around. "Does your business slow down around this time each day?"

"Jah, from three to five we usually have a lull."

"Do you mind if I kumme by tomorrow and chat again around three-thirty?"

She should tell him she did mind, but the words wouldn't form on her tongue. Her heart told him to please kumme back. "You can stop by anytime."

Esther returned from the apothecary. "Liza, I'm glad you're taking a break. Jacob, Liza has been on her feet all day. Danki for getting her to sit for a minute."

"My pleasure."

Stowing her bag under the counter, Esther grinned. "Jacob, you and Ellie are invited to join Abe, my husband, Hannah, and me for supper around six this evening. I've got leftover beef and vegetable pie to warm, and I'm taking home a loaf of fresh oat bread to go with it. What do you say?"

His eyes brightened. "How kind of you. I have to admit, I'm tired of the same three dishes I cook. Ellie can cook, but she's not been happy about it. She and her mamm used to make meals together. This would be a real treat for us. We'd be delighted."

"Liza, of course you'll join us."

She didn't miss the twinkle in his eye at Esther's invitation. What could she say? Esther hadn't given her much choice, asking her in front of Jacob. There she went again. Liza was hoping her schweschder would invite her to supper. She'd never been drawn to a man quite this way. Paul had been handsome, but she hadn't married him for love. It hadn't taken long before she'd struggled to tolerate him. Jacob had turned her life upside down the moment she laid eyes on him. But she didn't have time to sort this out now.

She leaned closer to Esther. "Do you want me to bring anything?"

"If the girls do a good job on the cookies, you could bring us some."

"If they don't, I'll bring my special molasses cookies. I have some stowed in the back room."

"Apple tarts are in a covered pan on the second shelf under the counter for tomorrow. I made plenty. We should have more than enough for patrons tomorrow." Esther walked to the back door. "I'm going outside to fetch some water in the washbasin to clean the pans I left inside." She disappeared through the other room to use the back door.

Jacob stood. "I should get going."

"We will take Ellie with us, because you'll be kumming to Esther and Abe's."

"I should tell her our plans have changed."

"I'll interrupt the girls and ask her to kumme speak

with you." She popped her head around the door. "Ellie, your daed would like to talk to you. Do you mind joining him in front?"

Ellie gave a disgusted sigh, washed her hands in the basin of clean water, and dried them. She joined her daed and stared at him.

He gave her a stern look. "Ellie, we've been invited to supper at Hannah's haus. Liza has offered to take you with them, and I'll arrive at around six. Respect Liza and behave."

Without a word, she whipped around and disappeared into the back room.

Red-faced, he bit his bottom lip. Moments later, he put his hand on the door. "I'm sorry you had to witness her disrespectful behavior once again. Are you sure you want to take her home? I don't want to subject you to her attitude."

"We'll be fine. Don't worry. We understand she may be difficult. Our goal is to befriend her in her own time."

"You're generous and kind to overlook her faults. I look forward to talking with you more this evening, Liza." He blushed and hurried out the door.

The man was broken. He loved Ellie, but his dochder wasn't giving him any glimmer of hope her attitude would improve. *He looks forward to talking to me more.* He didn't hold back. He said what was on his mind. Another trait she found attractive about him. She walked to the back and stopped shy of the open doorway and listened to the girls' conversation. She peeked in enough to watch them.

Ellie had removed her kapp and pins. She smoothed out her tresses. Golden locks cascaded down her back. "I get sick of wearing pins in my hair. They give me a headache. Why should we have to cover our hair with a kapp? It's silly. I ripped off my kapp the minute I ran away."

Liza stifled a gasp. Ellie's unpinning of her hair was quite defiant. She really had no regard for Amish law.

Eva stopped rolling the dough into a ball in her hand. She paused, as if someone had slapped her. "I like honoring our Amish traditions. I can't imagine leaving my family. Did you leave a note for your daed?"

"I wrote him a letter. I didn't tell him where I was going so he wouldn't find me."

Putting a hand to her open mouth, Liza was shocked. *Poor Jacob.* What anguish he must've suffered, unaware of where Ellie had gone or what was happening to her.

Hannah cut a piece of twine from a roll on the shelf and went to Ellie. "I'm going to tie your hair back, wind it in a bun, and put your pins back in it. We don't want hair in the cookies."

Pained regret came over Ellie. "I'm sorry. I forgot about getting strands in the food. Danki."

Interesting. Liza tapped a finger to her lips. Ellie hadn't shrugged off Hannah's insistence she tie her hair back. The frown of regret showed she cared what Hannah thought. Maybe her niece would have some influence on Ellie. She hid behind the doorframe and listened.

Leah diced peaches and added them to her cookie mixture. "Where did you stay and how long were you gone?"

Ellie beamed. "I met Jane and her bruder, Duke Patterson, in Indiana at the general store one day. Jane has a full head of golden curls and big, dark blue eyes. She was friendly and introduced herself and Duke to me. They lived close by in Sugarcreek. They agreed to meet me several times in Nappanee. I offered to go to town to buy supplies and Daed had no idea I was meeting them. I told Jane I was curious about Englisch life, and she invited me to stay with her and Duke. Their parents had died and Duke managed the farm and made furniture to sell in his friend's furniture store."

"Was Duke your beau?" Leah covered her open mouth.

Her tone matter of fact, Ellie said, "He was a friend, not a romantic interest."

Eva scooped a spoonful of dough from Leah's bowl and rolled it into a ball. "Did you tell your daed you'd left with them in your note?"

"I wrote I had met friends who would take good care of me and not to search for me. I told him I was curious about the world and I would write or return once I'd chosen the Amish or Englisch life. I told him my friends picked me up and provided transportation. I left it on the kitchen table when he was at a neighbor's haus, helping them put on a roof."

Biting her tongue, Liza crossed her arms. Ellie had left Nappanee with Englischers she'd barely known. She could've been abused or lost her life. This girl was fearless and foolish. She was too young and unaware of the dangers of the world. She'd been selfish to leave her daed wondering about her well-being.

"He must have been worried sick about you." Leah spoke barely above a whisper.

Ellie cocked her head and shrugged. "I suppose he was, but I was fine."

Hannah checked the molasses cookies baking in the wood-fired oven. "Were you hoping your friendship with Duke would grow into something more?"

Liza held her breath for a moment. She wasn't sure she wanted to learn the answer to that question. How intimate had Ellie gotten with this man?

"No, but I was comfortable around him. Jane and I became good friends. She showed me how to fix my hair in stylish pins and braids. She had button-down cotton blouses, tight-fitting belted dresses, and loose-fitting, everyday cotton dresses in red, blue, green, and yellow prints. She gave me some of her clothes. I enjoyed wearing them while I was there."

"Did you have your own room?" Leah squinted.

Breathing a sigh of relief, Liza bent her head and listened to Ellie. She could barely stand to peek now and then. This girl's nonchalant attitude in telling the others her story was maddening. She hoped Ellie's stories wouldn't negatively influence these naïve Amish girls.

"No, Jane and I shared a room. She had ribbons, bows, and fancy shoes. We dressed up a lot. We went dancing in town a few times. She taught me how to dance, and I caught on to the steps in no time. I loved the music and the way the full red skirt I wore swirled when I twirled on the dance floor."

"How long did you stay?" Eva leaned on the working counter.

Ellie poured flour and sugar according to the recipe into a mixing bowl to make her batch of peach cookies. "About a month."

Eva set her ball of dough onto the metal cookie sheet. "Why didn't you stay with Jane and Duke if you enjoyed the Englisch life?"

Head bowed, Ellie said, "Duke came home from the saloon one night and grabbed my arm. He pulled me to him, but Jane yelled at him and told him to stop. He did and stumbled to his room. I was petrified. She said he'd promised to quit drinking and he had for a while. She said he must've started drinking again. She was afraid of what he might do if she weren't there in the room with me to stop him. She offered to take me home the next day and she did."

Hannah gasped. "I'm glad Jane intervened. She was a true friend to keep you safe by bringing you home. Your daed must've been thrilled to lay eyes on you."

"We hugged and wept. I'd been homesick and I'd

missed him. I'm still confused about living the Amish or the Englisch life, but for now, I'll stay in Charm."

For now. Liza put a fist to her mouth. Ellie might leave Jacob again. He'd been through a boatload of heartache with the passing of his fraa and having his dochder leave once. She would do all she could to encourage Ellie to stay and seek God in her life.

Hannah washed her hands and circled an arm around Ellie's waist. "I'm glad you're here with us. We'd like to include you when we have gatherings like this one. Hopefully, we'll sway you into never wanting to leave your Amish life behind." She gave Ellie a merry grin.

Ellie bit her lip. "Your mamm may not want you to befriend me. The Amish in Nappanee found out about my running away. They spread gossip about me and thought the worst. The trouble I caused Daed is the reason we moved here."

Liza entered the room. She was shocked at what she'd overheard but didn't want to show it. Ellie was in danger of going down the wrong path again. Thankful Hannah had insisted on showing Ellie the Amish way was the better choice, she needed to join forces with her niece. They had to draw in this frustrated girl and give her confidence she could find happiness again in her Amish life. Hannah had used the right words to show Ellie she cared.

"You're wrong, Ellie. My schweschder, Esther, is a forgiving and loving woman. I hope you'll give my family and each of these girls a chance to become your friends. You came to Charm for a new start. Let us help you." Liza moved her hand toward Ellie's arm then pulled it back. She wasn't sure how Ellie would react. Better not to kumme on too strong with her.

Ellie remained quiet.

Liza would let it go for now. They hadn't known each

other long. She didn't want to push her to respond until she'd gotten to know Ellie better.

Whistling, Jacob strolled to the hardware store. As he unhooked a small knife, a man bumped into him. He whipped his head to look at the man. Eyes wide, he smiled. "Ezra, what a nice surprise!"

"Jacob, nice to run into you. I brought Annabelle to town to do a little shopping. Thought I'd stop in the hardware store and shop around to pass the time. Is your dochder with you?"

"Liza invited Ellie to a baking social this afternoon. I dropped her off, and Liza is taking her to Esther's for supper after her workday ends. I'm joining them at six."

"Sounds like you've made a good impression on Liza and her schweschder. I'm glad."

Ezra pointed to a worn pine bench outside the store. "Annabelle is picking up some material to make dresses for some of her elderly friends. Would you like to join me on the bench outside?"

"Sure." He followed Ezra to the bench, but they paused in front of it.

"Is Ellie adjusting to moving to Charm?" Ezra swatted at a fly that had landed on his sleeve.

"She's battling to overcome her grief over her mamm's passing. She's changed from a sweet and obedient child to a rebellious young woman. I'm hoping moving to Charm will give her a fresh start. She ran away from home in Nappanee, and that damaged her reputation in the Amish community. I'm afraid she'll do it again."

Ezra removed his straw hat and scratched his head. "I have a dochder. Her name is Martha. She met and married an Englischer. They live in Texas. Annabelle and I were heartbroken over her decision to leave the Amish life. She writes to us, but it's not the same as having her here. She'll never be wilkomed back in the community, and we wouldn't be comfortable making such a long trip. We're not supposed to speak about our loved ones who have left the community, but I thought it best you knew we understand your dilemma with Ellie. I hope Ellie will stay in Charm for her sake and yours." He swiped a tear from his cheek.

Jacob's heart hurt for his new friend. He would be lost without Ellie if she chose the outside world as her permanent home. Ezra's story was sad, but he was comforted that he could identify with what he was experiencing. Not many Amish would understand or be willing to discuss a child who had left the community. "I'm sorry, Ezra. Danki for telling me. It helps to talk to someone who understands my problem. Liza's been receptive to discussing Ellie with me too. I'm blessed to have met kind friends in the short amount of time I've been here." He sat.

Ezra started to sit.

A burly man with a thick mustache knocked into Ezra. "Watch where you're going, old man!"

Jacob reached out and grabbed Ezra to steady him. "Are you all right?"

"I'm fine. I should've been more careful." He glanced at the Englischer. "I'm sorry, Mr. Phillips."

"You should be." The bully harrumphed and walked away.

Jacob stared at the back of the arrogant man. His friend could've been hurt, and it hadn't been Ezra's fault. "That man was in the wrong, Ezra. He should've apologized to you."

"I don't want trouble. Chuck Phillips is an angry and dangerous man. I witnessed him hitting another man hard with his fist outside the hardware store a couple of weeks back. The man fought back in self-defense, and Mr. Phillips jumped on top of him and nearly beat him to death before a handful of men pulled him off."

"Did the sheriff arrest him?"

"No. The injured man ran away and didn't report him. I doubt anyone wants to cross Chuck Phillips."

Jacob frowned. Mr. Phillips's muscular, tall, and large size and menacing face would put off anyone. He hoped they wouldn't run into each other again.

A woman approached them, carrying an armload of packages. "Ezra dear, would you mind carrying these for me?"

Ezra took them from her and gestured to Jacob. "I'd be happy to. Annabelle, meet our neighbor, Jacob."

Jacob stood and tipped his hat. Her wide grin, big dimples, and round, rosy cheeks brought a smile to Jacob's face. She was the same height as Ezra but would make two of him with her round middle. She had the same sparkle in her eyes and cheerful voice.

He was relieved she hadn't noticed Mr. Phillips being rude to Ezra on her way to them. "It's a pleasure. Danki for the delicious food you sent over with Ezra the other day. Ellie, my dochder, and I really enjoyed it."

The three of them sat. Annabelle folded her hands on her lap. "You are wilkom." She elbowed Ezra's arm. "We should head back. So nice to meet you, Jacob. You and Ellie should stop over and visit us sometime."

"Danki for the invitation. Our door is always open to you both anytime too. Enjoy the rest of your day."

"Glad we had another chance to talk, Jacob. It's been good to learn more about you."

Jacob bid them farewell, retrieved his wagon, and headed home. He needed Ellie surrounded by kind and understanding Amish friends to encourage her to stay true to her faith in God and the Amish life. She was strong-willed and secretive. Would she give living in Charm, their kind neighbors, and making new friends a chance?

He arrived home, left food and water for his horse, and headed inside. Just enough time to get ready and go to Esther's. Ellie better have behaved this afternoon. Liza's friendship was important to him, and she and her family had gone out of their way to wilkom them. He didn't want Ellie or anything else to ruin it. He shrugged out of his clothes and boots, put on a clean shirt and pants, and snapped his suspenders in place. Getting out of sweaty, dusty clothes and changing into clean ones felt much better. He wiggled his toes and grinned. Time for shoes and socks. He sat and pulled them on.

He unhooked his hat from the peg on the wall, retrieved his horse and buggy, and went to Esther's. He couldn't wait to have supper with Liza at her schweschder's haus. Would they have time for a walk? He'd be grateful for any time alone with her. He sighed. Ellie might've ruined supper, depending on how she'd treated the girls at the social. He arrived and rapped on the door.

Liza surprised him. "You're right on time."

He stepped inside the haus. Her radiant smile resembled bright sunshine. "I'm punctual when it kummes to an invitation for a good meal." He grinned.

Abe stood and extended his arm. "I'm Abe Lapp. Call me Abe. We go by first names."

"A pleasure to meet you. Danki for inviting me into your home."

"I've met Ellie." He smiled. "She's lovely. She and Hannah are inside. They have been inseparable since they arrived."

Inseparable. This was encouraging news! Ellie must've

been on her best behavior at the social. Hope sprang inside him.

Liza gestured to a chair across from Abe. "Make yourself comfortable. I'll help Esther in the kitchen. You and Abe relax and get acquainted."

He nodded and she disappeared. "Your family has been very gracious to Ellie and me."

Abe chuckled. "Esther, Liza, and Hannah are the kindest and most generous women in the community. I may be prejudiced, but in time I think you'll agree. They have big hearts and are more understanding of awkward situations than most women."

"Ellie has been a challenge for me since her mamm died. She's finding her way, but it's been hard on me. She doesn't listen to reason and she's curious about the outside world. She's run away once and I worry she'll do it again."

"I'm sorry for your troubles. If I or my family can help you, please ask. I'd be a mess without Esther. Hannah and I would manage, but my dochder defers to her mamm about most things. Hannah hasn't questioned living the Amish life. I shudder to think what it would be like if she had. I don't envy you."

"I don't know if I'm too lenient or too strict. I've tried both. I'm praying and searching the scriptures for answers, but I'm not always clear about what to do."

"You're already doing it. You love her and you're listening to her. Give her advice and instruction whether she wants it or not. At least you have the assurance you've said what you need to."

Jacob studied Abe. The man's long arms rested on the maple chair arms and he had his legs up and feet propped on a footstool. Abe put him at ease. The man hadn't judged him but offered him sound advice. "It's reassuring to talk to another daed about it."

"Hannah has been an obedient child. We've been blessed thus far. I'm confident she'll influence and encourage Ellie to stay Amish."

"I'd be grateful. The thought of her leaving me and our community hurts more than I can say. The first time she left, I feared for her safety every day and night. The worry chewed my soul to bits. God and prayer were the only things that kept me sane. I don't want to relive it again."

"I understand." Abe leaned forward, his face serious. "Maybe you'll marry again and she'll be the right mamm for Ellie." He grinned. "Liza is available. Maybe you and she can form a friendship and let it grow. Just take building a relationship with her slow. I have no doubt she'd make any man an excellent fraa and mamm to kinner."

He had Abe's support to pursue Liza. All he had to do was convince Liza. He'd take Abe's advice. Take their friendship slow and hope they would both want it to turn into something more serious. He'd had indications she might be open to the idea. She'd sat and talked with him at the bakery and she'd accepted Esther's invitation to supper, knowing he'd be here.

He hoped Abe would share more insight about Liza. "Has she shown interest in a suitor since her husband died?" Jacob raised his brows.

"Since Paul passed, she has been quick to decline men's offers to get better acquainted with her for a possible future together. They have been honorable, respectable, and attractive. I wasn't sure if she'd ever open her heart up to another man, until Esther told me she had a sparkle in her eyes when she talked with you." He patted Jacob's knee. "I'd say you have a chance."

"The first time I met her I was drawn to her sweet voice, sunny blue eyes, and kind way about her. I plan to frequent the bakery and learn more about her. I had a close relationship with my fraa, Lydia, and I miss having a partner. Ellie needs a woman in her life, someone she can trust to discuss what she would have talked about with her mamm."

"If you and Liza progress into something more serious, you couldn't find a better mamm than her. Her patience is astounding, considering her unhappy times with her husband."

"Was he difficult?"

Abe cleared his throat. "He had a stellar reputation in the community. But Paul wasn't kind to Liza, and she shared examples. She kept his behavior toward her a secret from us until now. I'm shocked by what she confided to my fraa and disappointed she didn't tell us earlier about him."

"What examples did she give?"

"Forget I said anything. Liza wouldn't approve of me divulging to you what happened between her and Paul during their marriage. She should be the one to discuss her personal life with you. I've said too much already."

A red-faced Liza entered the room.

Abe paled and stopped talking.

Jacob cringed. She'd heard them. Her mouth in a grim line, she stared at her feet. He opened his mouth, then shut it. He didn't know what to say.

She whispered, "Supper's ready. Kumme in the kitchen and have a seat."

Abe gestured for Jacob to follow him to the kitchen. He whispered to Liza, "I'm sorry if I said too much."

Jacob's shoulders sagged. He hadn't meant to get Abe in trouble with Liza. Should he apologize too? He shouldn't have pursued the subject of Paul with Abe. Curiosity had gotten the better of him. This could destroy any chance of moving their friendship forward.

Ellie entered and plopped into her seat. "Daed, Hannah's showing me how to quilt."

The smile on Ellie's face erased his concern about Liza for the moment. Any glimpses of the dochder he had enjoyed before she turned rebellious was a gift these days.

"How generous of her." He addressed Hannah. "Danki for teaching her, Hannah."

"Quilting is one of my favorite things to do. I wish I had more time to devote to stitching them. I'm glad it's something Ellie and I can do together. She's wilkom here anytime."

Esther carried a basket of sliced bread. "Jacob, I'm happy you accepted my invitation to supper." She grinned and nudged her husband. "Did Abe talk your ear off?"

"We had a pleasant conversation when he arrived." Abe took the basket from her and put it on the table. He avoided Liza's frown.

"I love vegetable pie."

Esther's cheeks dimpled. "Fill your plate. We have plenty." She picked up a pan of vegetable pie covered with a golden crust and passed it to Hannah, then glanced at her guests. "Don't be shy. Take big helpings."

Jacob sat next to Liza. She remained quiet as she handed him the butter. She avoided Abe's gaze too. Later, he'd take the blame for asking Abe about Paul.

Esther bragged about Liza's most recent creation, her molasses cookie recipe. "They disappear as fast as we can put them in the showcase."

Abe held up his glass of water. "I can't get enough of them."

Liza blushed and whispered, "Danki."

Jacob and Abe discussed farming.

Esther rested her fork on her plate. "Liza, you're upset about something. What is it?"

Abe stared down at his plate.

Jacob glanced at her. A pang of guilt washed over him.

He had caused her pain. What could he say to erase her disappointment? Nothing came to mind.

"I'm a little tired, but I'm enjoying listening to the conversation."

Esther smiled. "All right." She switched her gaze to Ellie. "Did you enjoy meeting the other girls and baking this afternoon?"

Ellie smirked and stared at her daed. "I did. I may have shocked them with my story about my time in Nappanee with Jane and Duke Patterson."

Jacob dropped his spoon and shook his head. "Ellie, why would you bring up such a forbidden subject? No one needs to know of your reckless foray into the Englisch world."

"I didn't mean any harm." She gave him her usual dismissive shrug.

Hannah put her hand on Ellie's arm. "Ellie and I will become good friends and she'll forget all about the Englisch world. We've already made plans to quilt together."

Ellie's face softened. She patted Hannah's hand. "You're already a true friend, Hannah."

He envied Esther and Abe having such a wise and compassionate dochder. He was grateful to Hannah for her persistence in befriending Ellie, despite his dochder's insistence on sharing her life in the Englisch world.

Liza stood and stared at her empty plate as she carried it to the counter. "I'll serve dessert."

She and Esther carried over the empty dishes to the counter. Esther uncovered an apple pie. "I made this last night. No one wanted any, so I saved it for tonight."

"I love your apple pie." Liza smiled and cut and lifted out the slices onto plates and served them. Jacob listened to the girls talk about quilting. He nodded as Abe talked about the new saw he'd bought. Sitting with Liza's family, he hoped this would occur often. He liked them all.

Esther refilled everyone's water glasses. "We devoured dessert fast!"

"It was mouthwatering good!" Ellie grinned.

She and Hannah got up and carried away their dirty dishes.

Jacob noticed Liza had been avoiding him and Abe all evening. He had to correct his mistake in coaxing Abe to talk about Liza and Paul. He had to say something to her. "Would you mind taking a stroll with me after supper?"

Liza sucked in her upper lip and nodded. "I should help Esther with the dishes first."

"Of course, I understand. I'll help too." Jacob gave her a shy smile.

Esther waved a dismissive hand. "The girls and I will take care of the dishes. You two go for a walk and enjoy this beautiful evening."

Abe pushed his small plate aside. "I'll put extra chairs on the porch. We can all sit outside when you're done, Esther."

"Sounds good."

Liza and Jacob headed out the door.

She grabbed a blanket off the rocking chair on the porch. "We can spread this out near the meadow on the other side of the barn where there's a stretch of grass perfect for us to sit and enjoy the purple, white, and yellow wildflowers. They're beautiful this time of year."

He gently took it from her and strolled along beside her, then stopped. "This is a flat, grassy spot." He glanced over his shoulder to ensure they were out of Abe's view and gently put the blanket on the ground.

She sat and pushed her back against the big oak tree behind her. Her body was stiff, her face stricken.

He sat next to her. "Liza, did you overhear Abe and me discussing Paul?"

"Jah, and it upset me." She crossed her arms.

"I apologize. It's my fault. I shouldn't have questioned him about your late husband."

She heaved a big sigh. "He shouldn't have brought up the subject."

"He didn't share details. I asked him direct questions. Again, I'm sorry. You've been gracious, and I don't want anything to hinder our becoming friends."

She broke off a long blade of grass and snapped it in two. "I'm unhappy with both of you for discussing such a private matter. Our turbulent relationship is difficult to talk about. I kept it a secret for a long time. Esther insisted on telling Abe about my miserable marriage with Paul once I shared the information with her. I understood, but Abe knows how private I am. He shouldn't have spoken of it." She gazed at him. "I'm disappointed you pursued the matter with him."

Jacob stifled the urge to cover her hand with his to assure her he cared about her. She was honest and spoke her mind. Two more traits he admired about her. He had to win her trust again. "It wasn't for the purpose of gossiping about him. I care about you, Liza. I want to learn everything about you. You can trust me not to share what you tell me."

She glanced at him. "Paul paid the medical bills and gave food, horses, and did repairs for many of our friends. He listened to our friends' woes and showed them compassion. The Amish community assumes he treated me the same way. Esther, Abe, Hannah, and you are the only ones who know otherwise."

"I'll not talk about it with anyone. Would you care to tell me about your life with Paul?"

She didn't answer him right away. Had he overstepped his bounds again?

"Oh, Jacob, it was awful." She wiped at a tear wetting her cheek.

He was relieved she was opening up to him. He longed to hold her in his arms and console her. His heart broke for her. Why would her husband not love and honor such a beautiful and sweet woman? He moved his hand slowly to hers and covered it. She didn't pull it away. Joy rushed through him. He felt an instant attraction and connection with her he couldn't explain. "The man was a fool not to cherish you. We've just met, but I'd be blind not to notice your beauty, integrity, and giving heart. You're the first woman to give Ellie a chance. You've listened to my troubles. Share yours with me. Sometimes it helps to lighten your burden to speak about it."

She brought her knees to her chest and pulled her skirt down over her shoes and hugged her legs. "He criticized how I cooked, cleaned, sewed, and gardened. He punished me as if I were a child by sending me to my room. It was humiliating. His temper would flare over the silliest things and he'd hit the wall or table. Thankfully, he didn't lay a hand on me."

"Did you love him when you married him?"

"I never loved him. Our marriage was arranged. I assumed he was an honorable and respectable man because of his exceptional reputation in the community."

Jacob gazed at her. "Why did you agree to an arranged marriage? You have so many good qualities. Why didn't you wait to fall in love?"

"My family needed his financial support. Abe couldn't take care of my parents, his family, and me. Paul offered to hire Abe to manage his farm and oversee the field hands. My parents were ill and couldn't manage their property anymore. Amish men helped when they had time, but our crops suffered. It seemed like the right thing to do."

She had put her family's needs ahead of her own. Paul had trapped her in a miserable marriage. Had he forced her to work? "How did the bakery kumme about? I'm confused as to why he bought it for you."

"He inherited a lot of property from his parents. Paul's daed was a smart and wise businessman and grew his wealth. Paul took counsel from his daed and bought more land and made a lot of money with crops and gardens. He hired several Amish men to make furniture and sell it out of the store in town. I love to bake and I sold pies, cakes, and cookies to the general store. Englischers would ask for them. Paul wanted to keep all the money instead of sharing it with the general store, so he opened the bakery in a building he already owned. He sold the furniture store for a nice profit and the bakery brought in a substantial amount of money for him. I did all the work and he reaped the rewards."

This man had a long list of undesirable traits. "Were you happy he bought the bakery?"

"Jah. The bakery was my safe place. I could relax, bake, and enjoy my time there. I still do, but I can do all those things at home in peace now too." She lifted a small pebble from the ground at the edge of the blanket and gave it a toss. "Now I can do things my way without feeling inferior. I no longer have to listen to his constant criticism."

At least her late husband had given her something to enjoy. Perplexed as to why Paul had not cherished her, he wondered why the man had arranged the marriage. Her life with her husband had ended and there was no need to ponder it further. He had a chance to show her true male friendship. And if their relationship grew serious, what a loving husband was like. "I'm sorry you suffered such a tumultuous partnership with him. I hope it didn't turn you away from wanting to marry again. You're young and could enjoy a happy marriage and kinner one day."

She broke eye contact. "I'm afraid to marry again. I'm content to remain on my own."

Saying the wrong thing could tarnish their budding friendship. "I loved my fraa, and I told her everything. She offered advice when I asked for it, and we made decisions together. She was my best friend. I long to have another marriage where I can love and share life with a fraa someday."

"I'm happy you had a close relationship." She held up her palm and lifted her left shoulder. "Mine left me with too much fear to trust again. Maybe one day my mind will change."

"I pray so. Not all marriages are bad. You may fall in love again someday and have another chance at having a fulfilling marriage. I'm thankful for the time I had with my fraa before she passed."

She pressed her hands to her cheeks. "I don't understand why I'm talking with you about Paul. Maybe it's because you've been open with me. I appreciate your understanding."

He smiled. "I'm happy you're at ease with me."

She blushed and fidgeted with her hands.

Embarrassing her wasn't his intention. He shouldn't have been so forward. He'd change the subject. Ellie had made a spectacle of herself again tonight. He must address it. "On another topic, I apologize again for Ellie's snide remark at supper."

She tilted her head and smiled. "You don't have to say sorry for her. She's responsible for her actions, not you. She's old enough to know better and she is goading you to get you aggravated with her. Hannah and others will entice her to change her ways. We won't give up on her. We are here to help you with her."

What wonderful news! He didn't understand why this family was so accepting of them, but he was grateful. "I'm relieved we haven't exhausted your patience. I covet your advice and our talks."

Her cheeks pinked. Again, he'd embarrassed her. *Oh no!* He'd better go home before she asked Esther and Abe to throw him out. He glanced at the sun lowering behind the trees, its orange hue coloring the sky, and stood. He offered her his hand and she grasped his fingers to gain her balance, then quickly let go. The softness of her skin against his sent warmth from his head to his toes. She had a hold on him he couldn't explain.

"Ellie and I should head home. I don't want to wear out our wilkom." He grinned. "I'm hoping Esther and Abe will invite me back!"

She laughed. "Esther and Abe have an open door. She wouldn't mind if you dropped in for supper every night. The more the merrier to cook for is her motto."

If Liza would join them, he would never tire of being with her family. The days he didn't talk to her, his mind filled with her face and the sweet sound of her voice. "I've had a delightful time."

"Me too." She gave him a shy smile.

Beautiful music to his ears. She'd gazed at him as she said the words. Baby steps to growing their friendship, those two little words. *And they mean progress!* He shook out the blanket, folded it, and carried it to the porch. They greeted Abe and Esther, who sat in oak rocking chairs.

"Danki for the delicious meal and the hospitality, Esther." He extended his hand to Abe. "I'm grateful for our talk earlier."

Esther gave him a mischievous grin. "Don't be a stranger. You're wilkom here anytime." She winked. "If you let me know when you're kumming ahead of time, I'll make sure I invite Liza."

Abe shook his head. "Get used to it, Liza. Your schweschder is never going to stop trying to marry you off." He winked at Jacob. "I might help her if you consider this man."

Liza waggled her finger. "You two stop right now. You're embarrassing us both."

Jacob laughed with Esther and Abe. Liza raised her hands in exasperation.

Ellie and Hannah joined them outside. Ellie wrinkled her nose. "What's so funny?"

Esther circled around Liza and hugged Ellie. "Just having a good time. I expect you to stop by often. Understood?"

Hannah said, "I've already made plans with her to quilt after we close the bakery tomorrow."

Jacob wilkomed Hannah and Ellie's friendship, but should he punish her misbehavior by taking away time with Hannah? Something she enjoyed? On the other hand, Hannah's example of honoring her parents and God was what Ellie needed. He'd discuss her impoliteness earlier on the way home and not chastise her in front of them. "Danki, Hannah. Quilting is not something I can teach her."

Ellie rolled her eyes, her usual reaction. He abhorred it.

He and Ellie bid them farewell, untied their horse and buggy, and left.

The horse trotted at a comfortable pace. Jacob wanted time to address Ellie's comment at supper. "I'm disappointed in you, Ellie. This family has gone out of their way to befriend us and your belligerent remarks threaten to destroy it. Why?"

She stared out over the horizon. "You irritate me with your puppy-dog eyes admiring Liza. I want her to know if she even sneezes in your direction, I won't make it easy for her. If you pursue her and marry again, I'll lose you too. I don't want another mamm."

"Ellie, a fraa for me would also be at least a friend to you no matter what woman I might choose to marry someday. We would be a family."

"I don't believe you!" She tightened her mouth in a grim line.

His head began to throb. *Control your temper.* He gripped the reins tighter. "Ellie, if I marry again, no matter who she is, you are to respect and obey her. I would not tolerate you treating her otherwise." He pulled the mare and wagon to a stop in front of the barn doors.

She huffed and jumped out of the wagon and ran inside.

He took deep breaths to calm his endless frustration.

Chapter Three

Liza greeted and served pastries to a steady flow of customers from Thursday morning to afternoon. Not an empty seat was left in the place. Hannah and Esther had baked tarts, cookies, and pies to fill the empty spots in her display cabinet. She'd never had so many visitors at once.

Hours later, Esther walked from the back room to the front door and flipped the hanging sign to "Closed." She patted her apron. Puffs of flour decorated the air. "I don't have a clean spot left on this apron." She chuckled. "We haven't had a crowd passing through town like the one we had today for a long time. I did manage to bake enough treats for tomorrow."

Jacob and Ellie came in. "Good afternoon. Ellie and I were in town, and I brought her here to meet Hannah. They had planned to quilt. Do you mind taking her home with you?"

Esther chuckled. "I'm glad I forgot to lock the door and that you ignored the 'Closed' sign. I wouldn't want to miss seeing you or Ellie."

"Danki, Esther. I caught a glance of Liza in the window, so I knew she was still here." Jacob grinned.

Liza gazed at him. Each time she encountered him, her

heart raced. His eyes danced and his smile beamed. He couldn't hide his emotion if he tried. He could've easily dropped Ellie off at Hannah's later. He must've stopped here to chat with her. She couldn't deny she was happy he was here. *Think friendship. He has difficulties with his dochder.* Marriage scared Liza. Her head hurt with this back and forth.

She'd take things slow with him. "We'll take her home with us." She passed Jacob and Ellie oatmeal cookies. "Hannah's in the back, Ellie."

"Danki." Ellie skipped to the back room.

Esther followed her. "Pleased you stopped in, Jacob." She touched Liza's back on her way to the kitchen. "I'll tidy up in the back. You take a break."

Jacob pulled out a chair for Liza. "Talk with me for a bit."

She sat and yawned, covering her mouth. "I'm sorry for my rude yawn. We've had a long day."

"Ellie and I had to weave through the crowd on the boardwalk to get in and out of stores this afternoon. The town is bustling with activity." He leaned in and crossed his arms on the table. "I had an enjoyable time with you at Esther and Abe's last night. Danki for opening up to me. You're easy to talk to, and I'm not always the best at communicating."

She cocked her head. "I'm astonished. You share your thoughts with ease and I'm relaxed with you. I have a difficult time sharing things about the life Paul and I had together. Your gentle and nonjudgmental demeanor made it easier."

Esther, Hannah, and Ellie joined them.

Liza straightened her back. Her cheeks heated, as if she'd done something wrong. The special moment was broken. *Our attraction and conversation is getting too personal anyway.* She needed to back off a bit.

She stood and wrapped a loaf of apple bread. "Jacob, take this home and butter it for supper."

He accepted the package. "Danki, I appreciate it. I should go."

Esther herded the girls to the door. "Let's go home, everyone."

Jacob followed the women out and escorted them to their buggy at the livery. He paid the liveryman. "What time should I pick up Ellie?"

Esther shielded her eyes from the sun. "Would you like to kumme for supper?"

"I would, but I've got to finish shopping in town then head home to do chores."

"I'll bring her home a little after supper." Liza grinned.

"Danki. I'll look forward to it." He winked and headed for the hardware store.

Her face heated and she waved. The women bid him farewell.

Liza couldn't help herself. The man had woven his way into her life quickly, and she was enjoying him. No matter how hard she tried, she couldn't shake the giddy feeling she had around him. She had grown comfortable with Jacob in a very short time, but she must keep herself in check. Her marriage to Paul had been hasty. She wouldn't make the same mistake twice.

She glanced back at Hannah and Ellie. The bag in Ellie's hand puzzled her. A printed piece of material with a button peeked out of the bag. Was it an Englischer blouse or dress? Maybe she planned to show the fabric to Hannah and use it for a quilt. It made her uneasy. She didn't want to ask and be nosy. She'd wait until later, and maybe Ellie would show them what was in it.

Esther nudged her. "My dochder and Ellie are prattling away in the back. You'd think they'd known each other all their lives."

"I'm glad they're getting close, but I'm a little uneasy considering Ellie's past and present interest in the outside world."

"Hannah loves Charm and the Amish life. A hurricane couldn't budge her. Her faith in God could move mountains. I'm not worried." She rolled her shoulders back. "I'm stiff. I didn't get many chances to sit today. We had to bake extra tarts and pies for your display cabinet and still have enough to start the morning tomorrow. I'm fixing beef stew. I have leftovers in the icebox for an easy supper. Would you like to join us? It will give you a chance to spend time around Ellie."

Liza was determined to find out the contents of Ellie's bag. Esther trusted everyone to a fault. She didn't want Ellie to put Hannah in an uncomfortable position, bringing strife to her life. She worried also that Ellie might tarnish Hannah's reputation through her association with her. Liza would blame herself if that happened. "I would like to join you."

"Good. You can slice the bread for me." She pointed. "Mae Chupp is talking to Abe on the porch. Wonder if anything is wrong?" She tilted her head. "Her little boy, Peter, is with her. I can't believe he's five. I remember the day he was born. I wish she'd remarry. She needs a loving husband and Peter needs a devoted daed."

Liza could understand why Mae hadn't married. Her husband had dropped dead in the post office one afternoon three years ago. He'd never smiled and hardly said a word at church or when she'd observed him at the bakery. Mae had walked a few feet behind him each time she ran into the couple. The woman hung her head and frowned in the presence of her husband. It had always bothered Liza and, given her past with Paul, she'd assumed her friend also suffered from a bad marriage. She empathized with Mae.

She admired the widow. Her dochder, Naomi, had died two years ago. The girl had experienced terrible pain in her lower abdomen, gotten a fever, and passed two days later. The doctor couldn't pin down a diagnosis. Liza was sure it would break the woman, but she'd persevered with courage and strength to raise her son.

"He's adorable. He won't mutter more than a word or two when I talk to him since his schweschder passed. Let's find out why they're here."

The women went to greet their visitor.

Peter ran to Ellie and hugged her legs. He looked at her with his big brown eyes. "You remind me of my schweschder, Naomi."

Mae and the other women gasped.

Ellie knelt before him and put her hands on his shoulders. "Is she with you?" She scanned the yard.

"No, she died. I wish I could have her with me again. Mamm says she's in Heaven with God."

Ellie blushed. "I'm sorry, Peter."

"She did puzzles with me. Do you have any puzzles here? Would you play with me?"

Hannah knelt beside Ellie. "I've got some stowed in a trunk in the barn. They were mine when I was little. Let's go sort through them."

Peter took Ellie's hand in his. "Mamm, is it all right if I go with them?"

Mae wiped the tears staining her cheeks. "Jah, you can go." She dabbed her eyes with her fingertips. "He hasn't spoken in sentences since Naomi left this earth. Ellie does resemble my dochder quite a bit."

Liza hooked her arm through Mae's. "Hannah and Ellie will entertain him. Kumme inside with us. You and Peter stay for supper. I won't have it any other way."

"Absolutely. I've got more food than I needed to prepare.

Please join us." Esther stepped onto the porch. "Abe, my handsome man, how are you?"

"Had a satisfying day, but I'm hungry." Abe gave Esther a warm smile and flopped in a rocker on the porch.

"Supper will be ready earlier than usual. I'm making leftover stew." Esther waved them inside.

Mae coughed and covered her mouth. "I don't want to trouble you."

"It's no trouble, and I enjoy having a big crowd at my table. To see little Peter smile brightens my day." Esther reached over and patted Mae's shoulder.

Liza winced. The woman's deep cough concerned her. "Sit and relax. Take advantage of Ellie helping Peter to open up. He's content. Let's let him get better acquainted with her." She rested her hand on Mae's arm. She poured Mae a glass of water and passed it to her.

Mae sipped the water, then held the glass. "This cough kummes in spurts. I'm sure it's nothing. Let me do something."

Liza and Esther pulled plates and dishes out of the cupboard and set them on the counter. Liza handed her utensils. "You can set the table." Maybe Mae was right and she was making too much of the woman's cough.

Knife in her hand, Liza paused. "I'll cut the bread."

Esther checked the stove. "Abe has wood burning in the cook stove. I'll put the stew on."

Half an hour later, Liza called everyone to the table.

"I want to sit by Hannah and Ellie." Peter raced to an empty chair.

Abe stuck his bottom lip out for a moment. "I wanted to sit by you, Peter."

Peter looked at him. "Don't be sad. I'll sit by you."

He tousled the boy's thick brown hair. "I'm teasing you. You sit with your new friends."

Esther pulled out a chair for him and put a pillow on it. "There you go." She sat and bowed her head.

Abe prayed and thanked God for the food.

Peter grinned from ear to ear. "Ellie and Hannah had puzzles with pieces shaped like bears, rabbits, and goats. We raced to put the pieces in the holes and I won!"

Mae beamed. "Maybe now you can work your puzzles at home."

"They remind me of Naomi." Peter's eyes clouded. He sucked in his bottom lip, forked a bite of beef, and was silent.

Ellie drank her water and set the glass on the table. "Peter, what do you like to do when you're not doing chores?"

"I've been too sad to do much of anything since Naomi went to Heaven. It's no fun playing without her. We used to go fishin'. She put the worms on my hook. I'm too scared to do it. We played catch, or we dipped our feet in the water in the pond. She baked cookies and we made sandwiches together and had picnics." He lowered his eyes, then hung his head.

Ellie lifted his chin. "If it's all right with your mamm, I'll take you fishing, and we can stick our feet in the pond on a nice warm day. I might even bring some of Liza's molasses cookies to share. She made a new recipe for them and they're delicious!"

"You will?"

"Of course."

"Mamm, did you hear what Ellie said?"

"I did. We'd be glad to have you over, Ellie. Danki."

Ellie put her hand on Hannah's arm. "We must include Hannah."

"Jah, Hannah, will you kumme too?"

"Jah, I'd love to."

Esther sighed. "I had one too many slices of bread."

She carried a stack of dishes to the dry sink. "Ellie and Hannah, you take Peter and go play. His mamm, Liza, and I will wash and dry the dishes."

Abe excused himself and followed Peter and the girls out of the kitchen.

Mae pressed a hand to her chin. "I'm amazed at how he reacted to Ellie. He bubbled over with enthusiasm around her. He was chatty at supper. I can't remember the last time he was this happy."

Liza held her close. The woman wept in her arms. "You've had a hard time. First your husband passing, then your dochder. I admire your strength getting through it all."

Mae dried her wet cheeks. "I shouldn't spill my emotions out on you. Danki for being so tolerant."

Liza beamed. "We're happy for you and Peter. It's been wonderful to watch him with Ellie."

"Indeed." Esther grinned.

Mae cleared her throat. "I came here to ask if either of you had any suggestions for a young woman to watch Peter for me Monday through Friday from eight until two. I've been offered a job at the front desk of Maybelle's Inn. The sewing I take in and my crops aren't a steady enough income to count on for unexpected expenses. This will be money I can count on." She pressed a hand to her chest and coughed.

Liza handed her a clean handkerchief. "Would you like lemonade instead of water?"

She waved a dismissive hand and shook her head. "Danki. I'll be fine."

Esther lifted a basin off a hook. "Ellie might be available."

Could she be trusted? Liza wasn't certain. Peter, impressionable and young, didn't need any outside-world influences in his life. Ellie boasted and spoke without reservation about the things she liked that Englischers used but the Amish avoided. She didn't use discretion. She'd left the Amish life once. Would she again? It would break this child's heart. He'd suffered enough hurt. "We should ask Jacob's permission. I'd rather approach him before we mention it to Ellie."

Mae winced. "Leah said Ellie had a blemished reputation in Nappanee. She left, then returned."

Esther balanced the basin on her hip. "I don't condone Ellie leaving her Amish life, but she's young. Point being, she did return home. Caring for Peter would give her purpose and help her grow roots in this community. She's having a positive influence on Peter. He needs her. Give her a chance." She headed for the back door. "I'm going to get water for the washbasin."

Esther didn't analyze or compare the negatives and positives. Liza couldn't help it. She did most often. Envious of Esther's simple and straightforward way of arriving at conclusions without hesitation, Liza wished she was more like her. "She did run away, but she's back living the Amish life."

"Do you think she'll stray again?"

"We can't be sure. We're doing everything to inspire her to choose to stay in our community and adhere to our way of life."

"No one has been able to reach Peter before. He's enthralled with her. I'll hire her with her daed's permission. Would you ask him for me? I take it you know him because you've befriended Ellie."

"I'll speak to him about it when I take her home, and then I'll let you know what he says."

"Danki."

The women washed and dried the dishes and chatted. They bid Mae and Peter farewell. Hannah and Ellie went to Hannah's bedroom.

Liza plopped in a chair at the table, and Esther dragged one close to her.

Esther removed her shoes and propped her feet up on the chair beside her. "I wonder if Jacob will agree to Ellie taking care of Peter."

"It's hard to say. Ellie's unpredictable. Should he take a chance Ellie's caring for Peter might teach her responsibility or does he choose to wait until she's got her feet more firmly planted in Charm and matured?"

"Liza, you overthink things. Mae needs Ellie to take care of Peter to lift his mood. She's the only one who has brought a smile to his precious face in a long time. Maybe they need each other. It's worth the risk." Esther rose. "I need to make a trip to the outhaus. I'll be right back."

Liza went to Hannah's room. Printed button-down ankle-length dresses lay strewn on the bed. She backed out of the doorway and peeked around the corner. They had their backs to her, and she hoped they wouldn't turn around. The bag Ellie had brought lay open. She held a calico fitted round-collared dress to her body and twirled around. The tiny buttons went from top to bottom. "Isn't it beautiful?" She shoved it toward Hannah. "Try it on."

Hannah passed it back to her. "I'm not interested in these clothes. Please put them away, Ellie. I have no use for them, and you shouldn't either."

"Amish rules are ridiculous. No buttons, no printed clothing, no decorated straw hats, and no fun. What harm is there in adding a little color to our lives?"

"You know why. The Ordnung is for our protection. If we allow one thing, it will lead to another and another. Where would it end? Before you know it, we'd no longer be any different from the outside world. We don't need showy clothing or modern conveniences. God provides all we need."

"Blah, blah, blah. I've heard it all my life. You don't

understand what the outside world is all about because you haven't explored it. It's full of wonder, with men and women wearing fancy clothes, hats, and shoes. Piano music is beautiful when it vibrates in your chest. You want to tap your foot and sing along. I took a ride in a motor-car. It was fun! I could go on and on."

"I don't desire any of it. I'm happy here. You can be too, if you trust God and have faith He has a plan for your life."

Ellie flopped on the bed. "I do love God, but I can love Him in the outside world too. I'm torn between Amish life and the outside world. I find security and comfort here, but I enjoyed all the things I mentioned while living as an Englischer." She heaved a big sigh. "You're a good friend to me, Hannah. I don't want to upset you." She pushed herself up and put the clothing back in the bag. "I won't bring them here again."

"Ellie, please talk to me about anything on your mind, but understand, I'm firm in my faith in God and in living in this community. I won't be swayed to think otherwise."

"Understood. I respect the choices you've made. I'm not quite sure where I'll end up yet."

"I'm going to do my best to persuade you to stay. I like having you around. We never did stitch anything. Maybe we can get together again?"

"You can count on it."

Liza entered the small bedroom. "Ellie, are you ready to go? I should get you home." She wouldn't broach the subject of the clothes. Hannah had spoken her mind and been straightforward. Proud of her niece, she smiled.

Ellie grabbed her bag. "I'm ready."

Hannah followed them to the front door. "I'll walk with you to the buggy."

Esther kissed Liza's and Ellie's cheeks before they left.

"Good night, Ellie. Don't be a stranger." She waved to Liza. "We'll be ready in the morning for you to pick us up."

Liza nodded and got in the buggy. She waited for Ellie and then flicked the reins. "Peter hasn't spoken much since Naomi died. His enthusiastic response to you stunned us."

"Hannah told me about Naomi and her daed both passing so close together. Poor Mrs. Chupp. Peter is a smart little boy and full of energy. He made me wish I had a little bruder."

Was Esther right? Did Ellie need Peter as much as he needed her? She was curious what Jacob would have to say on the matter. "Mae bubbled over with joy at your interactions with her son. You brought hope and happiness to her life amid all her grief. You jumped in and took Peter under your wing. You could've ignored him."

"I love kinner. I hope to have girls and boys of my own someday. Peter is a darling child, and so full of wonder."

Liza arrived at the Grabers' haus.

Jacob greeted her. "Danki for bringing Ellie home. Please join me on the porch for a cup of coffee. I have it warming on the stove."

As she followed him to the chairs, she admired the freshly painted white haus and the straight two-story white barn and fresh vegetable garden planted in neat rows. The light evening breeze rippled the spring-fed pond's water over several large field rocks. His haus and farm painted a telling picture of a man who cared for his land. Two muscular black horses grazed in the field nearby.

She met his deep brown gaze. "I'll take half a cup. Danki."

Ellie skipped up the steps. "I'll go get it."

"I picked up some lemon drops for you in town, Ellie. They're on the counter."

"Yum. I appreciate it, Daed."

She went inside and quickly returned. She handed them each a mug. "Here you go. I'll be inside."

Jacob sipped his coffee and then balanced the mug on his knee. "Ellie's in a chipper mood. Did she behave?"

Liza shrugged and cocked her head. "I checked on them once while they were in Hannah's room. They didn't notice I was there, and after I listened for a bit, I quietly slipped back to the kitchen." She stared at her coffee. "Ellie brought over a bag of Englischer clothes and showed them to Hannah. The garments were spread on the bed."

He put his head back and closed his eyes for a moment, then focused on her. "I had no idea she had them. I didn't even think to ask what was in the bag she brought with her. I'll make sure she gets rid of them. I'm sorry. I don't understand why she won't stop talking about her fascination for worldly things. I'm taken aback you didn't scold her."

She didn't know what she'd do if she had a stubborn and obstinate dochder like Ellie. Jacob was doing the best he could for her and Ellie stomped on his heart over and over. She watched her struggle to choose which life to live. She suspected deep pain over the passing of her mamm had sent her into a whirlwind of turmoil and uncertainty. She hoped she and Hannah would succeed in assuring Ellie they were there for her. "I overheard Hannah say she wouldn't be swayed by Ellie's attraction to what the outside world has to offer. She made it clear she would like Ellie's friendship and hoped she would choose Amish life. Your dochder respected Hannah's position and put the clothes in the bag. I didn't need to intervene."

"Hannah is a wise soul for a young woman. You must be so proud of her. I'm grateful for her patience and willingness to befriend Ellie under the circumstances."

"She's got a soft heart but a strong determination. She has no problem standing up for what she believes in, and she's a loyal friend to those she loves. I am very proud of her." She held the handle of the mug and balanced it on the arm of the chair. "Ellie is a beautiful and smart young woman. God has a plan for her life. She'll find her way. We must have patience and keep her in our prayers."

"She wears me out with her up-and-down moods. I get glimpses of the obedient and sweet girl I raised, then her outbursts pierce my heart and scare me about what lies ahead for her if she leaves me and her Amish life again."

Her breath caught. His anguish lingered in his eyes and voice. It sent a stream of sorrow through her. She cared about him and couldn't bear to watch him suffer. She had to discuss Mae's request for Ellie to take care of Peter with him. Would he have the same reservations as her about the job? "I have some news. Mae Chupp joined us for supper at Esther's. She's a widow who lost her husband and her dochder, Naomi, quite close together. She has Peter, a young boy. He hasn't spoken much since Naomi's death. Ellie and Naomi have close to the same appearance. When Peter met her, he smiled and opened up to her. They talked and he beamed at her. It stunned us and was a wonderful sight to behold. Mae couldn't believe it. Ellie took him under her wing, talked to him, and played with him."

"What a tragic story about Mrs. Chupp suffering the loss of her husband and dochder. I'm thankful Ellie was wilkoming to Peter and has given his mamm hope he'll heal over the passing of his schweschder. Ellie's always been good with kinner. Is there anything I can do to make Mrs. Chupp's life easier?"

"She asked if I'd talk to you about Ellie watching Peter Monday through Friday from eight to two, while she works at Maybelle's Inn. She wasn't comfortable approaching you herself because she hadn't officially met you. She did say she'd pay Ellie."

"Did you or she mention this to Ellie?"

She shook her head. "I told Mae I wanted to discuss the offer with you first."

"Do you have reservations about it?"

She shifted in her seat and cleared her throat. This was his *dochder*. It was probably all right for him to have misgivings about her, but would he be open to her concerns? She didn't want to insult him or Ellie. She wanted what was best for both of them. To protect them from a potential problem if Ellie were to disappoint Mae or her son, considering her loose tongue about what the world had to offer.

"Mae is thrilled with Peter's openness with Ellie. She's hopeful he'll improve the more time he spends with her. Ellie enjoyed him too. I'm torn. They could both benefit. Ellie could mature and learn by caring for Peter." She paused and bit her bottom lip, then raised her eyes to meet his gaze.

"But . . . ?"

"She might be a bad influence if she shares her wonder about the outside world. He's impressionable." She may as well tell him her main concern. "I'm worried she'll leave and break his heart." She stole a glance at him.

His mouth in a grim line, he dropped his head to his chest.

Oh no. She'd hurt his feelings. Why hadn't she kept her opinion to herself? It wasn't worth ruining their friendship. She should've presented the offer and not expressed her point of view.

Jacob switched his gaze to the tall white barn. "I understand your concerns, but she's got someone who needs her. We all want to be needed. Peter is offering her unconditional love by choosing her to help him move on from his schweschder's passing. Not something you or I could do. I trust her with him. I'll discuss this with her."

She stiffened. He'd kept his voice serious. Had she overstepped her bounds? Her chest tightened. Opening up to him about Paul had been a relief and a surprise. She'd trusted him with her secrets about her past. He had a gentle but strong way about him that she found attractive.

Drawn to him, she was afraid of being hurt or pulled into a stressful situation between him and his dochder. A friendship was comfortable, but a future with him as something more seemed bleak. She'd have to tamp down her emotions. *Friendship, nothing more.* A friendship she didn't want to tarnish. "I understand and respect your position. It would be a shame to keep them apart. They make each other happy. Their instant connection was beautiful to behold."

His gaze drifted back to hers. "Liza, I'm relieved you're not fighting me on this. I could use a bit of encouraging news concerning Ellie. I'm confident Peter will enhance Ellie's life. He will show her love and wonder through his eyes, and she can nurture and enjoy him at the same time."

Maybe he was right. She'd put her doubts aside.

Ellie came outside onto the porch and joined them.

Jacob told her Mae's proposition.

She clapped her hands to her cheeks. "Please let me do this, Daed. Peter's a charming child. I'd love taking care of him."

Liza swallowed the worry that Ellie might flee the Amish life one day and scar Peter. She had to admit no one had succeeded in breaking through the barrier he'd put up since Naomi's funeral. "Peter does respond to you, Ellie. Your cheerful response to him encouraged him to discover his voice and laugh, and his eyes to sparkle. Priceless gifts for his mamm."

She noticed Jacob's warm smile toward her. Her stomach leaped with bliss. She didn't want to cause turmoil for him but rather to encourage him. She had to stop overanalyzing everything.

Jacob touched Ellie's cheek. "I'm proud of you." He leaned forward in his chair. "You're taking on a big responsibility. This child chose not to speak due to his heartbreak over his schweschder's passing. If you hadn't kumme along, he may never have broken out of this shell. You must be careful with his tender heart. Another loss of someone he loves would do irreparable damage."

Ellie sucked in a breath and clasped her hands tight. "I will take good care of him."

Liza didn't miss the nervous tension in Ellie's eyes or her white knuckles. She suspected a battle raged inside her to accept the job but afraid to make promises for the future. She'd pray Peter and Ellie would form a healthy friendship to fill a void in both their souls. "It's settled, then. I'll tell Mae you've accepted the job. Kumme to supper at my haus Saturday night around six. I'll invite her, Peter, and my family. You can get acquainted with the widow and her son and work out the details of Ellie's new job."

Ellie relaxed. "Danki, Liza." She shifted toward her daed. "You'll love Peter. He's obedient and you never know what he's going to say. He's so genuine."

"I'm sure I will find meeting him a pleasure." He winced. "Liza, I don't want to add work to your already busy schedule. Ellie and I can rustle up something here to serve for supper."

She waved a dismissive hand. "I have venison in the

icebox, and Esther will bring some of her vegetables. I'm happy to cook."

Ellie chuckled. "Your food will taste much better than anything we could put together. I'm relieved you're willing to have us over."

"Good. I'll stop by Mae's on the way home, invite her to supper, and tell her the good news." She stood. "I should be on my way."

Ellie waved. "Danki, Liza." She went inside.

Jacob accompanied her to the buggy. "You've been so kind to include Ellie and me in your family and social gatherings. Now you're acquainting us with Mrs. Chupp and her son. You're an amazing woman, Liza Schrock. I'm glad I've met you."

Touching her warm cheeks, she gave him a shy smile. "I'd like you and Ellie to feel wilkom in this community. I want to do all I can to help." It was much more of a personal mission for her, and her heart sang a different tune. Friendship had blossomed between them, and an attraction she'd never experienced for a man before. An attraction she couldn't shake.

She bid him farewell and headed to Mae's haus. She arrived and knocked on the door.

Mae swung open the door. "I'm stunned to find you on my doorstep at this time of day. Is anything wrong? Please kumme in."

"Danki, but I need to get back home. I just need a minute of your time. I delivered Ellie home and asked Jacob Graber about Ellie watching Peter. She's excited and her daed has given his permission. I've invited the Grabers and my family to supper at my haus on Saturday night to meet you and Peter and work out the details. It's short notice, I know. Does this fit into your schedule?"

"Oh, we'd be delighted to join you. How generous of you, Liza. Danki. Peter is in bed asleep or he'd be squeezing past me to greet you. He's talked nonstop about Ellie since meeting her. It's a drastic change, and a wonderful one. I'm glad she's agreed to care for him."

"Kumme over at about six on Saturday."

"We will. Danki again."

Liza got in the buggy and went home. The day had been productive, and she'd witnessed Peter speaking more freely again, Ellie connecting with the child, and Jacob being receptive to her concerns but taking a stand for his dochder. A position she respected. He spoke his mind but in a kind and compassionate way. She didn't take offense at his defending Ellie but rather admired him for it.

Friday, she'd have the evening to get her haus in order to prepare for her company kumming on Saturday. She'd have every chair occupied at her long oak table by people she cared about, and she'd learn more about Jacob Graber. What did it all mean? She wasn't sure, but she'd be curious to find out.

Chapter Four

Jacob glanced at the early morning dawn from the window Saturday morning and drank the last of his milk. His muscles ached from chopping up the two large oak trees on Friday.

Ellie came in with a fresh pot of water. "I'll wash the dishes, then mop the floors. I'm eager to go to Liza's this evening to finalize the plans for caring for Peter. I'll earn money and have fun doing the job."

"We should discuss your taking on this responsibility first." He pulled out the chair for her. "Please sit."

Her eyes wide with worry, she took slow steps and sat. "Please don't change your mind, Daed. You can trust me. I'll take excellent care of Peter."

"I don't doubt you will be a loyal nanny, but I'm concerned you may entice Peter to wonder about the outside world. It would be wrong for you to advertise the outside world in a positive light or as an option to Peter or anyone in this community. You need to put an end to this kind of conversation. Understood?"

Her mouth in a tight line, she shook her head. "I won't impress upon Peter my opinions of the outside world, but I will discuss it with Hannah and my friends." She went to the sink and poured the now-warm water she'd left on the stove before supper into the washbasin.

"Ellie, this conversation isn't over. Please return to the table."

She rolled her eyes. "What now?" She took a seat.

"Watch your tone, young lady." He crossed his arms against his chest. "Where is the bag you took to Hannah's?"

Her eyes narrowed. "In my bedroom."

"Go get it."

She went to her room, came back, and dropped the bag on the table. "These are personal. I'd rather not show them to you."

"Open it."

She narrowed her eyes and spread the bag wide open. "You didn't say a word when we were in the buggy on our way to Hannah's. Why now?"

"Why do you have these clothes and why did you take them to Hannah's?" He didn't want to betray Liza's confidence. He should've found out what was in the bag before they ever left home to go to supper at Liza's.

"I thought she might like them. She didn't and asked me to put them away. I abided by her wishes and I won't bring them to her again."

He stood. "I'm getting rid of them. You are well aware how inappropriate these garments are, and it's a disgrace for you to have them in this haus. I'm angry you put Hannah in an uncomfortable position. She's been nothing but gracious to you." He grabbed the bag, found a small box of matches, and went outside.

She hurried after him. "Please, Daed, don't burn them. Hannah and I came to an understanding. I haven't destroyed our friendship. Please, Daed, don't ruin them."

He went to the burn barrel, threw them in, lit a match, and dropped it on top of the pile. "Don't bring another thing in this haus you know doesn't belong."

She scowled, strode across the lawn with stiff arms and long strides, and then went inside the haus.

He mucked the stalls, worked in the fields and garden, and went inside a few hours later. The Englischer garments Ellie had in her bag were another reminder she might leave him again. She'd shown an attachment to them. The precious little girl had grown up and tested his patience often. To protect her had been his goal, but if she left, he would be powerless to keep her safe. Fear riveted through him.

He found her stitching a hole in one of his socks. He knelt beside her. "Ellie, I dread our hard conversations. The outside world is full of danger as well as wonder. You are important to me. As your daed, I want to shield you from harm. I love you. God loves you. He has a plan for your life if you'll listen to Him. Scriptures will guide you to what's right. Save yourself heartache, submit your life to Him, and stay and make this Amish community your home. You've made good friends. Hannah's family and Peter love you. You are happy around them. Give Charm a chance."

She went to the window and crossed her arms. "I'm torn. Hannah is a wise and true friend, even though we've only known each other for a short time. I trust her, and she truly cares about me, as I do her. Peter is a child who needs me and accepts me. You mean the world to me. I don't want to leave any of you, but I'm not sure the simple life is for me. I yearn for the modern conveniences, music, and clothing."

His chest ached at the words kumming out of her mouth. "You've gotten a taste of the forbidden. Please don't leave. It would break my heart." He grabbed his straw hat and went outside. The sun warmed his damp cheeks. He loved her so much. The sense of helplessness enveloping him overwhelmed him. He went to the barn and knelt by a bale of hay. "Dear Heavenly Father, forgive me for my sins. Danki for Your blessings. Please change Ellie's heart so she wants the Amish life without a doubt. I can't bear to lose her. Help me to say the right words and act in the way You would have me do. Amen."

He snatched a rag from the shelf and wiped beads of sweat from his forehead. Ellie scared him with her contrary nature. She would never be happy until she came to grips with a clear direction, centering on God's will for her life. She was letting materialistic and worldly things cloud her thinking. What a blessing to have met Liza and her family. They provided such an exemplary picture of a happy Amish lifestyle, friendship, and strong faith in God for Ellie and for him.

He strolled outside and scanned the property, then threw himself into hard labor. He rid the garden of weeds and replaced weathered fence posts and the latch on the corral. Hours later, he'd finished tending to the animals and walked over to the pump and ducked his head under the water to cool off.

Ellie carried out a clean towel and a biscuit for him. "Here's a rag for your wet face and a biscuit to hold you over. You missed dinner. We'll be going to supper at Liza's in an hour." She gazed across the meadow next to their place. "I love you, Daed."

Before he could respond, she hurried inside. Her love for him wasn't the issue. Miles wouldn't change her love for him or his for her. She didn't realize how agonizing it was for him to watch her suffer or make mistakes. One day, if Ellie had kinner, she would have a much clearer picture of what he was going through with her mood changes and indecisiveness about her life. He devoured his biscuit, filled the water and feed buckets for the animals, stowed his tools, and walked inside to his favorite chair.

Jacob fell asleep. He woke and jerked upright. How long had he been snoozing? He glanced at the clock. *An hour.* "Ellie, are you getting ready to go to Liza's? The last hour got away from me. I'll wash up and we'll be on our way."

Meeting him in the hallway, Ellie winced. "I'm ready. Sorry. I should've reminded you."

"No harm done. I'll hurry."

His dochder had a beaming smile on her face. He suspected her new friends, Hannah and the little boy, Peter, were responsible for her good mood. Liza was the reason for his excitement at going to supper. He washed, dried, and redressed.

Heading for the door, he heaved a big breath. "Let's go, Ellie!" He pushed open the door and a big smile spread across his face. She had readied the horse and buggy.

"I need one more minute. You go ahead and get in." True to her word, she finished securing the horse to the harness and jumped in beside him. "I intend to make a good impression on Mrs. Chupp. I don't mind earning a bit of money."

He patted her knee. "I'm sure Mrs. Chupp will be happy to have you care for Peter. He's attached to you, and he'll be your best supporter in encouraging her to hire you."

"I wish I had a little bruder."

He opened his mouth, then shut it. Telling her now that she might one day didn't seem right. Her objections to his remarrying might stir up an argument and ruin the evening. He stifled a chuckle at the thought that he was already contemplating any kind of a future with Liza. They barely knew each other, but it seemed as if they'd met years ago. They'd shared their pasts, they'd discussed issues with Ellie, and she'd helped him more with his troubles than anyone. He had to pursue her with patience. She'd been hurt by her husband, and if he pushed too hard, she might turn away from him. The thought jarred him. "Peter can fill in as your little bruder for now."

"Jah. I'm anxious to play with him and talk to Hannah again. She and I can differ in opinions without letting them interfere with our friendship. It's why I feel close to her."

He was optimistic about Ellie staying in Charm. Why would she leave if she had a job she enjoyed and Hannah, her close friend? It was important to him to strengthen his relationship with his dochder. He had moments, such as these, where he thought he'd succeeded in accomplishing this goal, but doubt crept in. She kept him guessing, that was for sure. He pulled up in front of Liza's, jumped out, and secured the horse.

Liza greeted them at the door. "Ellie, Peter and Hannah are in the side yard tossing a ball. I'll help Esther. You go join them."

"Danki, Liza." Ellie scurried off.

"You are lovely, as always." He met her beautiful blue eyes.

Her cheeks pinked. "You flatter me." She stepped out. "Why don't you sit in the rocker on the porch? Abe should be here anytime. Esther and Mae are in the kitchen helping me. May I bring you something to drink?"

He shook his head. "Danki, but I'll wait until supper." He settled in the rocker, then stood when Mrs. Chupp and Esther came to the door and stepped outside to join them.

Esther wiped her hands on a towel. "Jacob, good, you're here. Meet Mae Chupp."

"I'm Jacob Graber. Pleasure to meet you, Mrs. Chupp."

"Call me Mae. Mrs. Chupp is too formal. I told Esther, Liza, and the girls to do the same."

"Only if you'll call me Jacob."

"Agreed, Jacob."

Esther clutched the towel to her chest. "Oh no, I'd better check on the bread in the oven. It's been in too long." She ran to the kitchen and Mae bustled after her.

"There's Abe. I should get back to cooking. You and Abe relax." Liza grinned at Jacob.

"Don't worry about Abe and me. If you need anything, please ask. I'm happy to help."

"Danki." She went to join the women.

Jacob stepped off the porch and helped Abe with his horse. He slapped Abe's back. "How are you?"

"A little worn out but can't complain." He gazed at the kinner. A smile crossed his lips. "Ellie, Hannah, and Peter are having a jolly time. Their laughter is infectious."

"It springs hope in me to have her happy here. My conversations with her are still worrisome. She won't make up her mind to stay in Charm. It pains me to think of her making a life in the world. I pray she'll grow closer to God and choose an Amish life."

"Sometimes hard lessons are learned to steer us in the right direction for our lives. Ellie may stray, but God can still rein her back to Him and to the Amish life."

"I'm bothered she'll live in the world and encounter men with bad intentions or harm will kumme to her."

"Don't fret about the future. Trust God to take care of her. In the meantime, do all you can to guide her to choose the right path."

"Abe, danki for allowing me to discuss my problems with you. Sometimes you need to talk to another man about these things."

The man didn't judge him or dictate what he should do. He listened and gave him sound advice. Abe had a gleam in his eye anytime he had his eye on Hannah,

Esther, and Liza. He loved and cared for them deeply. The man was approachable, kind, and considerate.

"Anytime, friend. And I still say you need to consider Liza for a fraa." He beamed.

Jacob smiled wide. "I am."

The kinner ran to the men. Ellie bent over to catch her breath, then put her hand on Peter's shoulder. "Daed, this is Peter. Peter, meet my daed, Jacob Graber."

Peter held out his little hand. "Happy to meet you, Mr. Graber."

"You can call me Jacob."

He clasped a hand to his lips. "Mamm may not let me."

"I'll talk to her."

The little boy stood close to Ellie, who glowed with happiness around the child. His heart thundered with hope that this little boy would have a positive impact on Ellie's life. She would learn what it was like to have someone depend on and respect her.

Peter crooked his finger for Jacob to kumme closer.

Jacob bent closer to him. "What is it?"

"Could you tell Mamm that Ellie and I will be fine when she's working? She worries too much."

Jacob gazed into the precious little boy's eyes. "I'll do my best."

Peter jumped with joy. "Danki!"

Hannah smiled. "You made a new friend, Jacob."

"I understand why you and Ellie are so enamored with Peter. He's a sweet child."

Hannah tousled Peter's hair. "He's full of energy. He's got Ellie and me wrapped around his little finger."

Abe and Jacob laughed with her.

Liza called out to them, "Time for supper. Wash your hands and kumme to the table."

The kinner raced to pick up the ball in the yard.

Jacob and Abe waited for them to wash and dry their hands, then they did the same, drying their hands on the towel hanging on a hook beside the pump. The men followed the kinner to the kitchen.

Abe came alongside a flustered Esther. "Fraa, your cheeks are red and you're in a tizzy. What can I do to help?"

She gave him a playful swat with a rag. "I'm fine, husband of mine. Have a seat. Supper's ready." She gave him a quick peck on the cheek. "You know Mae Chupp."

"Jah, Mrs. Chupp, did these women work you too hard?"

"I'm happy to help, and *please,* call me Mae."

Abe pulled out a chair and sat. "If you insist, I'll abide by your wishes." He gave an exaggerated bow of his head.

Jacob grinned and exchanged a cheerful look with Liza. He enjoyed having suppers with Liza and her family. Mae and Peter chattering away with Hannah and Ellie added more joy to the mix. He had longed for a big family, but they hadn't been blessed with more kinner. Maybe he'd marry again and they'd have kinner. He wondered if Liza desired kinner and how many. He swallowed hard. Would she consider him for more than a friend? In time, he hoped she would.

Everyone sat at the table.

Abe reached for Esther's hand. "I'll pray for the food."

Jacob waited for Abe to finish his prayer, then he scooped buttered noodles, sliced tomatoes, and shredded pork onto his plate. "You women have cooked up a storm. The aroma makes my mouth water."

Peter wiped the milk above his lip with the cloth on his lap. "Jacob, this would be a good time to tell Mamm she shouldn't worry about me while she's working."

Mae's mouth flew open. "Peter, you address him as Mr.

Graber!" She grabbed her cloth napkin and held it to her lips as she coughed.

"He said I could call him Jacob."

Jacob held up his palm to defend his little friend. "In all fairness to Peter, I did ask him to call me Jacob." He concentrated on Peter next to him. "Parents worry about their kinner. We can't help it."

Peter shrugged. "I don't know why. We're gonna be fine."

Hannah and Ellie grinned endearingly at Peter. Jacob sided with them in adoring Peter. He'd captured his heart the moment he met him.

Mae said, "If it's all right with Mr. Graber, then you may call him Jacob. And mind your attitude. Be respectful and a good boy."

Peter nodded.

"Mae, we had an agreement to go by first names. Right?" Jacob glanced around the table for support.

Everyone nodded.

Mae put her fork on her plate. "Jacob, Liza tells me you approve of Ellie watching after Peter from eight until two Monday through Friday."

Peter stared at him with puppy-dog eyes. "Please don't change your mind, Jacob."

"I have no objections. She loves kinner, and we've discussed that your mamm is entrusting her with a very important responsibility. She has assured me she understands this is a serious commitment. Right, Ellie?"

"I'll take this job very seriously." Ellie reached for her water glass.

Jacob took a sip of his water, then set his glass on the table and glanced at Mae. "Do you need help with your livestock or property?"

"It's kind of you to ask. I have plenty of help. Danki."

Esther passed Abe the meat platter. "Take another serving. I brought this for supper tonight. We've got plenty more at home, and I have enough for everyone to take a second helping."

"Don't mind if I do." Abe scooped a small serving onto his plate.

Hannah sipped her water, then set down her glass. "Mae, I've been with Ellie and Peter playing games and talking. He's happy being with her. The timing couldn't be better with you being offered the job at Maybelle's Inn and Ellie being available for Peter. It's wonderful you've offered this job to her."

Peter wrinkled his cheerful face. "Ellie and I are going to have lots of fun together."

"We'll find all kinds of things to do, but we have to do chores too."

"I'll do my part. I promise." Peter gave her a sincere smile.

"Ellie, I'm depending on you to take excellent care of my son. Leah mentioned you telling her about your experience living in the world for a period of time in the past. You mustn't give him any notions about life in the outside world and don't express views opposing any of our Amish traditions or laws."

"I understand."

Mae paused, then heaved a big breath. "Ellie, I trust you won't let me down. I'm grateful to you for doing this for Peter and me. I'll pay you at the end of each week, depending on the number of hours I work. I've been told my hours may vary a little. Never more, just less."

"I'm fine with whatever and whenever you pay me. Danki for the opportunity." Ellie's mouth spread in a wide grin.

Peter jumped up and ran to his mamm. He kissed her

cheek. "I'm so happy, Mamm. I was scared you'd change your mind." He went to Ellie and crawled up on her lap. "I can't wait for you to kumme to my haus on Monday. You can meet my pet bunny, Snuggles."

Hannah poked Ellie's arm. "You have a new job."

"You helped, and I appreciate it."

"I meant it." Hannah giggled. "You'll have Snuggles to take care of too."

"I love bunnies." Ellie chuckled.

Jacob smiled at Liza. "Danki for your involvement in bringing Ellie this job."

Liza carried empty glasses to the counter near Esther. "Esther suggested Ellie. I tend to overanalyze everything. Esther doesn't hesitate to trust people immediately and doesn't worry about the repercussions. I should adopt her way of thinking. It's healthier. I drive myself mad sometimes, overthinking things. I'm sure Ellie will do fine with Peter. Forgive me for my reservations about the arrangement."

"There's nothing to forgive. You've brought the proposition to me and it has all worked out." Jacob smiled at Esther. "Danki for suggesting Ellie to Mae."

Esther stacked the dirty dishes to make room for more. "Of course. Ellie may have her doubts about Amish life, but I'm rooting for her. She and Hannah have formed a friendship. She's part of our family and you are too."

Liza grabbed another wash pan. "I'll go outside for more water."

Esther waited until the door shut behind Liza and whispered to Jacob, "I wouldn't be opposed if you and Liza tied the knot someday in the future."

Jacob lowered his voice. "I have to take things slow with Liza. She has to overcome her fears about marriage after the way Paul treated her."

Meeting his gaze, Esther grew serious. "You've barely met and I'm pushing you to her. But I have a good feeling about you, Jacob. And there's no denying the spark between you and Liza. I shouldn't have been so outspoken, but I can't resist. Abe and I think you'd make a perfect couple. You're absolutely right in your assumption. She's skeptical about a serious relationship with a man, but you're different. I can tell by the way she smiles when she says your name. You're making progress, Jacob Graber. Keep it up."

"I aim to please." He tipped an imaginary hat. Jesting with Esther brought a grin to his face. Her impish way and outgoing personality drew him to her. Liza was blessed to have such a loving schweschder. Abe and Esther bantered, exchanged endearing expressions, and loved each other very much. It showed in their expressions and how they addressed each other. He envied them. He'd had the same relationship with his fraa, and he longed to have it again.

Liza came inside and set the pan on the stove to warm. "What are you two conspiring about over here?"

"Nothing." Esther raised her brows and smiled.

Ellie, Hannah, and Peter brought their empty dessert plates to the sink.

Peter folded his hands under his chin. "May we go outside and play?"

Mae motioned to Peter. "We have to go home right after I help with the dishes. You need to get to bed early. It's been a long day for you." She coughed.

Liza carried more dishes to the counter. "Mae, I have plenty of help. You take Peter home."

Mae reached for Peter's hand. "Ellie, will you kumme at seven Monday morning so I can give you instructions?"

"Jah. I'll be on time."

"If you're sure my help isn't needed, I will take Peter home."

Liza smiled. "Danki for kumming. I enjoyed your company."

Jacob watched Liza. She was the perfect hostess, and so gracious. She'd wilkomed him and Ellie into her life, and she'd been warm and friendly to Mae and Peter. He'd noticed she greeted and served her customers with the same kindhearted manner.

Everyone bid the Chupps a cheerful farewell.

The women walked them outside.

Abe waved Jacob to join him in the front room. "Let's get out of the women's way before they put us to work."

"You don't have to tell me twice." He winked at Liza, then followed Abe. He'd gotten comfortable enough to exchange endearing glances and tease her. She hadn't protested. It was important she knew to trust him. A milestone for her after Paul's misuse of such an important part of marriage. A problem she'd have to overcome if they had a chance at a future together. He'd take it one day at a time with her.

Ellie's first day to watch Peter on her own would be a good and worrisome one for him. He couldn't predict if this job would keep her here. Taking care of Peter in the best way possible should be her priority. He trusted her not to disappoint him or Peter's mamm. Would she make him regret giving her this chance to prove her sense of responsibility?

Jacob waved farewell to Ellie early Monday morning. They'd had a good day together at the Sunday service and the afternoon meal yesterday, sitting with Liza and her family. Ellie and Hannah had been inseparable. He'd had a chance to chat with Liza, which always made his day brighter. "Have fun with Peter. Give him my best." He leaned against the barn and watched her back until she disappeared at the end of the lane. Full of vibrant energy, she'd done a couple of chores and readied to leave for the Chupps'. Ellie hadn't appeared this happy early in the morning for a long time.

Liza had proposed this job for Ellie at Esther's suggestion, despite her concerns. He worried Ellie might blindside him and show Liza's apprehensions were valid. His gut told him the risk was worth it.

Liza had become an important part of his life in such a short time. She'd captivated him the moment he met her. His interest in her hadn't waned, and he hungered to learn more about her. They'd both had their share of sorrow, Liza, with her troubled marriage, and his loss of his precious fraa.

Conversations with Liza had been frank and personal. She'd shied away from him at times, but he understood her desire to protect her heart after the way Paul had treated her. Liza might be the one for him. So far, she had the kind and compassionate demeanor he was searching for in a fraa. Her strong faith in God and importance of family were evident. He hoped her scars didn't run too deep. He mustn't prod her too much about Paul. He might have asked too many questions about her late husband in their past conversations.

He walked into the barn and clamped his hand on his toolbox. No time for distractions. The porch steps wouldn't repair themselves.

Hours later, Jacob held his head under the pump and drenched his hair and face with water. He raked both hands through his wet hair and pushed it out of his eyes. Pleased with the porch repairs and the work in the hayfield and garden, he went inside and fixed a cold leftover pork sandwich for dinner. Supper was a long way off and he was hungry. He opened a jar of peaches and dumped them in a bowl. He sat on the porch and admired the summer breeze swaying the trees a little and the cows grazing in the pasture as he forked a slice of his fruit.

His choices hit the spot. He enjoyed every bite. Scraping the bowl, he devoured the last of it. He couldn't sit still another minute. He had to check on Ellie and stop at the bakery.

Harnessing his horse to the wagon, he headed out to the Chupps'. Waving to neighbors, he scanned the properties in Charm along the way. Green grass, thick woods full of tall trees, and fat cows and muscular horses grazed in the distance. The community's appearance fit its name. Turning into the Chupps' lane, he waved to Ellie and Peter outside, secured his horse, and approached them.

Peter threw a ball to Ellie, then ran to Jacob. "We made butter cookies. Want some?"

Jacob smiled at Ellie and tousled Peter's hair. "I'd love a couple."

Ellie tossed the ball in a wooden box in the barn, then came alongside Peter. "This little one thinks he can have more cookies if you eat some."

"Please, may I have two more? Please?" Peter stared at her in anticipation.

Ellie pushed out her lips. "You're a big help."

He winced. "Sorry."

"No, you're not, but kumme on, you two. I'll give you both a snack."

"Yippee!" Peter hugged her legs.

Eyes moist, Jacob swallowed the lump in his throat. Pride sprang within him. His little girl had grown up. She'd taken on the role of caring for Peter as if she'd done this often. No need to worry that she had any trepidation about her caring for the child.

Ellie put two cookies each on plates for them and one for herself. They sat at the kitchen table.

Peter got up and dragged his chair closer to Ellie's. "Your dochder made me clean haus with her this morning." He groaned and rolled his eyes.

Jacob held his cookie in midair. "You did a fine job."

Peter's lip curled into a smile. "Mamm will be surprised. She was embarrassed for Ellie to find the mess I made at breakfast when I dropped my glass on the floor." He lowered his eyes.

Ellie patted his arm. "It's all right. Accidents happen. We threw away the broken glass and wiped up the spilled milk in no time."

"Mamm is still gonna be upset. She said her mamm gave her those glasses when I broke the other one."

Jacob tightened his lips to stifle his chuckle at Peter's confession and the worried expression on Ellie's face. He batted a hand in the air. "She'll realize Peter didn't mean to break the glass and she'll be happy not to have to clean it up."

Peter relaxed, and Ellie's mouth curled in a smile. "I'm glad you stopped by, Daed."

Jacob bid them farewell and went to the bakery. Town bustled with activity. Englischers and Amish entered and exited stores carrying their purchases from the general store, the milliner's shop, and the apothecary. A line of men and women waited for their turn at the post office.

He opened the door to the bakery and gasped at the number of customers waiting for service. He weaved his way through them to the back of the counter, next to Liza. "I'll wrap their purchases for you."

She gave him a wide grin. "Jacob Graber, you showed

up at the right time. I'd really appreciate it. You can wash your hands in the porcelain bowl behind you. Hannah and Esther are busy baking in the back, and I could ask one of them to help me, but your offering is better. You're a wilkom sight."

Jacob recognized Mr. Phillips. The rude man had bumped into Ezra, his neighbor, a while back. Ezra had told him the man had a bad temper. The young man behind him must be his son. The two resembled each other in their light brown hair and muscular build. The daed wore the same scowl he had the first time Jacob had encountered him. But the young man nodded and smiled. "Are you Ellie Graber's father? She mentioned your name was Jacob. Is Ellie here?"

Jacob's heart thudded in his chest. His eyes narrowed. "I am her daed. How do you know my dochder?"

The young man held out his hand. "I'm Bill Philips. She and I have bumped into each other in town a few times."

Jacob shook his hand and wanted to question the boy, but Bill's daed's huffs of impatience and glower stopped him. Ellie had often offered to go into town for food or supplies. Thankful she wanted to help, he hadn't suspected she might have other motives for doing so. Had Bill Phillips been the real reason she was so anxious to go to town? He should talk to her first before getting upset.

"Boy, I don't have time for this nonsense." Mr. Phillips elbowed his way in front of an elderly woman who was ahead of him in line. "Mrs. Grayson, I'm in a hurry. You don't mind, do you?" Not waiting for the woman to answer, he smacked his hand on the counter. "I'd like six oatmeal cookies and an apple pie."

Mrs. Grayson moved slowly with the help of her cane and backed away from him. "Go ahead, Mr. Phillips."

Bill hurried behind Mr. Phillips and put a friendly hand on his arm. "Dad, I'll stand in line. Let Mrs. Grayson order."

Mr. Phillips gave his arm a hard shrug and the young man's hand dropped. "Don't tell me what to do, son." The man's eyes glared at the boy, then he yelled to Liza, "What's the holdup, woman?"

Liza, red-faced, stammered, "I . . ."

Jacob swept in behind the counter, hurried to remove the man's requests, and wrapped and handed them to him. "Here you go."

The man shoved money at Liza and pushed customers out of his way to the door. Jacob winced.

The young man darted his regretful gaze to all of them. "I'm sorry."

Mr. Phillips grabbed the young man's collar. "You don't speak for me, do you hear?" he yelled, "Get in our wagon now!"

A burly, broad-shouldered man closed a firm hand on Mr. Phillips's shoulder. "You've been rude. You owe Mrs. Grayson and the woman behind the counter an apology."

Mr. Phillips glowered and huffed. "Take your hand off me, Clint, or I'll move it for you."

Hands on hips, Clint said, "Your son, Bill, is a gentleman. Not a word I would ever use to describe you. Now apologize. I'm sick and tired of putting up with your meanness around town. I've witnessed you too many times treating people unkindly and turned a blind eye."

Jacob came around the corner of the counter. Mr. Phillips's hands were balled. A fight was brewing. The patrons had stepped back and stared at them. He made his way to the door and opened it. "Please take your conversation outside."

Clint nodded and complied. Mr. Phillips and his son

followed. Jacob backed away from the door but kept an eye on them. Mr. Phillips reared a fist back and Clint held up his palms and made an abrupt exit. The son, Bill Phillips, sat in the wagon. Mr. Phillips got in the wagon, snarled, slapped his son's face, and then drove his wagon away.

Jacob pinched his lips and shook his head. How could a man be so full of hatred? He breathed a sigh of relief that the two men hadn't resorted to a fistfight and returned to Liza.

She penciled in the last purchase in her journal and bid the woman farewell. "I didn't know what to do. The man is such a bully. He sought a fight with the belligerent tone of his voice and his piercing eyes. I've noticed him in town and he's had the same glower on his face every time."

Jacob recounted the details of Mr. Phillips bumping rudely into Ezra. "Ezra stays away from the man. He warned me that Mr. Phillips is trouble. I hope you don't mind I didn't demand he wait his turn in line. It was better for everyone if he got out of here as soon as possible."

"I was grateful you took over and handled the matter. Mrs. Grayson understood what you were doing, and she agreed with getting him out of here. He kummes in periodically, but this is the first time he would've had to wait. This time, his temper got scary." She fluttered her hand. "Enough talk about Mr. Mean. Peter must be thrilled to have Ellie to himself today."

Busy and having had to deal with a difficult situation, she was thinking of Ellie and shifting the conversation to what she knew was of interest to him. The woman was remarkable. "Curious to find out how my dochder and Peter were getting along, I went for a short visit. They were tossing a ball outside, and they'd cleaned haus and made cookies."

Liza raised her eyebrows. "What kind?"

"Butter cookies, and they tasted like the ones you sell here."

"I wonder if Hannah gave her my recipe. I hope so. I'd be flattered."

Esther and Hannah came to the front of the store. Flour in her hair, Esther grinned. "Jacob, always a pleasure to have you here." She cocked her head. "What was the commotion out here? Nosy me wanted to peek out, but I couldn't take my eyes off the sugar pies in the oven."

Hannah nodded to Jacob and kept silent.

Liza gave a grateful glance in Jacob's direction. "Jacob took care of getting the angry man out of the bakery without a hitch until another man scolded Mr. Phillips. Thankfully, the men agreed to Jacob's request to settle their dispute outside the bakery."

Esther brought fingers to her lips. "Jacob, I'm glad you were here to help settle these men down. Your timing couldn't have been better."

Hannah flattened her hand to her mamm's back. "I'd have been very uncomfortable if I'd been here and Mr. Phillips had been rude to me. Danki, Jacob, for urging them to take their argument outside."

Liza distributed molasses cookies to them. "Have a snack. We all need a break. Jacob, you get two for rescuing me." She closed the counter's sliding door.

Jacob faced Hannah. "Mr. Phillips's son, Bill, introduced himself to me and asked if Ellie was here. He said they'd met in town a few times. Did she tell you anything about him or their meetings?"

Hannah jerked her head in surprise. "She hasn't mentioned him to me."

He gave her an apologetic grin. "I'm sorry to put you on the spot. I'll talk to Ellie about him tonight. I worry about her."

"It's all right. I understand." Hannah's smile faded and her eyes darkened.

Jacob's heart sank. Hannah's worried expression told him she really didn't have any knowledge of Ellie and the Phillips boy. Why was Ellie keeping this boy a secret? What did he mean to her?

Chapter Five

Liza waited on customers and wondered how Jacob was doing since he'd left the bakery an hour earlier. He'd been upset when Bill Phillips told him that he and Ellie had been meeting in town.

The door swung open and she smiled at the woman. "Wilkom."

The Englischer had a kind smile and a pretty flowered cotton skirt and blouse. Her hat matched with its white ribbon and pink flowers. "I'm Mrs. Phillips. I'm sorry for my husband's outburst in your bakery today. My son, Bill, shared with me what happened." She harrumphed. "If I had family near, I'd leave the man."

Liza's jaw dropped. The woman's personal comment shocked her. Trapped in a bad marriage herself before Paul died, she empathized with her. Mrs. Phillips smiled and had a much kinder demeanor than her husband. "You would've been proud of your son. He was quite the gentleman. All is well." She went behind the counter. "How about a cherry pie or rhubarb tarts?"

"I'll take a cherry pie." She quirked her eyebrows. "Bill told me he met Jacob Graber, Ellie Graber's father, when he was in the bakery with my husband. Jacob's daughter is such a sweetheart. Bill said Mr. Graber pitched in to help you when my husband had his outburst. Are you interested in him?"

This woman didn't hesitate to dive right in and ask personal questions, and they'd just met. She seemed nice enough, but much too forward. Liza's cheeks warmed. "We're friends. My niece, Hannah, and Ellie, Jacob's dochder, are close. How do you know Ellie?"

"Bill brought her to our house when he knew his father would be out of town. She mentioned her father's name was Jacob in conversation. I fed them dinner and we had a pleasant afternoon. She told me they'd moved from Nappanee, Indiana, to Charm not long ago. I was surprised she came with my son by herself. I didn't think her father would approve of her being alone with my son in the wagon or at our house, although I stayed with them the entire time she visited us."

"Did you ask her about it?"

Mrs. Phillips shrugged. "I didn't want to put her on the spot. She's a sweet girl. My son is smitten with her, but she seemed truthful, calling him a friend. I hope I haven't gotten her into trouble. Her father may not be aware she was at our house. Must you tell him?"

"I hope you understand. Jacob and I are friends and it wouldn't be right for me to keep it from him. If I were in his position, I'd want to know."

"As a mother, I agree with you. Ellie's such a dear, I wouldn't want to cause her any turmoil. I've never seen my son happier, gushing about her. My husband makes both our lives miserable, so I'm thrilled she and Bill have met."

This woman prattling on about her son's happiness and the joy Ellie had brought to his life showed her Mrs. Phillips hadn't considered the heartbreak it would cause Jacob if Ellie chose the Englisch life. As an Englischer, it was clear Mrs. Phillips didn't understand the Amish laws or lifestyle traditions. Otherwise, she would've understood how wrong it was for Ellie to meet Bill alone without her daed's knowledge and for her not to care who saw her with Bill.

Liza sucked in her lips. A surge of frustration mounted in her. Ellie had such disregard for her reputation and her daed's feelings. She didn't want to discuss this any further with Mrs. Phillips. She forced a smile. "We have fresh pies, an assortment of cookies, pastries, and many other desserts. Would you like any other offerings besides your cherry pie?"

Mrs. Phillips bent to peruse the goodies on the shelves behind the glass. "I'll take a dozen of your famous molasses cookies my neighbors are always lauding and a sugar pie." She opened her reticule and paid for her purchases. "Thank you, and it was a pleasure."

Liza wrapped her purchases and passed them to Bill's mamm and then walked around the counter and opened the front door. "Kumme in anytime."

She shut the door behind her. The back of her hand to her head, she groaned. Jacob would be distraught to find out Ellie had had dinner with Bill and his mamm. The action spoke volumes about her disrespect for Jacob and her Amish upbringing. She couldn't rest until she'd told him everything. He'd be devastated and she dreaded hurting him.

At five, Liza bid farewell to Esther and Hannah and they climbed in their separate buggies. She didn't speak to them about Ellie and Bill. *Better tell Jacob first.*

Jacob peered out the window. Liza had just pulled her buggy in front of his haus. He came running to her, flailing his arms. "Ellie's gone!"

"What do you mean, she's gone?" Liza clasped his hand and jumped down from the wagon.

Jacob grabbed the reins and tied them to the hitching post. He showed her a note. His heart raced. "I got home and found this. I'll read it to you." He couldn't stop his hands from shaking as he stood next to Liza and held the paper out in front of them.

"Daed, I'm going away with Bill Phillips. He told me you met him today. I didn't want to face you. I knew it was wrong to meet him in town without your knowledge, even though we have not even held hands. He's a friend, nothing more. I have met him in town a few times and even gone to his haus and met his mamm. He's a gentleman and I can trust him. I knew you wouldn't approve and I didn't want to argue with you. I'd planned on leaving at some point, and now seemed like the best time.

"I'm not going to tell you where we're going, and I don't want you to search for me. I must find out once and for all which path I will choose for my life. I won't commit to when, but I will write you when I've made my decision. I must do this for me.

"Please tell Mae and Peter I'm sorry. Bill had to get out of town in a hurry and I chose to go with him at the last minute. He picked me up at the end of our lane and we left. I didn't want to take a horse you may need. I hope you can find it in your heart to understand. I love you, Daed. Please tell Peter I love him too. Ellie."

He pressed the note to his chest and let tears cloud his eyes.

Liza opened her arms.

He cocked his head in question. He didn't want to show her disrespect if someone were to kumme down the lane and witness them in an embrace. Nothing would feel as good as being comforted by Liza, but not at her reputation's expense.

Liza fluttered her fingers to beckon him. "I don't care if it's proper or not."

He held her tight and wept, not caring about his vulnerable and distraught state. Moments later, he swiped tears with the heels of his hands from his eyes. "I'm a mess over this. What should I do?"

"Mrs. Phillips told me Ellie had had dinner with her and Bill one day. I don't know the exact date. Mrs. Phillips confirmed what Ellie has told you. She said Bill is smitten with Ellie, but she said Ellie thought of him as a friend."

"My worst fears have kumme true. She and Bill have been meeting behind my back and he has enticed her to discover all the world has to offer. Some of which could be dangerous. She's too trusting of this young man. Putting her life in his hands. So much could go wrong. I'm sick with worry." He darted his eyes to the barn. "I'm going to the Phillipses' to ask if they have any idea where Ellie and Bill could be headed. Then I'll stop by the sheriff's office and ask him to keep an eye out. Hopefully, I'll find out information from the Phillipses and I won't need to alert the sheriff."

Liza wrung her hands. Fear clawed through her. "Please don't go to Bill's parents' haus. Mr. Phillips scared me with his temper in the bakery the day you were there and he was too impatient to wait his turn. He may be angry his son left. You don't know what he might do. I'm afraid he'll turn his bad temper on you." She put a hand on his shoulder. "Do you want me to tell Mae about Ellie not watching Peter?"

"I don't want to put you in a difficult position. I'll speak with Mae." Sliding his palms one over the other, he said, "I must go to the Phillipses'. I have to try to find Ellie."

"Please stop by my haus before you go home. I won't rest until I know you're all right."

He nodded and kissed her cheek. He untied her horse's reins and waited until she'd left to ready his horse and buggy. Peter would be disappointed Ellie had run out on him. He gripped the reins tight. Ellie had certainly proved Liza's concerns about Ellie being unreliable with Peter correct. It would be a wonder if Liza ever considered a future with him after Ellie's abrupt departure.

He pulled his wagon over to the side of the road and bowed his head. "Dear Heavenly Father, speak to Ellie's heart. Guide her back to You and bring her home to Charm and her Amish life. Wrap Your arms of protection around her. Give me patience, wisdom, and understanding. Give me the strength to endure the heartache while I go through this. Danki, Heavenly Father. I love You. Amen."

Jacob rolled his stiff shoulders and took a deep breath. He flicked the reins and went to Mae's.

Peter kicked his ball to the side and ran to him. "Jacob!"

Mae set a pail of water next to the pump and approached him. "Jacob, Ellie left a while ago. She and Peter had a grand time today. He hasn't quit telling me what a jolly time they had together. Is anything wrong? You appear distressed."

Worry mixed with frustration festered in him. How could Ellie be so thoughtless as to get this little boy's hopes up and then let him down? Peter had opened up to her and his dochder hadn't considered what this might do to his fragile mental state, still getting over his schweschder's passing. "Peter, do you mind if I speak to your mamm a minute?"

Peter shook his head. "I have to go to the outhaus. I'll be right back."

Mae wiped her wet hands on her apron. "Would you like to sit on the porch?"

He shook his head. "I won't keep you. I'm sorry to have to tell you Ellie won't be available to care for Peter."

Wide-eyed, she gasped. "Why not?"

"She's left town and I'm not sure how long she'll be gone. I'm sorry she didn't give you notice."

Peter came up behind him, his eyes wide with worry. "Where did she go?"

His chest tightened. "I'm not sure, Peter. I'm praying she'll be back soon."

"How do you know she won't be back tomorrow?"

"She left me a note saying it might be a while."

"Did she leave a note for me?"

Jacob bent to meet his gaze. "She did say in the note to me to tell you she loves you and she's sorry to leave you."

Tears pooled in Peter's eyes.

Jacob knelt and drew him in a hug. "I'm so sorry, little friend."

Peter wrapped his arms around Jacob's neck. "Why would she leave me?"

Jacob hurt and could understand the boy's bewilderment. He didn't have answers why Ellie did or didn't do things. She puzzled him most of the time. He did understand she had put her desires before his or Peter's, without thinking of the repercussions or caring enough about him or Peter. Hannah would be upset too.

"She loves you. She said so in my note. She didn't leave because of anything you did or said."

Mae took Peter's hand. "Go inside and pick your toys off the floor in your room. You can have another candy cookie when you're all done. I'll be in soon." She bowed her head and put a hand to her mouth as she coughed.

Peter darted his eyes from her to Jacob. "I'm glad you came to see me, Jacob." He hugged his legs, then dragged his feet to the front door.

Mae crossed her arms and glared at him. "I shouldn't have trusted her. She's broken my little boy's heart. Leah said Ellie was too interested in the world for her liking when she met her at Liza's social a while back. I dismissed her remarks and gave Ellie a chance. Shame on me."

Jacob removed his hat and raked a hand through his hair. She had coughed each time he'd been around her. Was she all right? He didn't want to ask and get too personal. He might offend her. Maybe he'd mention it to Liza. This woman wasn't well on top of having to work and care for her child. He was frustrated his dochder was responsible for adding to Mae's burden. "I apologize for my dochder's actions. I don't approve of her decision, but I'm praying she'll realize the error of her ways and kumme back. Please include her in your prayers tonight."

Mae harrumphed and marched inside.

He didn't blame her. His news had left her with the task of finding someone to watch Peter while she went to work next week. Peter was so disappointed, and she'd have to console her son and hope he wouldn't withdraw from her and everyone again. Ellie thought only of herself. Liza had a business to run and was content with her life. She might not want to be associated with this quandary Ellie had created. Did she realize the effect of her actions? She'd left him to answer for her and he didn't know what to tell people.

He could handle the criticism and disgrace, but he couldn't handle Ellie slipping out of his life, not being there when she married or had kinner. Just being a part of her life as her daed.

He'd passed the Phillipses' place several times, and now he drove to the front of the big red haus with white curtains fluttering in the open windows. The property stretched far and wide, with several corrals teeming with cattle and horses. Two freshly painted large barns on the right side not far apart from each other would hold many animals and whatever else the man wanted to store. A pond with geese in a straight line paddling their feet presented a pleasurable sight. Mr. Phillips must be doing quite well for himself. Good for him. Why was the man so unhappy? He guessed there could be any number of reasons. He hoped he'd find Mr. Phillips in a better mood than when they'd last encountered each other.

Jacob secured his horse. He went to the door and knocked. A round and nervous-looking woman with silver hair opened the door halfway. "How may I help you?"

"I'm Jacob Graber. Ellie's daed."

She held up her palm to interrupt him. "I suspect you're here because of Ellie and Bill taking off. My husband is furious about it. Bill left us a note. I'm so sorry. We don't know anything, and I'm afraid my husband will take his anger out on you. I suggest you leave."

Jacob rose his brows in alarm. "Should I worry about you?"

"No. He yells and screams, but he would never lay a hand on me, though he doesn't hesitate to take his frustration out on my son or other men. Please leave. I don't want him to unleash his temper on you."

"You have no idea where they went?"

"No. I wish I did. My son is a good boy. He would never take advantage of Ellie, and he'll do his best to protect her. He has had enough of his father's outbursts, and he said in his note Ellie wanted to leave and have Bill show her more of what the outside world had to offer before she settled on what to do with her life. Bill said he loved me and he'd write when Ellie was comfortable with him telling me where they were. She probably knew you'd come here asking if I had information on their location."

"If you hear anything, please let me know. I live at Ten South Road."

"I will. Now please go. I'm afraid for your safety. My husband is a hot-tempered man." She shut the door.

Jacob stepped off the porch and froze.

Mr. Phillips was pointing a rifle at him. "What are you doing here talking to my wife?"

Holding his arms up in self-defense, Jacob took a step back. "Your son and my dochder, Ellie, are friends. I came to find out if you have any idea where they went. She wouldn't say in the note she wrote to me."

The menacing man squinted. "You were in town with Ezra one day, and at the bakery when I was with my boy, Bill. What's your name?"

"Jacob Graber."

"You're Mr. Do-gooder. Men like you make me sick. Always wanting to do the right thing." He sneered. "You Amish hide behind your Bible to avoid settling a dispute with your fists like a man."

Jacob glanced at the haus. Mrs. Phillips had shut the door. He was relieved she'd chosen to stay out of this. He didn't want her in trouble with her husband because of his visit. "Mr. Phillips, I mean no trouble. I'm only here to ask for any information you may have to help me find my dochder. Do you know where Bill might have taken her?"

He waved the rifle. "I don't know and I don't care. Bill has been a disappointment to me. Now he's gone off with an Amish girl of all things. You must have a wild one on your hands. She ran off without a word to you. Didn't think a respectable Amish girl would do such a thing. Now get off my property. The two lousy kids deserve what they get."

Jacob took a deep breath and left. No sense in trying to reason with this man. He'd have to pray Ellie would return to him. Frustration and worry swirled inside him. Why, why, why, couldn't she be content with her life? Could he have done something more to steer her in the right direction? He drove through town on the way home and talked to the sheriff, giving him a description of Ellie and when he'd last seen her.

He hadn't wanted to involve the sheriff. The Amish didn't like to ask for assistance outside their community, to involve Englischers. But the sheriff would know other lawmen, and he could ask them about Ellie. If she wore her Amish clothes, she'd stand out. He'd do anything to find her.

Sheriff Williams wrote a note about Ellie and left it on his desk. "I'll check with other sheriffs in surrounding communities and keep an eye out for her. It's the best we can do."

"I appreciate it." He tipped his hat and left. He drove outside of town, hoping to catch a glimpse of Ellie. Nothing. He drove to Liza's with a heavy heart.

She met him outside. "Did you learn anything from Mr. Phillips?"

"You were right. His temper had the best of him and he doesn't care about his son or Ellie leaving town. I talked to Mrs. Phillips. She said Bill didn't say where they were going. She urged me to leave before her husband discovered I was on their porch. I didn't leave in time and he pointed a rifle straight at me. He hurled insults and the visit wasn't productive at all."

"Jacob, we'll get through this together. I don't have kinner, so I can only imagine how painful Ellie's leaving is for you. I'm so sorry. Please don't give up hope she'll return."

"The last time she left me, I was alone in dealing with the constant fretting and loss of her from my life. At least this time I'll have you to talk to. I'm so grateful for you, Liza."

Her beautiful, empathetic expression and hand on his arm calmed him.

"I believe God will protect her and she'll kumme home to you. She loves you. She returned before and she will again."

Ellie had turned her back on him and God as far as he was concerned. It seemed harsh, given the fact that he'd provided a good home for her and he'd raised her with love and understanding. "God gives us free will. Ellie has to want to turn to Him. I fear she may not. I don't understand her decisions."

"I've gotten to know Ellie and I don't believe she'll stay away for long. If she does, I'll be shocked."

He loved Liza so much. The short time they'd gotten acquainted didn't matter to him. The kindness in her voice, the gentleness of her spirit, and the way she looked into his eyes, as if she could touch his soul, captivated him. Her wisdom and thoughtful ways continued to lift him up.

She could've reiterated her reluctance for Ellie to care for Peter. Instead, she'd comforted him and placed more faith in Ellie than he did at the moment. Her words of encouragement and support were what he needed to calm the emotional fury in his bones. He'd trust God to give him the grace to accept whatever path Ellie chose. *Not easy.* As Ellie's daed, he wished to protect her and force her to kumme home.

Shaking his head, he pressed his tense arms to his sides. Where would he search? His dochder and Bill could have gotten a ride with someone or taken a train. They could be anywhere. He gazed into Liza's eyes. "I can't even think straight at this point. Danki for standing by me."

"No need to apologize. Kumme inside. There's nothing you can do at present. Try to calm your nerves. Can I interest you in something to eat or drink?"

Food didn't sound good. Maybe something sweet. It was getting late. He should go home. But being alone would make things worse right now. He managed a half grin. "Pie would be a nice distraction."

"And here I thought my company would be a good enough distraction." She gave him a shy smile and opened the door.

Her attempt to flirt and lighten his mood brought a smile to his face. He couldn't help himself. It was so out of character for her. Her guard down and her sweet grin on those petal-soft lips took his mind away from Ellie for a moment. "You are always a wilkom distraction, Liza. And it goes without saying, my dear." He gently touched her cheek.

Asking Liza to make plans for the future, not knowing what Ellie would do or what he would be faced with if she did kumme back wouldn't be the way to start a marriage with Liza. He doubted Liza would want to consider a future with him knowing Ellie kept his life in turmoil. Would he ever lay eyes on his dochder again? The unknown answer stabbed him in the heart.

Chapter Six

On Monday morning, Liza covered nuts with a clean cheesecloth and crushed them with a rolling pin. She peeked out the window at the newsboy, whose orange-red hair was hard to miss.

"Read all about it! President William Howard Taft, born in 1857, talks about growing up in Cincinnati, Ohio!"

She raised her brows. *Interesting.* The president was from Ohio. She enjoyed tidbits of information about the presidents and world events, even though the Amish were not to concentrate on such things. Dr. Harrison and Sheriff Williams's discussions about politics and the latest inventions mentioned in their newspapers kept her somewhat informed. The owner of the newspaper office must be happy to have such a dedicated boy intent on selling their papers. He raised his voice and shook the latest news in his palm with vigor.

She paused before pouring the nuts into the bowl. Ellie had been gone three weeks without a word. The young woman should've written her daed to let him know she was alive and well. Jacob visited her each workday around three. Business was most always slow at that time, and she enjoyed having a cup of coffee with him. He'd not

dwelled on Ellie in conversation. She admired his trust
and faith in God. It was evident in his calm demeanor
when he talked about his dochder.

Not having kinner, she wasn't sure how she would
have handled the situation. She hoped she'd have faith
and trust in God like Jacob and not want to shut down her
life. Jacob worked hard every day, maintained his property, and asked how she was doing. His gaze and attention
to her were sincere. Her love for him had grown through
this time, but she wasn't sure if she wanted the turmoil
bound to kumme if Ellie returned. The young woman was
unpredictable and stirred up trouble consistently. It was
easier to have meals and discussions with Jacob while
they were living separate lives and she wasn't a part of his
family. Or responsible for Ellie. Even the idea frightened
her. She was glad he hadn't broached the subject of marriage yet.

She told him the gossip in town and listened to him
talk about his day to keep his mind off Ellie. Feeding him
supper and desserts had been easy.

Even though she had misgivings about being a mamm
to Ellie in the future, she'd grown fond of her. What was
Ellie doing this very moment? Did she have a proper place
to stay? Had harm kumme to her? She prayed to God for
His will in Ellie's life. She had to remind herself often to
trust God to take care of Ellie. Her heart would shatter if
something happened to the young woman. Each day she
hoped Jacob would say he'd received a letter from her.

Hannah and Esther had gasped the day she told them
Ellie had left town. Hannah had cried and said she
thought they were close friends. She didn't understand
how Ellie could go without saying farewell or leaving a
letter for her.

Dr. Harrison and Sheriff Williams wandered in, took
off their hats, and sat down on stools.

Liza lifted the coffeepot. "You're late today. You must've been busy this morning."

"Mrs. Timmons came to my office complaining about her neighbors' target shooting. They're on their own property way back in the woods and aren't doing anything wrong. The woman needs something to do. She grumbles too much."

Dr. Harrison grabbed a clean mug from the small shelf. "I'll take some coffee. Thank you, Liza." He shook his head. "Merry Lynn is five and she's been in my office for scrapes and gashes more times than any other child in this town. She loves to climb everything. She fell out of a tree and cut her leg bad enough to need a slew of stitches." He stretched his neck to peruse the top shelf of goodies. "I'll have an apple pastry."

"I'll have coffee and two sugar cookies." The sheriff licked his lips.

Liza served them. "Mrs. Timmons is a childless widow. She's hungry for company. You're a patient man to listen to her. You take good care of all of us and have more patience than most men."

Dr. Harrison chuckled. "I make every excuse to get away from her when she calls me. I need a little more patience." He opened the newspaper. "Steiff created twenty-inch curly mohair black teddy bears to sell to people to purchase as gifts for those mourning the sinking of the *Titanic*. They're making a limited number."

The sheriff peeked at the page. "I don't like the idea. Every time I glanced at the furry bear, I'd be reminded of the men and women who lost their lives."

"I like the cute button-nose bear. It's a thoughtful idea to comfort those who are suffering."

The sheriff shrugged. "You have a point." He pointed to the other pictures of their light brown teddy bears. "I like those better."

Liza wiped some crumbs off the top glass shelf inside the display counter. She would keep her mouth shut and not engage in this conversation. The sheriff and Dr. Harrison had often had different opinions and she had made a point not to get involved. This time she agreed with the sheriff. She was drawn more to the light brown bears too.

Dr. Harrison and the sheriff finished reading their paper, emptied their mugs and plates, and bid her farewell.

Jacob came in later in the day. "Good afternoon, sweetheart. Where are Esther and Hannah?"

"Gone for the day. I surprised them and insisted they take a day off now and then. I'm sure they're working hard at home." She shook her head and glanced out the window. "I can't believe it's May thirteenth. April passed in a flash. I'm enjoying the lush green grass and full meadows of colorful flowers in the pastures and on the way to work each morning."

"Were you busy today?"

"No, it's been calm for a Monday." She slathered butter on a piece of cinnamon bread and handed it to him. "It's still warm."

He lifted the slice to his nose. "Yummy." He ate the corner of the bread and smiled his approval. "I talked to the sheriff and stopped by the post office. No news."

The sad, patient man had lost weight, and the dark circles under his eyes told her he wasn't sleeping well. She'd lost weight and hadn't been sleeping through the night since Ellie left either. A naïve and confused young woman searching for the kind of life she wanted to lead in the outside world couldn't be good. The more time that passed without so much as a letter from Ellie, the more she feared something bad had happened to her.

Mae and Peter pushed the bakery door open.

Mae said, "Good afternoon, Liza, Jacob."

Peter tugged on Jacob's sleeve. "Is Ellie home yet?"

"I'm afraid not, little one."

Mae harrumphed and coughed. "The girl is trouble. Jacob, you'd be better off if she stays away. Young men and women turning their backs on our way of life shouldn't tarnish what we've built here."

Liza splayed her hand on the countertop. "We are to love and forgive those who have hurt us. I pray she'll return, and you should too. She's a beautiful and vibrant young woman who is unsure of herself. We need to wilkom her back with open arms if she returns."

"I don't agree." Mae coughed and held a fist to her mouth until she recovered. She hurriedly grabbed Peter's hand and bustled out the door without buying a thing.

Liza groaned. "I should have kept my mouth shut. I only made things worse."

"It's happening again. Ellie left Nappanee and it wasn't any time before the gossip started about her. A large part of the community didn't accept her when she returned. Ellie didn't help nurture their acceptance of her. The stories she told about the outside world frustrated me and fueled the fire against her, and I'll never understand why she did it or why she did the same here."

"Esther has invited us to supper. Kumme with me to their haus and take your mind off Ellie and what other people are thinking of her."

"I'd like to. Danki." He patted her arm. "I could use a diversion from my constant worry about Ellie." He snapped his fingers. "Mae's cough seems worse. Have you suggested she pay Dr. Harrison a visit?"

Liza sighed. "I did. She dismissed it. She's a proud woman. I don't want to anger her by prying."

"You're right. It's all you can do." He opened the door. "I'll be back. I've got to stop by the hardware store for some nails."

"I'll be here." She finished baking her nut bread,

washed her hands, and waited on customers trickling in the rest of the afternoon. Jacob had been gone for a couple of hours. Ready to close the bakery, she removed her apron and hung it on a wooden peg inside the kitchen. She stowed her remaining desserts in containers and put them away.

Jacob dashed inside the door an hour and a half later. "I went home for a little bit. I couldn't shop anymore today."

"Why?"

"I'm not myself. I'm distracted and unable to think straight since Ellie's been gone. The stores were crowded and I kept bumping into people. I stepped out in front of a shiny black Ford Model T. The driver shook his finger, smiled, and told me to be careful. I apologized and he gave me a friendly wave instead of the scowl I deserved."

"I'm glad you weren't hit by the motorcar! Did you run into anyone you knew?"

"In the general store I dodged several of the men and women I recognize from Sunday services. Two couples were talking about Ellie's exploits in the outside world the last time she left the Amish life, when we lived in Nappanee. They mentioned that Leah and Eva had told them about Ellie's past at your bakery social. I don't blame people for being appalled by her behavior. I have no response for them. I avoided them and left. You may not want to associate with me. It could tarnish your reputation. Two women commented I might not have been a good influence on Ellie for her to act in such a disrespectful way."

People could be so cruel. She'd had a dose of it from Paul. Fearful that if she told anyone what he was really like they'd have turned on her. He'd done a good job convincing their friends he was an upstanding and respectable man. Her problem with Paul had been a secret, and she didn't have to suffer ridicule, like Jacob. "I'm not distancing myself from you. Genuine friends in our community won't either. Many people have compassion for you and Ellie and will forgive her and wilkom her back if she returns. You're a wonderful daed. Pay them no mind."

Jacob brushed his lips against her cheek. "I'm glad you're a strong woman. I'm so sorry about all this."

"Other kinner leave and practice rumspringa to satisfy their curiosity about the outside world one way or the other. Most have returned and joined the church. Ellie has the same opportunity."

Jacob raised his shoulders and winced. "She's run off without having a conversation with me about it twice and both times young men who are Englischers have been involved. The kinner who return don't boast about how much they love the outside world, and they don't make known their indecision about staying in the Amish community. They just don't kumme back. She put us in jeopardy of being shunned in our previous town and now here."

He was right. She hadn't discussed this with him and she'd flaunted her past with Englischers to her Amish friends. There was no sugarcoating this. "You're right. I don't like judgment being placed on you for Ellie's indiscretions."

"I may have to move again to another Amish community if she returns, depending on her attitude. Would you ever consider relocating? I have to keep trying with Ellie if she returns. I know the bakery is important to you." He held her hands in his. "Liza, marry me. I love you with all my heart. The timing isn't ideal, but no matter if Ellie returns or not, I want to spend my life with you. We can discuss moving. I realize you may be against it."

This was his first hint about a possible future with her, but she wouldn't leave her life in Charm. It meant everything to her. She'd learned how important it was to have family by her side as she dealt with her loathsome husband. Life for her had become happy, and she loved working side by side with Esther and Hannah.

Hannah would probably marry and have kinner. She wouldn't want to miss any part of it. Even if Ellie came back and Jacob stayed in Charm, she wasn't sure she could handle being a mamm to a young woman as difficult as Ellie.

She loved Jacob, but the thought of jumping back into a marriage with constant turmoil scared her. The reality of not having a future with him scared her too. It was too early to consider this now. They had to wait. Ellie might or might not return. "We don't know what's going to happen. Let's be patient and have this conversation when Ellie kummes home. We both have much to consider."

Jacob nodded and stepped outside behind her and waited for her to lock the door. "I went to the livery earlier and got your buggy. I'll follow you to Esther's."

Liza drove to Esther's. Her request to delay their discussion had upset Jacob. His furrowed brows and lips in a grim line were evident this was true. A smart man, he knew she had doubts. A pang of regret at causing him more pain ratcheted through her. Being truthful with him and herself was important to build a solid foundation of trust between them. A commitment to love, honor, respect, and resolve problems for a lifetime with Jacob switched back and forth from fear to trust. She'd longed for a peaceful life and she finally had it. And then Jacob had swept in and captured her heart.

She'd learned marriage wouldn't always be easy even in the best of times. Ellie, if she returned, might not agree to their union, and that would be the end of her and Jacob. She wouldn't kumme between him and his dochder. It wouldn't be wise, and the turmoil to kumme would be more than she was willing to handle. She hoped the problem would be resolved if Ellie returned.

The horse stopped in front of the hitching post and Jacob stood ready to take the reins. "You go on in. I'll take care of your mare and mine."

She nodded and strolled inside. "How is everyone?"

Abe grinned. "Hungry."

Hannah set plates on the table. "Did Jacob kumme with you?"

"He's taking care of the horses. He'll be in shortly."

Esther passed Liza platters laden with food. "The potatoes, turkey, and vegetables are ready. Would you mind putting these in the center?"

"I'd be happy to." She sniffed the scent of warm comfort food and couldn't wait to satisfy her hunger. She crossed the room and centered the food for easy passing.

Hannah skipped to the door. "I'll tell the men supper's ready."

Jacob came in behind Hannah and greeted everyone and took his same seat at the table. "The turkey must've been a big one, Esther. The bird had big legs and thighs, which are my favorite. The meat is falling off the bone. Danki for inviting me."

"Consider this your second home, Jacob." Abe spread a tattered napkin on his lap.

Hannah chuckled. "Daed, you should let me get you

another cloth. You've asked for the same napkin for years. It's worn thin."

"Your mamm made two of these for us before you were born. I used the other one until it had holes in it. I'm being careful with this one. It's a special napkin to me." He winked at Esther.

Her cheeks pinked. "You're an old softy, Abe, and I love you for it."

Liza admired Esther and Abe's relationship, speaking openly about their feelings for each other. Most Amish men wouldn't do such a thing. "Esther worked hard on those. She wanted them to be perfect."

Hannah covered her mamm's hand. "I hope my future husband treasures the gifts I make him as much as Daed does the ones you make him, like the napkin."

"Consider everything about the man you want to marry before taking the big step. Love isn't everything. Commitment, communication, and putting each other's needs before your own are what make a happy marriage." Esther reached for her water.

Liza reflected on Esther's advice to Hannah. She applied the wisdom to herself and Jacob. There were so many unknowns for them. "We all want the best for you, Hannah. I'm sure God has the perfect man for you when the time is right."

Abe forked a small piece of turkey. "Hannah, don't be in a hurry to leave your daed. I can't bear not having you around here."

Hannah gave him a warm smile. "No one can take your place, Daed."

Jacob kept silent and ate quietly.

Liza glanced at him. This topic must be hard on him. He might never know what Ellie was doing, if she got married, had kinner, or was even alive.

Hannah lowered her fork. "Jacob, why do you think Ellie didn't tell me she was leaving? I've been contemplating this ever since she left. I don't understand why she wouldn't have confided in me."

Liza jerked her head back. "Hannah, Jacob doesn't want to speak about Ellie. It's painful for him. Let's talk about something else."

Esther gasped. "Hannah, you shouldn't put Jacob on the spot. He doesn't want to answer for Ellie. You'll have to ask your friend why she didn't tell you when she returns."

"She may not return and I really want to know." She heaved a heavy sigh. "Jacob, you don't have to answer."

Holding up his hand, Jacob smiled at Hannah. "She said in her letter that Bill had told her about meeting me in the bakery earlier in the day. She didn't want to face me knowing I'd be upset she'd met him in town several times without telling me. It's no secret she's been deliberating leaving us for a while. I hoped she'd been swayed to stay due to your friendship, along with the rest of your family and especially Peter. I don't think she could face you. You meant too much to her."

Liza's eyes watered with tears. She was grateful to him for his honesty and care in answering her niece. Hannah considered Ellie a close friend and the loss of her had been difficult for her niece.

"I had assumed I meant nothing to her because she didn't share her news with me. You shed a different light on the matter. Danki, Jacob. I pray she'll kumme back to Charm. I miss her."

Esther shoved a plate of still-steaming potatoes in Jacob's direction. "We all do, sweetheart. I have faith she'll kumme home with a clear mind soon. Now, I don't want anyone leaving this table not utterly stuffed. I made enough food to have second and third helpings. Don't hesitate to empty these serving plates."

Esther offered food to smooth over hurt or sadness, to divert the injured party's attention, Liza supposed. She remembered her schweschder fetching cookies for her when she had tears from an injury or had gotten in trouble with their parents. She had such fond memories of their times together. They'd hardly fussed as kinner and their friendship had grown deeper with every year.

Jacob and Abe pushed their plates away.

Abe gestured to Jacob. "Let's go out on the porch."

Jacob thanked Esther and Hannah for the meal and smiled at Liza on his way out the door.

Liza joined Esther and Hannah at the sink in the kitchen.

Esther nudged her. "What's wrong between Jacob and you?"

Hannah gently swiped at her with the dish towel. "I noticed it too."

"You're both too observant."

"Jah, so, answer my question." Hand on her hip, Esther stared at her.

"Jacob's worried if Ellie kummes back, the Amish community may make life awkward for her in Charm. He and Ellie experienced that in Nappanee. He's afraid if that happens, he'll have to move again."

"Why move again? The idle talk will pass if she asks for forgiveness from God and the church congregation." Hannah slung the towel over her shoulder and held the dry plate to her chest.

Esther sighed. "The Amish are guilty of gossiping. We should know better, but we're human. It will take a while for the people to accept and trust her again. No one wants had in the yard on the damaging fire to extinguish the oxygen feeding it.

The men worked until the fire diminished and smoke filled the air.

Ezra wiped sweat from his forehead with the back of his sleeve. "It's not too bad. We caught it in time. I'll help you replace the back section. It won't take us long."

Jacob thanked his friends for their help and bid them farewell. He was grateful to the kind, good men for their fast response and willingness to rescue his enclosure.

"Do you have any idea how this fire got started?" Ezra bent to wash his hands under the pump.

Jacob handed him a clean rag from the unaffected shelf in the barn. "Danki, Ezra." He slid one palm over the other. "I don't want to accuse Mr. Phillips and get him in trouble, but I'm almost certain it was him I saw heading away from my place in a hurry on his horse. Ellie left with his son, Bill. Not long ago, I approached the Phillipses to ask if they knew where my dochder and their son might have gone. Mrs. Phillips said she didn't, but she asked me to leave for fear her husband would start something with me. He came out and pointed a rifle at me, demanding I leave. He's so unreasonable. The man doesn't show an ounce of happiness in his life."

"I passed him on the way to your place. I don't know why he's so obstinate either. I'm sorry about Ellie." He stared at the ground. "I should've told you this earlier. I didn't know whether to get involved or not. I realize I did the wrong thing, keeping it from you."

"What is it, Ezra?"

"I'd seen Ellie and Bill together a few times. They didn't notice me fishing in the woods. They weren't doing anything inappropriate, other than being alone, with her being Amish and him an Englischer. I'm sorry for keeping this from you."

Jacob put a hand on Ezra's shoulder. "Don't apologize. I understand. I wish I would hear from Ellie. I haven't the slightest idea where she went or how she is. She's on my mind constantly."

"I'm sad to know you're suffering like Annabelle and me. God has given us an unexplainable peace about our dochder, Martha. We remain disappointed in her decision. But it's relieved our minds to know she's healthy and safe whenever she writes to us." Ezra pointed to neatly stacked wood, perfect for replacing the damaged fence. "You've got what we need to rebuild the corral's fence already. Let's repair it while we still have daylight."

"I had them left over. Good thing I did." Jacob nodded.

They replaced the damaged portion and stood back to admire their work.

"You're much better at this than I am. I appreciate your help and friendship, Ezra."

"Always glad to help, my friend." Ezra bid Jacob farewell.

Jacob walked to the haus and went inside. He fixed leftover potato soup and slathered butter and raspberry jam on fresh bread as he mulled over what Ezra had told him. Ezra and Annabelle had to live without their dochder near. He hoped not to have to settle for the same situation with Ellie.

Why would Mr. Phillips do such a thing? Does he blame Ellie for his son's departure? The man is unpredictable and vengeful. Jacob wouldn't go to the sheriff about his suspicions. He had no proof, and he didn't want any more trouble or to antagonize the menacing man any further. Mr. Phillips searching for Bill and Ellie terrified him. Mr. Phillips had proved he was prone to senseless violence. The Amish abhorred violence. It sickened him that he couldn't protect his only dochder from this man.

She could be anywhere. He feared Bill wasn't a match for his daed but hoped he was wrong.

Jacob rose Tuesday morning missing Ellie so much. Each day he stared at the door or at the lane, hoping she'd return home. As time passed, he grew more anxious about her safety and wondered if he'd ever lay eyes on her again. He blinked away tears. Stiff and weary from yesterday, he peeked out the open window. The sun played hide-and-seek with the puffy white clouds floating overhead.

He would visit Liza later. They'd gotten into a comfortable routine, having coffee or tea in the afternoon at the bakery, even if it was just for a few minutes. He'd go around three, which was her slowest time of day for business. He didn't hold back anything from her, and she had been frank with him about her feelings and reservations about considering him for a potential husband. His faith in God and Liza's love for him kept him from going mad fretting about Ellie.

Swinging open the front door, he took a fresh cup of coffee out on the porch and sat in his rocking chair. The birds chirped and the slight breeze sent the water rippling over the stones on the pond's edge. He'd paint the new part of the fence.

A buggy was traveling on his lane. He stood and squinted. "Ellie!" He jumped off the porch and opened his arms wide. Bill Phillips jumped out and tied the horse to the post.

Ellie ran into Jacob's arms.

Tears fell onto his cheeks as he held her tight. "Ellie, I was so worried about you." He gently pulled away from her, his hands on her shoulders. "Are you all right?"

She glanced at Bill, standing a short distance away. "I'm fine, Daed. Bill watched out for me. We did nothing inappropriate together. He's an honorable man and no more than a friend."

Jacob swallowed the frustration and relief in his throat. Ellie had chosen to go with this young man. She was as much at fault for their abrupt departure as Bill. "I don't condone you taking my dochder with you, but I'm glad you've brought her back to me."

Ellie walked to Bill's side. "Don't be upset with him. I coaxed him to take me away. He had to get away from his daed. Mr. Phillips has berated him and not shown him an ounce of love." She stared at her shoes. "The opposite of the way you treat me."

"Kumme inside. Tell me where you've been."

Bill wrung his hands. "Mr. Graber, I'm sorry for upsetting you by taking Ellie away. I can assure you I haven't laid a hand on your daughter in a way that would be displeasing to you. I would like to stay and explain where we've been and answer your questions, but I must get going for all our sakes. My dad may ride by and recognize our quarter horse and wagon. If he does, I don't know what he'll do."

"Don't worry, son. I'm concerned for your safety too. Let's put your buggy and horse in the barn in case your daed passes by, then we'll talk inside."

They put his animal and buggy out of sight in the barn, then went inside to the kitchen.

Ellie touched the coffeepot. "Coffee's still warm. Would you like some, Bill?"

"Yes, please."

She poured them each a cup and joined them at the table.

Jacob crossed his arms. "Where did you stay?"

Bill traced the top of his mug. "My aunt Delores and uncle Glen Phillips live about thirty miles outside of town. They own forty acres and my uncle raises a large any turmoil here. We love her and we'd embrace her, but others may not for a long time."

Hannah put the plate in the cabinet. "Liza, it's no secret Jacob loves you. What would you do if Ellie came back and Jacob asked you to leave with them to start a new life somewhere else?"

Liza put up her palms. "Wait a minute. Let's not invite trouble. God is the only one who knows the future. I have no intention of leaving Charm. I hope Jacob and Ellie won't either. As far as a possible marriage with Jacob, there's a lot at stake for me. He asked me to marry him, but I squelched it. We both have a lot to consider. It's only been three weeks since Ellie left. She's our focus right now."

Esther pushed a stray hair near Liza's eye and tucked it back under her kapp. "Correct answer. We love you. Take your time."

"I love you both very much and appreciate your watching out for me." Liza kissed each of them on the cheek. She had only concentrated on Ellie not accepting her if she did go forward with him in the direction of marriage. It hadn't entered her mind they might move to avoid Ellie facing constant tittle-tattle and for another fresh new start for them. This was a much bigger rut in the road for her and Jacob if his decision to leave became a reality.

Liza, Esther, and Hannah joined the men on the porch.

Jacob rose. "I should head home. Liza, do you mind walking me to my wagon?"

She strolled with him and stopped to pet the beautiful horse. "You've been unusually quiet this evening."

"Liza, please look at me."

She faced him. His voice low and serious perked her ears. "I hope I haven't driven a wedge between us with my talk of moving if it becomes necessary. I shouldn't speculate at this point."

She shivered. Waiting to discover what happened with Ellie was all she wanted to do right now. Her decisions weighed heavily on Ellie's choices in life, and if she returned, her reaction to Liza as a potential part of their family. "Jacob, if Ellie has a change of heart and kummes home, her attitude about us matters."

"Ellie's not here. She's my child and I'm the parent. She has to accept decisions I make in my life and trust what I do is best for both of us. If she doesn't approve of you being my fraa, she'll have to respect and be kind to you. I won't have it any other way." He lowered his chin and raised his gaze to hers. "Am I a potential husband for you? Liza, again, I want you to marry me. The circumstances aren't good, but why wait? Ellie may never kumme back."

"What if Ellie kummes back to Charm and then runs away again because of us? I don't want this unrest in a second marriage. I also don't ever want to destroy whatever positive relationship you may have with Ellie."

"We can't wait forever for her to act on our plans."

"Not now, Jacob. Please understand. It's important to me to wait. Let's give Ellie more time. Let's talk about this in a few months."

"A few months? In the short time we've been acquainted, I've had no doubt you are the woman I want by my side for the rest of my life. Please, Liza, don't put our lives on hold." Jacob pinched his eyes closed for a moment, then opened them. "Everything is about Ellie. She'll have to grow up and accept what decisions I make for my life and hers if she returns."

"Please, Jacob. Accept my request to put this subject aside for now. I have my reservations about the dissention it would bring to our lives. I love you, but love isn't enough. I won't commit to thinking of marriage anytime soon. I'm sorry. I hope you'll let us continue to be content with what I'm offering you now."

"I'll not coax you anymore for the time being. I understand your reservations." He glanced around. "Everyone has gone inside." He pulled her close and kissed her softly on the lips. "I love you, Liza. Sweet dreams." He smiled.

Her heart beat with joy. She should've shoved him away, but she couldn't do it. His strong arms around her and his kiss reminded her how much she loved him. Then she stiffened. His earlier forlorn expression sent a twinge of guilt through her. The man was suffering and she hadn't helped by rejecting his suggestion they marry. He wanted some type of commitment she would marry him soon and she couldn't do it. Ellie would have to accept her first, and she didn't foresee that happening. She'd pray for God to speak to Ellie's heart and give the young woman peace of mind and clarity. Maybe then Ellie would be in the frame of mind to accept Liza as Jacob's fraa and at least a friend to her.

Jacob went home burdened, got his horse settled in the barn, and crossed the yard to go inside the haus. He slumped in the big oak cushioned chair and stretched his feet out on the matching footstool. The softness of Liza's lips from their farewell kiss lingered on his. Her past would keep her from committing to marry him. She was afraid they couldn't overcome Ellie's attitude if she returned. He couldn't blame her, but together, and with God's help, he was certain they could conquer any problem they encountered, including whatever Ellie threw their way. Ellie might surprise them and be happy to include Liza in their home. Either way, he was ready to commit to a date to marry Liza.

A dark cloud hung over him while he went over his conversation with the sweet woman he wanted to call his fraa. Why couldn't she let her inhibitions go and trust him?

One minute he found himself frustrated with Ellie and the next he was wrought with sadness. He'd give anything to have her home safe. If she did kumme home, he'd have to have a frank conversation with her about Liza. He believed Liza would be good for Ellie, even if his dochder didn't agree. She'd have to follow his rules and he'd have to stop being too lenient. If she refused and left again, he'd have to accept her decision and realize she had to learn from her mistakes. There was only so much he could do.

He sniffed the air kumming through the open window. *Smoke!* He hurried to the window. Fire blazed near his corral fence. He caught sight of a man on a horse riding away. Running outside, he squinted to identify the stranger too far away to identify. *Mr. Phillips?*

He rushed back inside, unhooked his rifle above the front door, and fired in the air twice, alerting the neighbors there was trouble. He grabbed his coat from the hook, rushed to the mare, and jerked open the corral gate. The flames licked closer to the boards, and he breathed deeply to calm the storm of worry rising inside him. His voice soft, he soothed the horse, reassuring the animal all would be well. He inched closer to the horse, threw his coat over his horse's head, and grabbed a handful of mane, then guided his four-legged friend to the barn. He was so thankful the workhorses were already in the barn.

Ezra and other neighbors jumped out of wagons and fetched pails from the barn, pumped water into them, and doused the mean and angry orange-hued blaze snapping and threatening to destroy part of the corral fence.

Jacob snatched a shovel and threw dirt from a pile he

She could be anywhere. He feared Bill wasn't a match for his daed but hoped he was wrong.

Jacob rose Tuesday morning missing Ellie so much. Each day he stared at the door or at the lane, hoping she'd return home. As time passed, he grew more anxious about her safety and wondered if he'd ever lay eyes on her again. He blinked away tears. Stiff and weary from yesterday, he peeked out the open window. The sun played hide-and-seek with the puffy white clouds floating overhead.

He would visit Liza later. They'd gotten into a comfortable routine, having coffee or tea in the afternoon at the bakery, even if it was just for a few minutes. He'd go around three, which was her slowest time of day for business. He didn't hold back anything from her, and she had been frank with him about her feelings and reservations about considering him for a potential husband. His faith in God and Liza's love for him kept him from going mad fretting about Ellie.

Swinging open the front door, he took a fresh cup of coffee out on the porch and sat in his rocking chair. The birds chirped and the slight breeze sent the water rippling over the stones on the pond's edge. He'd paint the new part of the fence.

A buggy was traveling on his lane. He stood and squinted. "Ellie!" He jumped off the porch and opened his arms wide. Bill Phillips jumped out and tied the horse to the post.

Ellie ran into Jacob's arms.

Tears fell onto his cheeks as he held her tight. "Ellie, I was so worried about you." He gently pulled away from her, his hands on her shoulders. "Are you all right?"

She glanced at Bill, standing a short distance away. "I'm fine, Daed. Bill watched out for me. We did nothing inappropriate together. He's an honorable man and no more than a friend."

Jacob swallowed the frustration and relief in his throat. Ellie had chosen to go with this young man. She was as much at fault for their abrupt departure as Bill. "I don't condone you taking my dochder with you, but I'm glad you've brought her back to me."

Ellie walked to Bill's side. "Don't be upset with him. I coaxed him to take me away. He had to get away from his daed. Mr. Phillips has berated him and not shown him an ounce of love." She stared at her shoes. "The opposite of the way you treat me."

"Kumme inside. Tell me where you've been."

Bill wrung his hands. "Mr. Graber, I'm sorry for upsetting you by taking Ellie away. I can assure you I haven't laid a hand on your daughter in a way that would be displeasing to you. I would like to stay and explain where we've been and answer your questions, but I must get going for all our sakes. My dad may ride by and recognize our quarter horse and wagon. If he does, I don't know what he'll do."

"Don't worry, son. I'm concerned for your safety too. Let's put your buggy and horse in the barn in case your daed passes by, then we'll talk inside."

They put his animal and buggy out of sight in the barn, then went inside to the kitchen.

Ellie touched the coffeepot. "Coffee's still warm. Would you like some, Bill?"

"Yes, please."

She poured them each a cup and joined them at the table.

Jacob crossed his arms. "Where did you stay?"

Bill traced the top of his mug. "My aunt Delores and uncle Glen Phillips live about thirty miles outside of town. They own forty acres and my uncle raises a large number of beef cattle to sell. I've visited them often through the years and they've been very good to me. Glen is my dad's brother."

Ellie reached over and put a plate of shortbread cookies on the counter in the center of the table. "Glen is nothing like Bill's daed. It's a mystery how Glen could be so kind, giving, and thoughtful and Mr. Phillips is so hateful and mean having grown up in the same haus together."

Jacob wrinkled his brow. "It is a mystery." He cocked his head. "Didn't Mrs. Phillips question your bringing a young Amish woman to stay with you, and you being unmarried?"

Bill sat back. "No. They've asked me to live with them. They've witnessed my dad's temper directed at me. Uncle Glen visited us several times to check on me. Dad didn't lay a hand on me while he was around. Yet his harsh demands and shouts at me let my uncle know my mother and I were afraid and unhappy around him.

"Uncle Glen tried to take me with him one time, and my mother begged him to leave me with her. I didn't want to leave my mother and Uncle Glen didn't have the heart to separate us. He begged her to leave my dad more than once. I'm going to convince her to come with me. I suspect she's ready."

Jacob shook his head. "I'm sorry you've had such a tough time. I went to ask your parents if they knew where you and Ellie had gone right after you left. Your mamm was kind and told me she didn't know, and she warned me to leave before her husband caught sight of me."

Bill sat ramrod straight. "Did you get away in time?"

"He found me as I headed to my wagon."

"What happened?" Bill's eyes held fear and he scooted to the edge of his chair.

The concern Bill showed touched Jacob's heart. The young man truly wasn't the same hard man as his daed.

"He pointed a rifle at me. I tried to reason with him, then thought it best if I left and did."

"I apologize, Mr. Graber. I should've had Ellie warn you in her note not to approach him. He's a belligerent person."

"I'm so sorry, Daed." Ellie stared at Bill in wonder.

"I would've gone to ask the Phillipses if they knew your whereabouts anyway." Jacob cast her a reassuring smile. "Has your daed always been an angry man?"

"My mother said he fooled her with his charm at first. After they were married, he turned gruff and mean. He doesn't bother her much or lay a hand on her. They steer clear of each other, are quiet at mealtime, and discuss only what they need to. He provides a good living for us. I learned to leave him alone and do what I was told."

Ellie frowned. "How sad."

Bill glanced at Jacob. "Ellie told me what a good father you are to her. She's blessed to have you. Again, I apologize for any pain we caused you."

"You've returned her safe, and I'm grateful to you." He sipped his coffee and set his mug on the table. "What did you do while you were at your relatives' haus?"

Ellie held an oatmeal cookie. "Bill's aunt Delores taught me how to knit a blanket. I helped her in the garden and kitchen. Bill worked with his uncle, caring for the cattle and property." She bit her bottom lip and paused. "We slept in different rooms. Again, we're friends."

Jacob noted the disappointment on Bill's face. Ellie had repeated this statement more than once, he supposed to reiterate it to Bill. The young man must wish Ellie thought of him as more than that. As her daed, he was relieved she hadn't fallen in love with an Englischer. "What brought you back to Charm?"

Ellie rested her hand on her daed's arm. "I missed you and our new life here. Delores urged me to reflect on my faith, family, and friends. The values you, Mamm, and Amish life have taught me. I'm weary of running away from the pain of losing Mamm. I fell on my knees and prayed to God to forgive me for all the hurt I've brought on you and my friends, for turning my back on Him, and for running away from Him.

"I opened my Bible to read Matthew, 11:28–29. *Come unto me, all ye that labour and are heavy laden, and I will give you rest. Take my yoke upon you, and learn of me; for I am meek and lowly in heart: and ye shall find rest unto your souls.* The same verses I'd read many times before jumped out at me and seared my heart this time. I asked God for peace in my heart. He answered my prayers."

"Does that mean you're staying in Charm and you've chosen to live as Amish?"

"Jah, Daed. I'm home for good." She kissed his cheek. "I am ready to join the church when I reach eighteen."

His heart burst with gratitude as he pulled her into a hug. "I'm so relieved and happy. This is an answer to my prayers."

Bill pulled back his chair and stood. "I should be on my way."

"Please, sit for a few minutes."

Bill sighed and took his seat again.

Jacob noticed the worry and agitation on the young man's face. It was tragic that Bill was afraid he'd run into his daed and had to sneak to talk to his mamm to avoid a confrontation with him, the man he should be able to discuss anything with without fear.

"Where will you go?"

"I'll return to my aunt and uncle's. I need to get away from here as soon as possible. My dad won't come there. My uncle is the only person my dad won't cross. He knows he's no match for his brother and the ranch hands who work for him. He also won't want to face my uncle."

Ellie went outside and returned with jars filled with water, and she grabbed some containers of food and put it all into a clean flour sack. She handed it to him. "I'll walk you out."

Jacob stood and went with them. "I'll be right back." He hurried to the bedroom and took out some money, returned to Bill and Ellie, and handed the young man the coins.

Bill raised his eyebrows and gasped. "Mr. Graber, thank you very much."

"Be careful, young man." He opened the door, and they stepped outside.

Jacob blocked the sun with his hand above his eyes. A fast-galloping horse headed toward them. The man riding the animal held a rifle in his hand.

"Oh no!" Ellie gripped Jacob's arm. "It's Mr. Phillips! He's got a rifle!"

Bill froze.

Mr. Phillips yanked the reins, jumped off his horse, grabbed Bill's arm, and swung his son around. "I knew you'd come here to your simple Amish woman's house. You knew her dad wouldn't lift a finger to you. The Amish men don't have the guts to bring harm to anyone. They're weak and foolish. He might give you money, though. Is that the reason you're here?"

Bill jerked his arm from his dad's grip. "I brought Ellie home. I didn't ask Mr. Graber for money."

"Don't run away from me, you coward!"

"Dad, I don't want any trouble. Let me go and leave the Grabers alone."

"You're not going anywhere and neither are they."

Jacob motioned to Ellie. "Go inside and lock the door."

Ellie shook her head, holding fingers to her quivering lips. "I'm afraid to leave you and Bill."

"Please, listen to your father, Ellie. Go inside."

Jacob faced her. "You must obey me now, Ellie. Go."
She fled to the haus.

Jacob took a deep breath to calm the anxiety welling up in him. The man had a volatile temper. Anything he said or did could set Bill's daed off and he didn't want anyone hurt. "Mr. Phillips, please put the rifle down."

Mr. Phillips raised the Winchester double-barreled rifle and aimed it at the center of Jacob's chest. "I'm not afraid to use this and it wouldn't be the first time. No man crosses me. Got it? Now keep your mouth shut." He swung the rifle and shoved it in Bill's chest, hard enough to knock his son to the ground. "You're an embarrassment, running away from me like a scared rabbit. You're a disgrace, and a weakling. You make me sick."

Bill scrambled to his feet, dusted his trembling hands and stood ramrod straight.

Mr. Phillips shoved the rifle against Bill's chest again.

Jacob stepped in and grabbed the Winchester barrel, diverting it from Bill.

Mr. Phillips fought to hold on to it. Jacob didn't loosen his grip, struggling to wrench it away from him.

Boom!

Jacob stumbled back, then regained his footing as warm blood trickled down his arm, staining his shirt. The bullet had grazed his shoulder. The need to protect Bill and his dochder overrode any discomfort. He had to stop this man from killing them.

Mr. Phillips jumped back, dropped the rifle, and stared at Jacob in disbelief.

"Father, what have you done to this innocent man?" Bill dashed over and grabbed the double-barreled rifle from the dirt, snapped the lever; the next bullet slid into the chamber. With a steady hand and keeping a safe distance from his daed, he pointed it straight at his stomach.

"Get on your horse and leave. I won't allow you to hurt them."

Mr. Phillips regained his composure. "You won't shoot me. You don't have the guts."

"I *will* shoot you if you keep up with your threats to harm my friends. I wish I knew why you're such a bully. Mother and I would like nothing better than to have you change your despicable ways."

"My dad raised me tough and stern. You're soft, like your uncle Glen. I'm done with you." He pointed at Jacob's bleeding arm and smirked. "And you've learned not to cross me. I wish my aim had been better. Lucky for you, it wasn't. Don't cross me again." He got on his horse, kicked the animal, and galloped away.

Bill put the rifle down and rushed to Jacob, helping him to his feet. "Let's get you inside and check your shoulder."

Ellie swung open the door and dashed to his side. "Daed, I was so scared. I thought he was going to kill you and Bill." She gestured them to the kitchen table.

Jacob held a hand to his shoulder and took a seat. Blood seeped through his shirt. Pain throbbed around his gunshot wound. He pulled the shirt over his shoulder and glanced at it. "It's not serious."

Ellie snatched up a clean cloth, dabbed the blood, and then examined the spot. "The bullet must've grazed you. The doctor should examine it." She pressed the cloth to stop the bleeding.

Bill hovered over him. "I'll go fetch Dr. Harrison."

Jacob waved a dismissive hand. "I'll be fine. If I keep pressure on it until the bleeding slows, then clean and bandage it, the wound will heal without any problem."

Ellie smacked her lips in disgust. "You talk about me being stubborn. I must've inherited the trait from you."

Bill smiled. "He's right. I'd do the same thing. I suspect there's nothing more the doctor would do."

"Both of you are exasperating." She lifted the cloth. "The blood is clotting. I guess you're right." She helped him out of his shirt and cleaned and bandaged the wound.

Bill wrung his hands. "Ellie, I really must talk to Mother. It's no secret I love you, Ellie, and I'm not ashamed to say so in front of your father. I understand you don't think of me as more than a friend, and I don't regret falling in love with you. You're a sweet and kind woman. I wish you the best." He grimaced and faced Jacob. "I'm sorry my dad threatened you, Mr. Graber."

"It's not your fault." He smiled at Bill. "Son, danki for taking care of my dochder. Please understand, I have no ill will toward you and I wish you a good life." He gave him a serious nod. "Please travel safe."

Ellie wiped a fresh tear from her face. "Bill, please tell your aunt and uncle danki again for their hospitality and kindness to me. I'll never forget what they and you did for me."

He gave her an endearing look. "I'll tell them. I hope Mother will pack a quick bag and come with me. My aunt and uncle would be thrilled if she did."

"Your daed will be irate! You mustn't put yourself in danger again." Ellie clutched his arm and stared at him in disbelief.

"I'll keep out of sight and wait until he leaves. He goes to the saloon every afternoon. I have a sneaking suspicion he headed there after leaving here, and I'll be able to talk to Mother alone."

"Bill, please don't linger at your haus. Your daed could show up unexpectedly."

"I won't. Thanks for the food and water. I'd dropped it in the buggy before Dad caught me. Take care, both of you." He waved and shut the door behind him.

Ellie rushed to the window and remained unmoving for a few moments. "Bill's a trustworthy and honorable man. If he'd been Amish, we might have had a chance. He has no interest in living our simple life.

"His uncle is wealthy and was proud to show us his new motorcar when we arrived. He reads the newspaper and keeps abreast of the newest tools and inventions. I'm no longer interested in those things. As much as I went on and on about the outside world, I rebelled and lashed out, hiding my real pain over Mamm's death. Once I realized that, I found solace in my faith in God, Amish values, traditions, and my life in Charm. I can't wait to see Hannah."

This was the thinking of the dochder he'd raised. She had kumme full circle and realized she had run from the compassion, love, and comfort of God, him, and her friends. The blessings of Amish life were right in front of her. He hoped she could reestablish her close friendship with Hannah. "She was hurt and disappointed you left without telling her."

"Do you think she'll forgive me?"

Hannah had a big heart, like Liza. She'd befriended Ellie despite her wild ways, had faith she would change. He suspected Hannah would be happy Ellie was back with a new attitude. "Jah, I do." He cocked his head. "You need to nurture your friendship with her. You've put yourself before her since you've met. It's time to listen and be a friend to her now."

"I've been a horrible friend to her. She stuck by me and I let her down. I'll do whatever it takes to win her trust in me again. Hannah's the best friend I've ever had. Maybe I can even work on becoming friends with Leah and Eva. I was terrible, boasting to them about when I left you the first time to explore the outside world at the baking social

Liza invited me to when we first came to town. They must think I'm terrible. I didn't even try to befriend them."

"Peter is crushed. His mamm trusted you, and you let her and him down. She's bitter."

Ellie's chin dropped. "I'm disappointed in myself for abandoning him. I'll apologize to him and Mae tomorrow. I doubt either of them will ever want to speak to me again. I ache thinking about it."

Jacob gazed at his dochder. "There'll be consequences to your actions, and some hard lessons are kumming your way. Mae, Peter, and others in the community may need time to trust you again. They may not be wilkoming. Don't get discouraged. Depend on your faith in God to get you through this trial in your life. You were distraught when you left, but the good thing is that you came back and chose God and the Amish life." He moved his arm to get more comfortable. "You need to make amends with Liza, Esther, and Abe too."

"I'm sorry I put you through such heartache, Daed." She fidgeted with the cloth napkin on the table. "Of course they're first on my list of apologies. They've been so good to me and I've shown them such disrespect. I'm afraid the damage I've caused will make them weary of ever befriending me again."

He wouldn't coddle her. She'd have to win her way back into their hearts. He doubted Liza, Esther, Hannah, and Abe would make it a hardship. They'd be thrilled she'd seen the error of her ways when she showed them her pleasant and loving side, rather than the rebellious one.

Liza might refuse his offer of a future with him if Ellie didn't accept her into their lives as a potential fraa. She might also want to observe Ellie for a time to make sure she was committed to God and the Amish life. His troubles might not be over with Ellie yet. "They care about you, Ellie. They'll be happy you're home."

Ellie lifted her head. "We have company. I heard a horse's gallop. Oh no! I hope Mr. Phillips hasn't returned." She ran to the window.

Jacob grabbed a shirt from the stack of his folded laundry. He winced, shrugging on his shirt, then followed her. He glanced at his rifle but left it on its hooks. He wanted to avoid any altercation with Mr. Phillips. He peeked out the window and wrinkled his forehead. "I wonder why Sheriff Williams is here."

Ellie opened the door. "I hope it isn't because Mr. Phillips hurt Bill!"

"Let's find out what he has to say before you get upset." A stab of fear went through his chest at the man's sudden arrival.

Sheriff Williams stepped out of his wagon and tied his horse to the freshly painted post. He stepped onto the porch. "Mr. Graber, I understand Mr. Phillips may have set fire to your fence."

"Did someone tell you this, Sheriff?"

"Mr. Phillips was bragging at the saloon about the damage he caused your property because he blamed your daughter for coaxing his son to leave town with her. Mr. Phillips got into a brawl with some men, and a friend of mine was there who came to my office to tell me what was going on."

Ellie's hand flew to her open mouth. "Daed, why didn't you mention this to me?"

"I didn't want to upset you. You just got home. Sheriff, please kumme in."

Thumbs tucked in the gun belt on his hips, Sheriff Williams shook his head. "I won't keep you. Would you please verify it was Mr. Phillips who damaged your fence?"

"I don't want any trouble."

"Please, Mr. Graber, I understand the Amish avoid trouble at any cost. I need to know. Mr. Phillips went to the saloon, threw glasses at the wall, then shoved the men and women who work there for no good reason. He threw a few punches at two men, shattered another glass, and stabbed a man in the shoulder with a shard of it. Three men wrestled him to the floor and sat on him until my friend fetched me. You don't need to fret he'll come here. He's in jail. I came to make sure you're all right."

Ellie shivered. "Bill, Mr. Phillips's son, left here a few minutes ago. He went to persuade his mamm to leave his daed, for her safety, and go with him to his aunt and uncle's haus in another town. Would you check on them? And how's the man who was stabbed?"

"The injured man will be fine. The wound didn't look deep. His friends took him to Dr. Harrison's office. He was able to walk there. I went to the Phillipses' place first. When no one answered the unlocked door, I went inside to make certain Mrs. Phillips was unharmed. Her clothes are gone and she left a note on the table. She told her husband she was leaving him and joining her son to live with relatives. I'll let Mr. Phillips know when he calms down. He'll not be returning home. He's done enough to land him in jail for quite a while." He hitched his hat back on his head. "Please tell me about the fire in detail. I'll add it to the list of offenses committed by Mr. Phillips, giving him more jail time."

"I was home when the fire caught my attention last night and I ran outside. A man on a horse took off. The man could be Mr. Phillips's twin. Today, he returned, and Bill, his son, was here. He was livid that Bill had left town with my dochder for a time. He brandished his rifle and threatened to shoot us."

Ellie stepped closer to Jacob. "Sheriff Williams, my

daed isn't telling you the whole story. Mr. Phillips shot him. The bullet grazed his shoulder."

"Thank you, Miss Graber. I appreciate your forthrightness. Mr. Phillips has been a burr in my side for a long time, causing havoc in this town with his hot temper and perpetual bad disposition. He's a danger to everyone."

"We'll pray he reflects on the pain he's caused his family and others and chooses to become a better person during his extended time in jail. God is all-powerful. He can make all things possible if we let Him."

"I hope you're right, Mr. Graber."

Ellie eyes widened. "Sheriff, shouldn't Bill and his mamm know Mr. Phillips is in jail? Who will take care of their livestock and property?"

"I spoke to the man in charge of running Mr. Phillips's farm. He was outside. He said he'd write to let Bill know about his father. Bill trusts him and left him their address. I told the man he could visit Mr. Phillips in jail to discuss care of the property. Mr. Phillips is a wealthy man and he had an agreement with his main man, Mr. Russell, to take over in case something happened to him. I got all this from the man when I went to the property. He said he'd asked Mr. Phillips to make a plan when he witnessed his boss's tendency to get in fights in the saloon. He figured he would be thrown in jail someday for injuring someone. He wasn't startled by the news."

"Did Mr. Russell mention Mrs. Graber or Bill?"

Sheriff Williams rested his hand on his holster. "He was relieved Mrs. Graber and Bill were leaving. He often worried about them."

"Why does he work for Mr. Phillips, given the man's cantankerous disposition?"

"I asked him. He said his boss pays him more than any of his friends who work in the same position earn. He also lives in a house behind the property as part of his compensation. And Mr. Phillips treated him decent."

Ellie rested a hand on her hip. "Mr. Phillips sounds like a complicated man. I'm happy Bill and his mamm are safe and away from him. Danki for stopping by, Sheriff."

"You're welcome, Miss Graber." The sheriff gave her a friendly smile. "I'm glad you're home safe."

"Danki, Sheriff. Please call me Ellie."

"And call me Jacob." Her daed held out his hand to the round-bellied, gray-haired man.

Sheriff Williams shook his hand. "It's been a pleasure to meet and speak with you again."

Ellie stared after Sheriff Williams as he guided his horse and buggy down the lane. "The sheriff is a kind man. I can rest easier knowing Bill and his mamm are away from Mr. Phillips."

"Me too."

Silence hung between them. Ellie grimaced and met his eyes. "Daed, I'm nervous about facing Liza, Hannah, Esther, and Abe. I've bragged about the outside world and how much I desired what the Englischers have to make tasks convenient. I'm embarrassed at how selfish and impolite I've been to you and to them. Why would they trust me again?"

"You'll have to face consequences with some of the Amish in the community. It may take a while for people to warm up to you again."

"Will you ever trust me again?"

"Your eyes and demeanor tell me you're the sweet dochder I recognize, but things will be different for us now."

"How different?" Her brows rose.

"I won't stand for disrespectful remarks or your dismissal of my authority. I overlooked your bad behavior and was lax in putting my foot down because of your sorrow over your mamm's passing."

"Daed, I've changed, and I'm determined to prove it to you."

He wanted to believe her, but she'd left him twice. Trusting her would kumme if she was respectful and responsible to him and others. Jacob had Liza's name on his tongue. The moment might be right to bring up his love for Liza. He bit his lip. He would treasure this heartwarming conversation with her, but he didn't want to spoil it. He hoped Ellie would be happy about his news, but his stomach clenched. He didn't have a positive feeling about it.

Chapter Seven

Liza added assorted fruit pies to the top shelf under the counter. The bakery door opened. She rose and spread her arms wide. Jacob and Ellie stood in front of her. "Ellie, you're home! How wonderful!"

Ellie walked into her arms.

Liza embraced her. "Jacob, you must be thrilled!" She hoped Ellie had returned to them a changed young woman, ready to obey God and her daed and return to Amish life. Jacob's dochder had a sparkle in her eyes and a glow, telling her this might be true.

He beamed. "I'm very happy. She arrived this morning."

Ellie's cheeks pinked. "Danki for the warm reception, Liza. It's really good to see you." She scanned the bakery. "Are Esther and Hannah in the back?"

Hannah ran to her. "Ellie, wilkom home!"

Hannah and Esther circled Ellie in a hug. Esther wiped a tear from her eye with the corner of her apron. "Ellie, you mustn't leave us again!" She kissed her cheek. "Our hearts couldn't take it. You're like family. It wasn't the same without you."

Ellie's lips quivered and her face paled. "I apologize

for any pain I caused all of you. I'm blessed to have you in my life. I realized this while I was away. Please forgive me, and I want you all to know, Charm is my home. I won't be leaving again." She gently squeezed Hannah's hand and exchanged an endearing grin with Jacob.

Liza's heart thumped with joy. Jacob's lips couldn't stretch any farther in a smile. She had ached for him during the time Ellie was absent from his life. "Please sit and have dessert."

Esther poured them each a glass of milk and served them lemon candy cookies. "I'm glad we've got a break from customers. Hopefully, we'll have a few minutes to visit. Ellie, what happened to change your mind about Amish life?"

The room became silent. No one moved. Liza leaned forward. Ellie's answer would determine how deeply she'd thought about her decision. She glanced at Jacob. He was the only one relaxed and confident, appearing as if he knew what Ellie would say. She assumed the Grabers had already had this conversation.

"Delores and I worked alongside each other almost every day, doing laundry, cooking, working in the garden, and feeding the chickens and livestock. She's soft-spoken, wise, and loving. I'll miss her. She's close to God and reads her Bible every morning and evening. She offered advice and reminded me how much God loved me. I think I was more receptive to her because she reminded me of Mamm.

"God pricked my conscience about my wayward thinking and reminded me I'm His and I lived according to my preferences. I was ignoring God's principles. No wonder I was miserable. I'm grateful for God's forgiveness and for yours."

Hannah rested her elbows on the table and put her fists

under her chin. "Did you wear Englischer clothes while you were away?"

"I didn't choose to wear the clothes Delores offered me. I'd packed clothes from home before I left. I'm not sure why, but I had no desire to change from my Amish clothes this time. I didn't have the same desires I did the first time I left, but I had to squelch even the smallest doubt about living in the outside world before I could commit once and for all to Amish life."

Liza wished she could thank Delores for taking the time to coax Ellie to kumme home and find her way back to God. If Ellie hadn't returned, she doubted she could've committed to a future with Jacob. She would've always wondered if Ellie would kumme home and be angry her daed had remarried, causing friction between her and Jacob. She wouldn't forgive herself if that had happened. She was almost sure she was barren. Paul's rants about it being her fault they had no tiny feet pitter-pattering around their haus haunted her. She didn't know if she could live with the guilt again.

Liza hugged herself and sighed. Jacob stirred hope, a bit of trust, and love in her heart. She'd tempered it with the fear of getting hurt. The bakery and her family and her faith in God fulfilled her. Maybe she should keep her friendship with Jacob simple. Could she stop the love she had for him from growing? She'd have to concentrate and stifle the spring in her step and the smile on her lips each time her gaze met his.

Would it be fair to marry Jacob and rob him of having kinner? She didn't think so. He could eventually find and marry a woman who could expand his family if he wanted. Siblings would be good for Ellie, as they'd witnessed with her caring for Peter. "Peter will be happy you're home."

The door opened. Peter rushed to Ellie, halted, and crossed his arms in front of him.

She rose and opened her arms, a happy smile on her face. "Please, Peter, kumme to me."

Peter squinted and wrinkled his nose. "You left me."

She knelt and held his elbows. "I won't leave you again. I promise."

He shuffled his feet. "Did you miss me?"

"Oh, Peter, I missed you so much. I thought about you every single day. Will you please forgive me?"

Mae stood back, her lips pinched. "You broke his heart, Ellie. He's barely spoken and reverted to gloominess. How does he know he can depend on you?"

Peter wrapped his arms around Ellie's neck. "Because she promised she wouldn't leave me again, and I believe her, Mamm."

Ellie held Peter. "From the bottom of my heart, Mae, I apologize for the pain I caused your son and the mess I left you, having to find another nanny for him. Please give me another chance."

The picture of Peter's confrontation with Ellie turning to his defense of her touched her heart. She swallowed. She waited for Mae to respond. All eyes were on the woman.

Mae fidgeted with the empty cotton sack under her arm. The same bag the Amish carried to take their goods home from shopping. "I was angry with you for leaving, and I've prayed about my bad attitude. I'm glad you're home, and if Peter believes you and is willing to forgive you, I should too."

Peter left Ellie and went to his mamm. "Would you let her take care of me again?"

Mae didn't respond for a few moments. Her face ran the gamut of emotions.

Liza bit her bottom lip. The silence was awkward.

Jacob rubbed the stubble on his chin. "Ellie, perhaps Mae needs more time to ponder your request."

Peter bounced on his toes. "Mamm, please! I don't want to go to the Millers' while you work. Matthew picks on me."

"You have made quite a positive impression on my boy, young lady. How can I refuse his sweet little face? He'd never forgive me." Her face softened. "I'm glad you're home safe and I would like you to watch Peter for me. Please, Ellie, don't disappoint us again. I can't stand to have Peter in such dismay. When you have kinner of your own one day, you'll understand how helpless I've felt to cheer him."

Peter clapped his hands. "Ellie, did you hear Mamm? You and I can play ball, make cookies, fish, and feed the animals together! Yippee!"

Ellie tousled his hair. "I'm as happy about this as you are, little one."

Mae studied the desserts on the shelves under the counter. "I'll take two peach tarts and a dozen of your butter cookies." She bent and coughed.

Liza made her way behind the counter and selected Mae's choices, accepted payment, and wrapped them for her. She opened her mouth to ask her about her health, then changed her mind. "Here you go." She moved from behind the counter, crouched down, and gestured to Peter. "Do I get a hug?"

He grinned and hugged her.

Mae opened the door. "Kumme along, Peter. Ellie, I'll expect you at seven in the morning sharp."

"You can count on me. I'll be at your haus early."

Peter shook Jacob's hand and wrapped his arms

around Esther's waist, then Hannah's. They bid him and his mamm farewell.

Hannah chuckled. "Mamm, why were you quiet while the Chupps were here?"

She held a hand to her neck. "I had a lump in my throat, observing the sweet exchange. Peter is so taken with Ellie. He bounces with joy around her. I'm used to his foot-dragging, bent head, and frown, and he never hugs us. His transformation around her is a wonder."

Liza smiled at Ellie. "His reaction to you is astounding. He shines as bright as the sun around you."

"I'm grateful Mae is trusting me again. I love being around him. He brings me as much joy as I bring him."

A couple came into the bakery. Liza greeted them with a smile. "How may I help you?"

Hannah and Esther beckoned Ellie to join them in the back room.

Jacob stood idly by while Liza waited on the couple.

Liza filled their order and bid them farewell. She smiled at Jacob. "I'm so happy for you. Your face mirrors Peter's."

"I'm relieved, thrilled, and relaxed now she's home." He told her what had happened with Bill and Mr. Phillips's confrontation.

Her mouth opened. "I'm shocked." Her eyes went to his shoulder. "I had no idea you'd been shot. Are you in pain?"

He shook his head. "My shoulder is sore. The bullet grazed the skin and left a deep gash. The bleeding stopped and I suspect a scab will form soon. I'm keeping a clean bandage on the ugly spot."

Jacob could've been killed. The revelation shook her to the core. The love she had for him swirled in her chest. And Bill Phillips . . . The young man deserved a daed he could respect and create fond memories with to last him a lifetime. Instead, he'd been put in the position of protecting his mamm and fleeing their home to seek refuge with relatives. "What a terrifying story. My heart goes out to Bill and his mamm. The young man must be overwhelmed and fearful."

"Bill stands tall and speaks with a strong voice. He's far from weak, and he doesn't shy away from speaking his mind. Unlike his daed, he's kind and thoughtful. He and Mr. Phillips couldn't be more opposite. He has a close relationship with his relatives, and I'm certain he and Mrs. Phillips will be happier there."

"Did Ellie say whether she had fallen in love with Bill? I'm baffled they aren't together, considering she agreed to run away with him."

"Ellie desired friendship with Bill and nothing else. His lovesick eyes showed his hurt as he left without her. He didn't push her for more than friendship when she made her wishes clear." He brought his fingers to her cheek. "I'll talk to Ellie about you and me tonight. She's home, in Charm to stay. I sense you won't consider a future with me without her approval."

"Jacob, allow her time to settle back down in Charm and life in the community. Most of the Amish will wilkom her back. Some may gossip and shy away from her for a while. She doesn't need any added pressure from you about us. Ellie isn't the sole reason for my reservation about us."

Jacob sucked in a breath. "What other reason?"

She glanced over her shoulder toward the back room. The women's chatter buzzed. They weren't paying attention to her and Jacob. "You may desire more kinner, and I'm almost certain I'm barren." She gripped her other hand and held it tight. Her gaze dropped from his.

"Liza, I choose you. It doesn't matter to me if you can have a boppli. I'm fine without more kinner."

Paul had ridiculed her for not giving him the family he desired. Jacob and Paul didn't have much in common and she shouldn't blame him for her late husband's mistakes. Her husband had called her worthless, an embarrassment, and impure. He'd accused her of committing a sin, causing her barrenness.

She couldn't envision Jacob doing the same, although she cared for him enough and wanted him to have kinner. Ellie had been a challenge for him, and he'd impressed her with his unwavering love and support for his dochder.

He deserved more kinner, and they would be blessed to have such a compassionate daed. "Jacob, I love you. If Ellie would accept me and I could give you kinner, I would contemplate a future with you. I suspect you could have your pick of any available Amish woman in the community. One who can provide you with a happy home as a fraa and bear you kinner."

He dropped his hand to his side. "Liza, please. Don't cause a problem where there is none. I'm talking to Ellie before I go to bed tonight. I'm ready for us to move forward." He reached for her fingers and squeezed them. "If my dochder shows any disgruntlement about us, my pursuit of you will not stop. My child isn't going to dictate what I can and cannot do in my life with regard to you and many other things."

"Jacob, take her home, relax, and laugh with her. Don't confront her and upset her. You should enjoy each other after having been apart and afraid you might never lay eyes on her again. I'm not ready to forge ahead with you."

"You said you loved me."

"I do, but love isn't enough for us. We have Ellie's

possible objection, which could prove difficult. Give me more time. Let's enjoy what we have for now."

His chest heaved with a deep sigh and his gaze dropped to their hands. "I'm upset you aren't driven like me to move ahead like a freight train to wed."

Her stomach churned. Her mind muddled with fear of losing him and love as deep as the sea for him, and confusion about the decision ahead of them shook her to the core. "I don't want anything to change between us."

"The difference is, I do."

Ellie came from the back room.

Liza dropped his hand and stepped back.

Squinting her eyes, she skipped to her daed. "You do what?"

Cheeks warm, Liza bustled to the back of the counter and fussed with the desserts on the top shelf to avoid Ellie.

Jacob opened the front door. "I'll tell you later. We should go. Have you bid everyone farewell?"

Hannah and Esther came out and circled their arms around Ellie's waist. Esther kissed the girl's cheek. "You should work with us again in the bakery when you're not caring for Peter. What do you think, Liza?"

Liza put her hand on her hip, then crossed her arms. "Of course. We'd be thrilled to have Ellie's help. Ellie, you don't need to rush. You let me know when you're ready and we'll work out a schedule."

"Danki, Liza. I could work on Saturdays." Ellie exchanged grins with Esther and Hannah.

Hannah grinned. "Good. I'm anxious to have time with you. I've missed you."

Liza met Ellie's gaze. "It's settled. We go in at about five in the morning."

"I'm excited to work with all of you, and I'll be on time." Ellie dropped her gaze from Liza's.

Esther wrapped her fingers around Ellie's. "We'll make it fun."

Liza rubbed her own arms. Her nerves on edge, she hadn't wanted to disappoint Hannah. She wondered if hiring Ellie had been a mistake. Her discussion with Jacob had ended awkwardly. Would they have time alone to speak again before he left? She didn't know what else to say. Jacob's forced smile and stiff demeanor told her he wasn't happy with her.

"Jacob, may I take you aside and speak with you for a minute?"

He avoided her gaze. "Maybe tomorrow. We'd better head home."

Liza's cheeks warmed. "I understand. No rush."

Esther gestured to Jacob. "You and Ellie take care going home. Have a good rest of the day." She tightened her loose apron ribbons and went to the back room.

Hannah waved as the Grabers left. She lingered. "Liza, are you nervous about something? Your voice sounded tense and you've got a tight grip on your arms. What's wrong?"

"Jacob and I had a difference of opinion and I'm conflicted about the matter."

"What matter?"

"He insists on speaking with Ellie about us marrying sometime in the future if I agree. I asked him to wait."

"I agree with Jacob. Why wait? You two love each other. It's as clear as a windowpane. The man adores you. Ellie no longer leaves one foot in the outside world. She's here to stay. She'd be blessed to have you as a mamm." She wrinkled her nose. "Maybe you should inch your way into being a mamm and start out as her friend. Let the relationship between you grow naturally."

"Again, your wisdom for such a young woman is astounding. I might consider your advice, although there's more than Ellie upsetting the apple barrel. I need time."

"What more could there be?"

"Enough about this now, my sweet Hannah."

The door swung open and three customers strolled in.

Liza greeted them. "What may I offer you ladies today?" Thankful for the interruption, she smiled at Hannah before the young woman joined her mamm in the back.

Liza wrapped the patrons' selections, accepted payment, and bid them farewell in time to greet and wait on the small crowd coming into the bakery. Hours later, she flipped her sign in the window and locked the door. She hoped Hannah wouldn't tell Esther about their discussion. She'd rather ponder this herself for a while. She emptied the counter and carried what she could to the back. "Are you two ready to leave soon?"

Esther blew a stray hair hanging from her kapp. "I am!"

"Me too!" Hannah hung her apron on a sturdy wooden hook.

The women tucked the filled dessert containers in the maple cabinet along the side wall in the back room and left. On the way home, Liza nodded in response to Hannah's comments about Ellie kumming home and her enthusiasm on growing their friendship.

Liza couldn't concentrate on the conversation. She pictured Jacob and Ellie at home. What would Ellie's reaction be if Jacob discussed his proposal of marriage? What would she do if Ellie was thrilled? She hadn't freed herself from the past enough to believe she could trust any man fully for a lifetime.

* * *

Jacob scratched his ear, then adjusted his hat. He sat fully clothed on the edge of the bed and stared at the dust-free floor on Wednesday morning. He'd kept a clean haus while Ellie was away. Something she had prided herself in before she left. He'd be happy to let her take over those duties now she was back.

His mind drifted to his conversation with Liza. She had set his teeth on edge. Her being barren didn't change his mind about marrying her. He'd told her that. Why wouldn't she take him at his word? Whether Ellie put up a fuss about his marrying someday or not, he wouldn't let it stop them from putting their plans in motion. Liza should understand you didn't let a child dictate who you chose to marry. As far as he was concerned, they didn't have any problems, except for Liza's excuses. He was frustrated at having to pay for Paul's past wrongful treatment of her. He had to convince her that waiting would be silly. He'd start with having a word with Ellie.

He followed the bacon aroma to the kitchen at five in the morning. "Bacon and scrambled eggs?"

The smile crossing her petal lips and bright blue eyes lifted his mood and brought hope that he was all wrong thinking she might put up a fuss about Liza. He took a seat.

She placed a full plate of food and a cup of warm coffee in front of him and joined him at the table with the same for herself. "I loved waking up in my own bed." She squeezed his fingers. "I'm glad I'm home with you."

His deep brown gaze met hers. "Ellie, I was empty without you. You're my sunshine and you mean more to me than I could ever fully express in words." He held a strip of bacon in his fingers, then set it back on his plate. "Ellie, I love Liza. She loves me too."

She twisted in her seat. "What did you say?"

He raised his voice. "I'm not going to mince words. Liza and I are in love. I've asked her to marry me, but she insisted we not talk about the future until we gave you time to return. Now that you're home, I don't want to wait. I'm going to ask her again."

"Daed, you're moving faster than a fox in a chicken coop. I haven't been home any time and you're ready to plan a wedding. Bringing a woman into our home is a lot to take in. I need time to digest all that you've told me. And I'm not happy about it. You don't need a fraa to take care of you while I'm here to do it."

He glared at her. "This isn't up for discussion." He forked a clump of eggs. "I realize this may be a big change for you to accept, and I would like us to have a civil conversation about your concerns, with the understanding Liza will be joining this family."

Her head cocked, she lifted her shoulders. "And if I won't?"

"I will expect you to treat Liza with the utmost respect. She's a kind, compassionate, and easygoing woman who you know who has been very accepting of you, despite your past behavior."

He sighed and covered her soft hand with his callused one. "Ellie, please be happy for me and for you. I'll always love your mamm, and I believe your mamm would want me to marry again and provide you with a woman who will love and offer you wisdom as she did. Please don't make one of the happiest times in my life difficult."

Ellie stuck out her bottom lip and stared at the cloudless sky. "I'm upset you're choosing her over me."

"I'm adding Liza to our family, not choosing her over

you." His dochder's pouted lips and sad eyes sent a stab into his heart, and her selfishness at insisting on having him to herself he understood. But he wouldn't succumb to her wishess. He'd help her adjust. In time, he was certain she would be grateful for Liza and a family.

Ellie rose and carried her plate to the sink, half her breakfast still on it. "Do you want my eggs and bacon? I'm no longer hungry." She grabbed her things. "I'm heading to Peter's."

"Give him a hug for me." He'd let her stew about his declaration. He was disheartened about her lack of enthusiasm for including Liza into their circle. Her reformed attitude hadn't eliminated all her selfishness.

She gave him a curt nod, readied her horse and buggy, and left.

He fed the animals, painted the fence, and worked around the property most of the day. The warm air and clear sky provided the perfect weather for doing chores. Soon the scent of rose bushes, sweet honeysuckle, and hyacinth would fill the air and color spots of his place with yellow, red, pink, and purple. May was his favorite month, with its introduction of summer, blooms on flower bushes, green lush grass, and leaves on trees. Liza in his life made everything seem more colorful, vibrant, and happy. He'd persevere to erase any fears she had about marrying him. Marriage had its ups and downs and it was work. The happy times had far outweighed his trials with his deceased fraa, Lydia. His one regret was not getting to spend the rest of his life with her. Being a partner suited him, and he was thrilled to have found Liza to fill the void of not having a fraa to share his day, laugh over the silly things, have their secretive, endearing exchanges, and hold each other during times of hurt or sadness.

Jacob strolled to the pump and let the water douse his

hair and run over his face. Slinging back his wet brown hair, he combed his hands through it, the droplets falling to the ground. He smiled and went into the haus, grabbed a towel, and dried off. He redressed in a pair of plain black pants, shrugged into a white cotton shirt, and snapped his suspenders in place, then rode to town.

He couldn't wait to tell Liza tomorrow he'd spoken with Ellie about them. Ellie's reaction hadn't been as positive as he'd hoped. Time with Liza and her family would change her mind soon. If not, he wouldn't live his life according to his dochder's rules. As much as it would hurt if she left to live elsewhere, either outside or inside the Amish community, he wouldn't succumb to her wishes that he not marry Liza.

He breathed in the warm air. His light heart had grown heavy while rehearsing what he'd recite to Liza about Ellie's response when he'd told her that he'd fallen in love with Liza. God had given him the strength and fortitude he needed in times of trouble. He bowed his head and prayed. "Heavenly Father, Psalms 121:1 and 2 kumme to mind. *I will lift up mine eyes unto the hills, from whence cometh my help. My help cometh from the LORD, which made heaven and earth.* Please give me patience and the right words to say to Liza and to Ellie as I try to bring us together as a family. Guide Ellie as she seeks You and Your will for her life. Help her to accept and be open to Liza's friendship and wisdom. Danki for Your love and power. Amen."

He rolled his shoulders back and peace enveloped his heart. God had directed his path and given him solace many times, and he was certain, no matter what the outcome, He would again. Liza concerned him with her stubbornness and holding on to the pain Paul had caused her. She could rob them of having a future together, and it would be a shame for both of them. Determined to win her over, he would wait for as long as it took for her to trust him fully. He hoped he wasn't old and gray before she did.

He had faith God had brought them together, and God would give Liza peace and clarity about choosing him for a husband if she'd let God take over. He'd prayed and given his problems to God and it had all worked out much better.

The rattle of buggy and wagon wheels, chatter from the crowds of men and women strolling in and out of stores showed town was busy this fine Thursday morning. The hunched-over peddler shouted to anyone who would listen as he waved his beautifully woven basket for sale. Jacob parked his buggy in front of the bakery and tied his horse to the hitching post. He opened the door, squeezed between five women waiting for service at the bakery counter, and grinned at Liza.

Liza smiled wide at him. "Take a seat. I'll be with you in a minute."

He nodded. "May I help?"

"I can handle it. Grab the coffeepot if you'd like and pour yourself a cup while you wait."

He watched her. Liza wrapped each selection, accepted money from her patrons, and sent them on their way with a smile. She gave each customer her undivided attention. The patrons gushed about her treats and expressed their thanks.

He'd had the hardware store clerk grow anxious, shove his purchase at him, and push him out the door when the store was overrun with customers. Liza knew the importance of servicing her patrons and leaving them with a pleasant shopping experience.

He waited for the last customer to leave, then poured Liza a cup of coffee and waved her over to the small white metal table. "Are Hannah and Esther here? I usually hear a spoon hitting a bowl or the oven door opening and shutting."

"Esther stayed home today to help Abe. He strained his back, and she's doing the necessary chores. A day of rest and heavy liniment on the area will give him relief and a better day tomorrow. Hannah went to the general store for me. I needed some flour, and I gave her money to buy some fabric. She wants to make a new white cotton baking apron for Ellie." She held her coffee cup. "How is Ellie?"

"She went to care for Peter all smiles and chipper." He licked his lip and forced a smile to hide the bundle of nerves rolling in his stomach. "I told Ellie we love each other."

Liza inhaled and choked on a sip of coffee. She patted her chest and swallowed hard, clearing her throat. "What was her reaction?"

He shouldn't have brought this subject up until Ellie had worked with Liza and her family at the bakery and she and Hannah had reunited to have fun together outside of work for the next couple of weeks. "She resents me wanting to marry you so soon after her return to Charm and needs time to adjust."

Liza glared at him. "I agree with her. I expressed my reservations about Ellie and about being barren. Jacob, you're ploughing ahead with plans for us without listening to me or Ellie. Please slow down and take a breath. Let's go on with our friendship and allow Ellie and me time to become friends."

"Does this mean you not being able to have kinner is no longer a stumbling block?" A small spark of hope warmed his heart.

"It's still a problem for me. Dig deep into your soul and

know for sure you're all right with not having more kinner if you marry me. I believe you've skimmed over this important fact because our love is making our world more colorful, happy, and exciting. Months and years down the road, we'll encounter issues to resolve and have spats about our silly differences. That's the time when you may resent me for not giving you a boppli."

"Don't be ridiculous, Liza. I'm a man of my word. I'm saying I can accept you not bearing me a child." He wouldn't want another child at the expense of losing Liza.

"I believe you mean what you say at this moment."

He stood and pushed his chair back. His blood pumped hard in his veins. Heat rose to his cheeks. "Liza, please don't question my integrity."

He rushed to the door, wiping beaded sweat above his brow. She didn't understand him. He suspected she had made this assumption based on Paul's blaming her for not bearing him a child. He could only hope she would reflect on their time together and kumme to appreciate his trustworthiness.

He had to leave her to settle the thunder roaring in his chest. The love he had for her had no bounds, even though she kept insisting her barren condition was a problem. He didn't know what else to say to convince her it wasn't an issue for him. He bid her a curt good day and left.

He passed by the Chupps' place and turned onto their lane.

Peter bounced on his toes. "Yippee! Ellie, your daed is here!"

Ellie turned and raised her brows. "Is anything wrong?"

"Everything is fine. I came to find out what you and Peter are doing."

She cocked her head and folded her arms across her chest. "You came scouting for cookies."

"I confess."

Peter grinned and rubbed his tummy. "We made ginger cookies and I had four." He held up four fingers and giggled.

Ellie scrunched her face. "I told you three and no more."

He put two little fists to his mouth and lifted his shoulders. "I snuck one when you went to the pump." He stared at his feet. "I'm sorry."

Jacob pivoted his gaze to Ellie. Her gaze bore into Peter with her finger pointed in the child's direction. He swallowed the chuckle in his throat. The frustration she showed at the sweet little boy brought back memories of when she was a little girl. This was her first time being the disciplinarian and facing a challenge. This job would test her patience, rejoice in Peter's victories over the simplest tasks, and be disappointed when they didn't agree. He fought to conceal the laugh begging to escape. She was about to learn some valuable lessons.

Gently tugging on Peter's earlobe, Jacob smiled. "I'd like two, please."

Ellie rolled her eyes. "You can have three." They went inside, and Peter pulled his chair close to Ellie. The acceptance and desired closeness shown by Peter to his dochder squeezed his heart and gratitude oozed from his pores. The boy had no idea how much his genuine love for Ellie meant to Jacob. Peter might be the best medicine for Ellie, to encourage her and give her the fortitude to find peace with living the Amish life in Charm.

Ellie reached over and rested her hand on his arm. "I'm sorry I was short with you yesterday."

He didn't want to discuss her problem with his proposal to Liza in front of Peter. "Enjoy your day with this little one." He patted the child's head.

Would Ellie allow Liza to show her the mamm's love she so desperately needed?

Will Liza want the challenge of becoming a mamm to Ellie? He shook his head. He would do all he could to persuade her to become his lifelong partner. He needed someone by his side on a day-to-day basis to encourage him, challenge him, and love him. He wanted to cherish, protect, and laugh with Liza every day. Hold her whenever he wanted, and kiss those sweet lips.

Ellie would work at the bakery this Saturday. He'd be anxious to find out how she and Liza got along being together since he'd told her they were in love. Maybe his dochder helping at the bakery wouldn't be a good idea. Could be too much togetherness too soon for Ellie and Liza. He sighed. *Too late now.* She'd made a firm commitment. He rubbed his aching forehead.

Chapter Eight

Liza tucked her feet beneath her skirt on the stuffed feathered cushion of her favorite wide maple chair. Her supper lay heavy in her stomach and the lantern flickered in the dark sitting room. She closed the Bible on her lap. Jacob's last statement to her before he left the bakery earlier that day repeated itself, and her mind fought to push it out. Guilt trickled through her. The strong and compassionate man had been diligent to kumme to the bakery to talk to her. He'd been honest from the start about how much he cared, and he'd wormed his way into her heart and soul.

He had every reason to set his sights on some other woman after the way she kept him at bay. Her home, family, and bakery were all she'd needed until he'd shown her what she was missing. These things were no longer enough. His sincere brown eyes and handsome face filled her mind most of the time. She'd never forget his lips touching hers or the brush of his fingers, igniting the love she held close in her heart for him.

She had to wait to find out if Ellie would wilkom her into their haus as part of their family. If not, she'd suffer through the pain of losing him. She wouldn't put any of them through the unnecessary heartache and turmoil they'd face living together in an unhappy home. Everything would be a struggle. Tension would be thick, and she wouldn't put herself in that position ever again.

Jacob had his dochder back, and they would enjoy a renewed relationship with Ellie obeying God and Amish law. This didn't mean she would want a new woman loving her daed, cooking in her kitchen. A woman she'd have to respect and obey. We all had our flaws, and not accepting her might well be Ellie's.

Liza went to bed and tossed and turned through the night.

"Cock-a-doodle-doo."

She opened her eyes and laughed. She could always count on her feistiest and loudest rooster to wake her. She stretched her arms and got out of bed Friday morning. Esther and Hannah would be joining her today. While alone to man the bakery at times when Hannah and Esther had things to do, she preferred having her family there for the companionship and help. Since meeting Jacob, Liza'd found having time to herself at the bakery gave her time to ponder their relationship, and privacy when Jacob came in to have coffee with her. This would end if she let him go.

She stopped by Esther and Hannah's as they were getting in their buggy. They hadn't talked about going together to work this morning. "Kumme with me today. I'll bring you home."

They smiled wide and climbed in. Esther rubbed shoulders with her. "Good morning, sweet schweschder."

Hannah scooted to the edge of the backseat and stuck her face between them. "Danki for taking us to the bakery. I hope I see Ellie after work. Peter must be over the moon to have Ellie caring for him. I can't wait to hear all about it from her."

Liza chatted with Hannah and Esther on the way to the bakery. She gasped. "The door's been kicked in!" She held her breath and pushed it open.

Esther followed close behind her. "Be careful. The person who did this may still be here!"

Hannah rushed ahead of Liza. "No one's here. What a mess. Why would someone do this?"

Liza shook her head. "I don't know." Flour covered the floor, the chairs and tables were turned over, and the fruit jars lining a high wooden shelf were broken, with sticky peaches, apples, and cherries spreading on the wooden floor.

"This is cruel and mean." Hannah picked up two metal baking trays.

Esther snatched a mop and pail. "We've got to clean and organize this place before we open." She bustled to the door and peeked out. "We can surmise who may have done this later. It could've been unruly and destructive kinner. We may never know who's responsible."

They lifted their long skirts and stepped gingerly over the gooey mess to the back room and gasped. Containers of fruit pastries, loaves of white and flavored breads, assorted cookies, cooking trays, bowls, and utensils were strewn across the floor and counter.

Liza, Esther, and Hannah picked up the shards of glass, mopped and cleaned the floors, and worked hard to put the bakery back in order.

"Do we have anything to sell?" Liza rubbed her aching temples.

Esther opened a corner cabinet in the back room. "These containers of oatmeal, ginger, and butter cookies are all right. We can arrange those on front-room counter shelves."

Hannah untied her apron and hung it on a sturdy maple peg. "I'll fetch the horse and buggy, pick up our extra canned fruits, and ask some of our friends if they can spare a few to hold us over."

Liza nodded. "Danki, Hannah. We'll take them goodies to show our gratitude in the next day or so." She watched her niece leave.

Esther slid the cloth curtain below the big centered working table in the kitchen. "Oh, good! The culprit didn't find the sacks of flour and sugar I had under here."

"What about our other ingredients?"

Esther's cheeks dimpled and she opened the door to the right-sided cabinet standing on her tippy-toes. "I had extra. We've got plenty for now."

Liza closed her eyes for a moment. "Esther, you're an angel. You saved the day, hiding these things. I'm thankful you both came with me today or I would've been facing this disaster alone."

Esther squeezed her hand. "If this ever happens again and I'm not here with you, you fetch us, Hannah and me. We're always available for you."

"Danki. I'm blessed to call you my schweschder." She blew out a breath. "I'm glad I remembered to take the cash home last night."

Jacob entered and lifted his brows. "What happened?"

Liza's heart thumped in her chest. She had no control over it when it came to Jacob. She loved him so much it hurt. "We arrived to find the bakery in shambles. The door had been kicked in. Jars of preserves broken and splattered on the floor, chairs and tables toppled over, and spices, flour, and sugar sacks broken open and tossed on the counters. The place was a mess."

"You should've kumme to get me. I would've been glad to help you clean up. Who could've done this and why?"

Liza put her hands to her cheeks. "You're kind to offer. Esther and Hannah grabbed mops and rags and whipped the bakery back into shape with me in time to open." She frowned. "Mr. Phillips is in jail or I would've suspected him. No one else kummes to mind."

Scratching his chin, Jacob appeared in deep thought. "I'll go talk to Sheriff Williams. Maybe other store owners have had break-ins and reported the damage to him."

Again, he'd offered to help. Always kumming to her aid. She found comfort in knowing he was available and willing to assist her with whatever she needed. She didn't want to grow dependent on him. She bit her lip. It was too late. "I'd rather not involve the sheriff. I don't want to draw attention to our community. We should avoid involving the law in our Amish lives if at all possible."

Hands on hips, he heaved a big sigh. "Liza, we need to know if this was an isolated incident. If so, this attack on your business is personal. I'm worried about you, Esther, and Hannah here alone."

Esther's mouth flew open. "Liza, Jacob's right. Please let him speak with the sheriff. We must know what we're facing."

Hannah carried in a bag. "Jacob, greetings." She shifted the bag to her other arm. "The general store had preserves, sugar, flour, and everything else we need for today."

Jacob reached for the bag and set it on the counter. He smiled wide. "Always a pleasure, Hannah." He nodded to Liza. "I'll fetch tools and lumber and fix your door. On the way to the store, I'll speak with the sheriff."

"Danki, Jacob."

Liza watched Jacob leave. He had a knack for showing up right when she needed him. Something she would miss when she told him she couldn't marry him. She had a stack of reasons why she was dreading that conversation and was putting it off. Could the love, respect, honor, and his integrity, along with the overwhelming love she had for him, outweigh her concerns? She pressed a hand to her forehead. She'd give herself more time before putting an end to their relationship. She hoped they could remain friends. "I'm anxious to find out what the sheriff will say." Hand to her cheek, she stared at Esther.

Esther patted Liza's shoulder. "Jacob swoons each time he sets eyes on you. The man's eyes betray his emotions. I find it an endearing trait. Put the man out of his misery, Liza. Tell him you feel the same. You blush, smile wide, and get giddy around him."

"You make it sound simple. It's not." She pushed desserts closer together in the case. "I don't want to talk about this, Esther."

Hannah leaned back against the wall. "Why not? This should be a happy conversation. What could be wrong with him? He adores you."

"Please don't push me."

"We'll let you off the hook for now." Esther put a finger under Liza's chin, lifted it, and stared into her eyes. "Don't let him go. I believe you'll regret it if you do." She patted her schweschder's shoulder and went into the kitchen.

Hannah kissed Liza's cheek. "Listen to Mamm. He's nothing like Uncle Paul."

Liza dabbed her tears with the corner of her apron. Her family didn't understand. Ellie's reaction and not being able to have kinner concerned her. Issues she considered too big to overlook. She cared about Jacob so much, she would let him go. No matter how much it hurt or scarred her.

* * *

Liza served customers and Hannah and Esther baked goodies until Jacob and the sheriff arrived. "Would either of you like lemonade and a slice of wheat bread?"

Sheriff Williams sat on the stool in front of the side counter. The same one he sat on every time he frequented the bakery. "I'd love both."

Jacob sat next to him. "Me too. Danki."

Liza served them.

Minutes later, Esther and Hannah joined them.

Esther said, "Do you have any information about who ransacked the bakery?"

Hannah stared at the sheriff with wide eyes.

Sheriff Williams took off his hat and put it on the empty stool next to him. "Two young male Englischers aged sixteen broke into your bakery to steal some goodies and money. They created a mess out of anger because you didn't have anything in your cashbox."

"Did they kumme to you and confess?" Liza couldn't imagine why the boys wouldn't keep their identity a secret.

"The boys are twins, and their father, a good man, overheard them bragging about their bad behavior. He brought them to me, as part of their punishment. Will you press charges?"

"You know I won't, Sheriff. We Amish don't like to cause trouble, no matter what the cost."

"I'm obligated to ask." He clasped his glass. "The boy's father insists he compensate you in some way."

"How?" Liza held her breath a moment. She didn't want to contend with mischievous boys working off their debt to her.

"He suggested his sons work for you without pay for a

couple of days." He patted Jacob on the back. "Jacob didn't want the young men around you, and I don't either. Jacob agreed to have them work for him for a day, and the father took him up on the offer. They were still present when Jacob came to my office."

Esther grinned. "Jacob to the rescue again! Danki."

Hannah nuzzled close to her mamm. "It's a good idea. We don't know these boys and they could cause us more trouble."

Liza blew out a breath. "I'm relieved and grateful to you, Jacob. I agree with Hannah." She gave Jacob a shy smile. "Danki."

Jacob held her gaze for a moment. "I'm happy to do it for you."

Those big brown eyes flowed with love for her. She was sure of it. Would she have the courage to break both their hearts and end the future they both so desperately wanted together? She shouldn't put off letting him go for good, but she didn't have the strength to discuss it with him. He'd understand after he found someone else. *Ouch!* The thought of him with some other woman sickened her. She managed a weak smile. "Danki, Jacob."

The sheriff gobbled the rest of his bread and drank his lemonade. "I shouldn't dally. Thank you, Liza. If you need anything, give me a holler."

Esther and Hannah bid him farewell and went back to the kitchen.

Jacob shook the sheriff's hand. "Danki for all your help, Sheriff."

"Good day, Sheriff." Liza watched the door close behind him. "He's a dedicated lawman. This town is blessed to have him."

"I like him." Jacob stood. "I'll repair your door."

She glanced at him while she cleaned and straightened

the bakery. The man had breezed into her life like a breath of fresh air. She didn't want to let him go, but she must.

An hour later, he packed his things. "Is there anything else I can do for you?"

"You've done enough and I've taken up too much of your time with my problems. The door looks as good as new. Danki. I appreciate everything." She avoided eye contact and stared at her feet.

He came around the counter and faced her. "Liza, what's wrong? Did I overstep taking matters into my own hands? Is it about the way I left in a huff the other day? I'm sorry. I get exasperated that you won't budge on accepting my proposal."

She shook her head. "It's not you. It's me. I have a lot on my mind."

"Tell me." He touched her shoulder and dropped his hand.

"Not now. We'll talk later." The warmth of his fingers lingered.

A young Englisch couple entered. Liza forced a smile. "Kumme in. How may I help you today?"

Jacob stepped aside and waited.

The woman pointed to a shoofly pie. "I'll take the pie and a dozen of those cute little cookies. What are they called?"

Jacob grinned. "Molasses cookies. They're Liza's specialty."

"Give me two dozen." The woman's full cheeks dimpled.

Liza packaged the order, accepted payment, and thanked the couple. She waved to them as they left.

Jacob waited until they were alone. "Liza, please tell me what's on your mind. Kumme have supper with Ellie and me tonight."

"She needs time alone with you. She's been home such a short time."

"Please, Liza. I want the two of you to talk and establish a friendship. Bring Hannah." The break-in at the bakery had taken precedence over him telling her about his discussion with Ellie. He was glad he hadn't mentioned it to her and would wait until Liza and Ellie had opportunities to get better acquainted. He was sure Ellie would find Liza irresistible to confide in, given time. Tonight, Hannah and Ellie could visit apart from him and Liza after supper, giving him a chance to confront Liza about what was bothering her.

Hannah joined them. "Bring me where?"

"I would like you and Liza to kumme for supper tonight. I'm sure Ellie would love to talk to you."

A big smile crossed Hannah's lips. "We'll kumme for supper. Right, Liza? I'd love to see Ellie." She grinned. "Mamm and Daed are going to the Yosts' for supper, and I was going to stay home and knit. This works out perfectly."

"It's settled. Six o'clock." Jacob hurried out the door before Liza could answer. He chuckled and patted himself on the back for his abrupt escape.

He sensed she was afraid of Ellie's rejection, considering his dochder's past bad behavior. Liza must be worried about how Ellie would take the news of their relationship. He'd handled problems for her to prove she could depend on him. He'd not let anything interfere with their planning a future, Ellie included.

He'd put the women together as much as possible to foster a friendship between them. He was certain Hannah and Esther would join him in this endeavor, without him having to say a word. They'd been supportive to him from the time he'd met them. He was confident God had brought him to Charm and chosen Liza for his fraa.

He went home and worked in the barn and garden. He washed his hands under the pump, then shielded his eyes from the sun at the buggy turning onto the lane. He waved to Ellie.

She halted the horse, jumped out, and plopped the reins in Jacob's outstretched hand. "How was your day, Daed?"

"Good afternoon to you. My day could've gone better. I've got some disturbing news. Two young men broke into the bakery and made a mess."

Eyes wide, Ellie's jaw dropped. "Englischers?"

He gave an affirmative nod. "They were after free dessert and money. They'd planned to rob Maybelle's Inn. They thought better of it when they noticed the owner still inside."

"How did you find out who they were?"

"I went to the bakery to visit Liza and she told me about the incident. I hurried to the sheriff's office to ask if any other store owners had had trouble. The daed and his twin sons were there. He didn't know if anyone witnessed them breaking into the bakery, and he thought it would be better if they confessed. Liza won't press charges, but the daed insisted they compensate her in some way."

"She shouldn't put herself at risk with them working at the bakery. They may get out of hand. She doesn't know them."

"I made arrangements for the twins to work for me tomorrow."

"Good. I wouldn't want them to cause any trouble for Esther, Hannah, or Liza."

"I've invited Liza and Hannah for supper tonight."

"Why Liza?" She narrowed her eyes.

"You know why Liza."

She shrugged. "I'll be happy to have Hannah here. Maybe we'll take the canoe out on the pond after supper."

"Whatever you would like to cook."

She avoided his eyes. "We have leftover ham. I'll make a big pot of ham and beans and bake some corn bread."

"Sounds delicious." He wouldn't allow her to ignore Liza. Ellie must've had a happy day. She was in a good mood. "How was your time with Peter?"

She beamed. "He's a curious little boy. He asks lots of questions about animals, food, you name it. I enjoy him. I almost feel guilty getting paid to care for him." She paused and sucked in her upper lip. "I think it will take time for Mae to restore her confidence in me again."

"You can appreciate her perspective. Peter is everything to her. You disappointed him, and her too."

"I didn't realize when I left how much my actions would wound you, Hannah, and Peter. I'm so sorry. In time, I'll win over Mrs. Chupp and restore your and my friends' faith in me. I wish I hadn't left in the first place."

"We don't need to rehash your mistakes. I'm glad you had a change of heart." He walked toward the haus.

She joined him, and they stepped inside. She plucked her apron off the hook and tied the strings behind her back. "I'd better get busy preparing the food or we won't have anything to serve for supper."

Jacob smiled and went outside to feed and water the animals. He strolled to the barn and dropped to his knees. "Dear Heavenly Father, forgive me for anything I've done or said to disappoint You today. Danki for returning Ellie home. Please open Ellie's heart to accept Liza into our family. Danki for bringing us to Charm and for all the blessings You've bestowed on Ellie and me. Amen."

He stood and grabbed a water pail to fill for the horses. He was falling more in love with Liza each day. Nothing would stop him from persuading her to marry him. Ellie was back, and he'd give them time to get better acquainted. Ellie hadn't given Liza a fair chance to know her or have a reason to cultivate a closer relationship with her. Ellie now knew he loved Liza, and she would benefit from a friendship with her. He hoped she'd understand this.

At six, Jacob answered the knock at the door. "Wilkom, Hannah and Liza. Ellie's whipped up ham, beans, and corn bread. She's setting the table."

Hannah took a deep breath. "Yum! I'll head to the kitchen and help her."

Liza gave him a shy smile. "Yum is right. The cooking aroma in your haus is wonderful. It was thoughtful of Ellie to provide supper."

He rubbed his forehead. He should wait until they had more time to talk. He bit his lip. He couldn't wait. He had to get this off his chest now. The other women were busy in the kitchen. They would be far enough away on the porch for them not to overhear their discussion. "Please join me on the porch. We have a few minutes before she's ready for us to sit at the table." He followed her to two rocking chairs on the porch.

She leaned back in the rocker and met his gaze, then stared at the pond.

He sensed her uneasiness and covered the hand resting on the arm of the chair. "Liza, do you still love me?"

"Of course I do. But Jacob, love isn't enough."

"Are you saying you don't want us to build a life together, to solve our problems together, to take care of each other in sickness and health?"

Ellie popped her head out the door. "Time for supper!"

Liza jumped to her feet and rushed inside.

Jacob gripped the arms of the rocker and closed his eyes for a moment. Ellie's timing had been horrible. Not her fault. He had a battle on his hands with Liza. He was determined to win. He'd speak with her again about their future after supper.

He joined the women in the kitchen. "You did a superb job cooking this meal, Ellie."

Liza poured water in glasses for each place setting. "I'm grateful for the invitation to share this beautiful array of food, and I'm not unhappy about not having to cook tonight."

Ellie gestured to the chairs. "Everyone sit and, Daed, please pray for our food."

Jacob bowed his head. "Dear Heavenly Father, danki for the food we are about to eat. Danki for bringing Ellie home safe, and for Liza and Hannah becoming such an important part of our lives. Amen."

He listened to the women discuss the robbery, recipes, and Peter. He hung on Liza's every word and cheered inside when she and Ellie had a pleasant conversation without a hint of tension. Pushing his plate aside, he stood and carried his plate to the sink. "Ellie, what did you make for dessert?"

"I have apple cookies."

Jacob motioned to her. "Don't get up. I'll serve them."

"Danki, Daed."

Her sweet smile encouraged him as he placed a platter of cookies in the center of the table and then handed small white porcelain plates to each of them. "Here you go."

"Ellie and Hannah, do you mind if Liza and I take ours outside?"

Hannah glanced at Ellie. "I'll help Ellie wash and dry

the dishes. It will give us more time to catch up on our news."

Liza covered a yawn. "Danki, girls. Hannah, we have to head home soon."

Ellie darted her gaze to Jacob, then Liza. "Liza, Daed and I can take care of the dishes if you and Hannah need to leave."

Jacob clamped his mouth shut. He saw the hint of panic on his dochder's face. She didn't want him and Liza to have time alone together and was determined to prevent it from happening. He held his plate of cookies and gestured to Liza. "I'm sure she can spare a few minutes."

Ellie frowned and went back to the kitchen.

Liza's cheeks pinked. "I'll stay a few minutes." She hurried to the door and stepped onto the porch.

Jacob followed her. His heart plummeted at his dochder's obvious interference. He'd remind her to respect him and Liza. She should remember the manners Lydia and he had taught her. He abhorred her manipulative and disrespectful manner.

He left his plate on the end table and followed Liza to the porch. "Liza, have you thought about my proposal?"

She leaned forward and gazed into his eyes. "Jacob, I must reject it. Ellie doesn't want us to make plans for the future. It was apparent in her hurried attempt to make it easy for me to leave tonight. I didn't miss her glance to you first."

"Liza, Ellie isn't going to prevent me from marrying you. I'm appalled with her intervention right before we came out here. I'll not allow her to make this decision for us. You shouldn't either."

"Ellie needs siblings. Her affection for Peter has proven she'd benefit from kinner."

"She'll be fine without a sibling, and I'm fine too. It's

you I want, Liza. I don't know how to convince you of this." He waited for her to answer.

She stood staring at her shoes.

"Liza, your choice not to marry me frees you of having to help me parent Ellie. Is this the real reason you don't want to become my fraa? It seems selfish." He held up his hand in answer. "Your barrenness isn't an issue. Are you saying you don't want kinner even if you could conceive?"

She shook her head and pressed a hand to her heart. "I do have reservations about becoming a parent to Ellie. I think it's only natural because I haven't had experience in raising kinner." She slid her hand to her stomach. "Of course I would love to have a boppli."

"So the problem is parenting Ellie with me?"

"My causing friction between you and Ellie is the problem. I'm sorry, Jacob. I've made my decision." She stood and rushed inside.

He followed her. "Liza, wait."

"Hannah, sweetheart, it's time to go." She managed a weak smile. "Ellie, danki for having us. I'll be anxious for you to arrive on Saturday."

"I appreciate your job offer. Take care."

Liza and Hannah left, crossing the yard to the buggy.

Jacob and Ellie walked with them. He avoided Ellie's gaze. He didn't have anything to say to her until Liza was gone. "Liza, Hannah, be safe going home."

Liza fixed her gaze straight ahead. "Danki again for supper."

Hannah waved to Jacob and Ellie.

Jacob watched the buggy disappear at the end of the lane. He cringed. He'd called her selfish. He hadn't meant it. His frustration had gotten the better of him. If Ellie didn't ever approve of Liza, he wouldn't regret taking her as his fraa. Ellie didn't have any say in who he chose for a fraa. She would be blessed to have Liza care for her as a mamm.

He whirled around to his dochder. "Ellie, I'm disappointed in you. You claim to have changed your life, yet your determination to keep Liza and me apart tonight showed you have more work to do to convince me. Don't let it happen again. I expect you to help me prove to Liza I'm the man for her, not to do everything in your power to keep us apart. Understood?"

"Did you propose?" She wrung her hands. "Did she turn you down?"

"She did. And you are the reason."

"Maybe she doesn't want to remarry, Daed. She appears happy working in the bakery and living alone. Taking care of a family may not appeal to her. I doubt I'm the sole reason."

"Don't be coy with me. You do your best to let her know you're opposed to our union."

"Daed, I was polite and included her in conversation at supper. I wasn't rude when I suggested you and I would wash the dishes so she and Hannah could leave. I don't deny I wasn't overjoyed at the two of you having time alone outside. I assumed it was to plan a future with her as my new mamm."

"Not your new mamm until you're ready. A friend is all I'm asking for now."

"I'll be polite."

Polite was not what he wanted from Ellie. He wanted her to open her heart to Liza and support him in his decisions.

Thunder rumbled in the sky. Lightning cracked, and they ran inside.

Ellie ran to her room. "Good night, Daed."

He'd had a long day. Enough said on the matter of Liza

and him. He was confident she'd grow to accept and love Liza given time. They'd gotten along fine until Ellie felt threatened by his attention to Liza. Ellie would most likely marry one day soon and have a family of her own. She was approaching the age where she'd start thinking about it.

Until then, Ellie would be expected to obey his and Liza's rules. He'd write them out, if necessary, for his dochder. Their discussion was far from over.

Chapter Nine

Liza blinked back tears. Her horse's hooves pounded the mud in the rain and the buggy wheels hit ruts in the road. Her body swayed to and fro. "I'm glad we only have a short ride to your haus."

Hannah grabbed her arm and winced. "The lightning is fierce!"

Crack!

Liza winced and flicked the reins. Her horse picked up his pace. Her heart ached. The deep sadness in Jacob's brown eyes tormented her. He'd probably never speak to her again. She wouldn't blame him if he ended their routine chats at the bakery and pursued another woman. She'd miss his voice, the brush of his hand across her fingers, his help, his wisdom and counsel, and his selfless love.

Hannah kept a firm grip on her arm and prattled on about Ellie working at the bakery on Saturdays. Her niece's voice echoed in her ears and she couldn't focus her attention on the conversation.

She brought the horse to a halt in front of Esther's haus. "I'm as close as I can get to the front door. I'm afraid you'll still get drenched."

"We're both wet from the rain kumming through on

the sides of the buggy. I'll race to the door to get out of the downpour. You be careful." She quirked a brow. "What's wrong? You're a million miles away."

"It's been a rough day."

"Want to talk about it?"

Liza stopped the buggy close to Hannah's porch. "I appreciate your offer to listen. We'll talk about it some other time. You get some rest."

"I wish you'd confide in me."

"I appreciate your concern, Hannah." She gave Hannah's hand a gentle squeeze. "I'm confused and need to sort out my thoughts. Understand?"

Hannah kissed her cheek. "Be careful, Liza. Jacob won't wait forever. Good night." She got out and ran inside.

Liza cried during the short distance home. The pelting rain seemed appropriate for her overwhelming despair. The hurt traveled through her veins and wouldn't stop. Losing Jacob was like losing a limb. He'd been a part of her life from the day she'd met him. Their connection immediate. She was certain there would never be another man who would measure up to Jacob. She'd end up living her life devoid of a husband and kinner to share special moments, hugs, laugher, and create memories with. Her plan to remain a widow had been simple and happy, then Jacob had swept her off her feet and she'd fallen in love. He'd given her a picture of what it could be like if she married again. Then her world shattered when she had to push him away.

This horrible wound on her heart would never heal. The memories of his laugh, his smile, and those big brown eyes filled with love for her had seared her mind. Part of her held on to them. The other part pushed them away, to no avail. Love could be cruel. She should've remained true to her plan to protect herself from falling in love. It hadn't been hard until now.

Liza separated the horse from the buggy harness and finished securing her horse in his stall. She dragged her feet to the haus, oblivious to the steady rainfall, changed from her wet clothes into her dressing gown, and crawled into bed. She turned down her lantern and lay her head on the pillow. "Dear Heavenly Father, take this pain from me. It hurts so much. Give me the strength to get through this trial. Forgive me for causing Jacob pain. Give him peace. Danki, Heavenly Father. Amen."

She buried her aching head in the pillow and wept. Ellie could relax and befriend her now without any threat she'd marry Jacob. Liza knew it was the right thing to do. She'd be helping Jacob much better by taking this approach. If she married him, the tension would rip the three of them apart. Now he had a chance to rebuild a close relationship with his dochder since her mamm's death. An unexpected blessing she wouldn't ruin for him.

Liza listened to Hannah and Ellie whisper and giggle Saturday morning. This was the second Saturday Ellie had worked at the bakery. June first already. May had brought unusually warmer temperatures and the flowers she'd planted were already blooming. She couldn't wait for the temperatures to get hotter this month. The young woman had been a joy to have around. She worked hard, had a cheerful disposition, and made them all laugh, telling stories about young Peter while under her care. Ellie shared Jacob had put the twins who robbed the bakery to work, and they had been polite and obeyed him. She'd been surprised.

Liza was grateful to Jacob for all he'd done for her. He'd left after the last church service on May nineteenth, claiming to have a headache, according to Abe. He'd talked to the men and had given her a nod and a faint smile before he departed. She envisioned running after him like a bumbling fool, not knowing what to say if she caught up with him.

She'd missed him again this week. Yesterday was their Sunday off from a church service, and she had hoped he'd stop by. It'd been over two weeks since they'd had their disagreement.

Hannah interrupted her thoughts. "Liza, Mae has been offered a job by two wealthy Englischers she met while working at Maybelle's Inn. The women want her to do their laundry, mend their garments, and bake for them. They'll drop the garments off to her and pick them up at her haus. She's thrilled to stay home with Peter and earn money at the same time."

"I'm so happy for her and for Peter."

Ellie sighed. "I'll be out of a job. I'll miss my time with him."

"Liza, would you hire Ellie to work here during the week?"

Esther clapped the flour off her hands and wiped them on her apron. "Before you answer, Liza, I have something to tell you."

Liza whirled around. Esther's serious expression was hard to read. Something about it made her heart race. "Should I be worried?"

Hannah winced. "Mamm, what is it?"

Ellie stood silent.

"Abe's knees are bothering him more and more. Dr. Harrison told him there's not much he can do. He has the men do the heavy lifting and hard labor under his direction. He takes care of the bills, supplies, and bookkeeping. I could do it for him if I wasn't working here. Ellie's timing couldn't be better. She's proven she's capable and dependable."

Liza raised her hand to subvert Esther's decision. "I

could hire someone to keep the financial records." She'd lost Jacob and now she'd miss her schweschder helping her at the bakery. They had time to chat and bake at the same time.

Esther patted Liza's arm. "Abe chooses to keep your and our property maintenance income and expenses private. He prefers he or I handle the money side of things. You understand."

"I do." It wouldn't make not having her there any easier, though. "I love you, dear schweschder. I will miss having you here."

Esther dabbed her eyes with the corner of her flour-dusted apron. "I've put off this decision for months. I have a good time with you and Hannah, and now Ellie. I'm available when you need help in a pinch."

Hannah shot her mamm a worried look. "I'll miss baking side by side. Should Liza find someone to take my place? I could help you and Daed."

Esther shook her head. "I'm all the assistance he needs, dear. You are good to do chores for us when you're home. We'll be fine. You stay and help Liza and grow your friendship with Ellie. It warms my heart to watch the two of you have fun working together." She darted her eyes from Liza to Ellie. "Both of you must promise me you'll visit often or I'll be hurt."

Ellie kissed Esther's cheek. "I promise."

Liza blinked back tears. "I do too." She tilted her head to Ellie. "Are you interested? Monday through Saturday from five until five will be quite a change." She would take a chance on the young woman. Ellie had been known to run away on a whim. A replacement on short notice would put her and Hannah in a bind. Would Ellie let her down? She'd give her the benefit of the doubt.

"I am happy to accept the job." Ellie wrinkled her nose. "I've got big shoes to fill, taking Esther's place. I'm more worried about letting you down than the increase in days or hours."

"I'm confident you'll do an excellent job. I'm already impressed with what you've done since joining us." Liza winked at her. "When can you start?"

"Right away!"

Esther grinned. "Then this will be my last day. Abe will probably cook me supper tonight, he'll be so happy. I told him I would ask you to find someone to replace me soon. I don't imagine he thought I'd ever really follow through on it."

Liza and the girls circled Esther in a hug.

Ellie squeezed Esther's arm. "Kumme in to see us. I'll miss you."

"I'll expect you to visit often!" Esther caressed Ellie's cheek.

Hannah smiled. "Daed will be happy. I'm glad for you both. I'm blessed to have parents still so much in love."

Hannah took Ellie's hand in hers and swung them back and forth. "We've got pastries to create and bake."

Ellie grinned. "I'll take Hannah home after we close, Esther. You go ahead and tell Abe your news."

"Danki, sweetheart. I'll take you up on your offer. Tell your daed to visit us, Ellie. I promise to feed him. Abe enjoys Jacob's company."

"I'll tell him."

"Hannah, will you stay at the counter for customers. I'd like Liza to walk me out."

"I'd be glad to, Mamm."

Liza and Esther walked to the livery. "I'm sad about you making this decision. At the same time, I love you for it. You're doing me a favor as well as Abe, taking care of the money."

"I have something else on my mind and it's Jacob. Hannah said she thought something happened between you and him while she was at their home for supper last time. She said you didn't want to talk about it." Esther gave her a hard stare. "I've waited a week for you to mention it to me to give you time to sort out whatever it is. I won't wait another minute. Why hasn't Jacob been to the bakery? He was kumming in quite often. Why didn't the two of you talk Sunday at the after-service meal?"

Liza cast her eyes on the livery door in front of them. She'd delayed this conversation for as long as she could. She had to tell Esther something. Her schweschder deserved an answer to her questions. She would've expected an explanation since they had shared so much since she and Jacob had fallen in love. "He asked me to marry him, and he wanted an answer. I told him no. My answer left things awkward between us."

"Why did you decline his proposal?"

"I'm convinced if I marry Jacob, it will ruin his chance of rebuilding the kind of relationship he desires with Ellie. She'll resent him for bringing me into their home. He wanted to talk to me in private after supper at their home the evening Hannah and I were there. Ellie piped up and said she and her daed would do the dishes if I needed to leave. I did want to leave to avoid talking to Jacob. I wasn't ready to tell him no yet. She didn't know that. It was obvious she would do anything in her power to break us apart."

"You're basing your future lifetime on one incident. Is Ellie's opinion about you a concern for him?"

She shook her head. "He's the head of the haus, and he said he'd require her to treat me with respect."

"Then you're being foolish not to accept his proposal. He's so smitten with you, he'd drink your bathwater."

Liza laughed and leaned into her. "You kumme up with the funniest and most disgusting analogies."

"I get them from Abe. He makes me cry, I laugh so

hard." Esther pointed her finger in Liza's chest. "You'll not change this conversation, my dear. Give me a better reason why you're not planning a wedding with Jacob."

"He didn't know if he'd ever see Ellie again. She's back and she's turned her life back to God. He can rebuild their relationship. One with the sweet dochder he's longed for and not the rebellious one he's been raising since his fraa's passing. I won't rob him of that."

"Ellie will grow to love you while working at the bakery. You two will have plenty of time to establish a healthy relationship."

Liza lifted her shoulders and clasped her hands together. "Because I'm not marrying her daed, she'll relax and trust me. We'll have a friendship and I'll help her as much as she'll let me, in turn, help Jacob. It's the best I can do for him now. Our other problem is that I'm barren."

"Knowing Jacob, I'm sure he's happy with Ellie. He doesn't need another child. Liza, these are excuses to protect yourself from changing your life. Jacob won't treat you like Paul did. I'm certain of that. They aren't the same men. Granted, I never thought Paul would treat you the way he did, blaming you for not having his child and belittling you. Jacob hasn't an arrogant bone in his body. He's not shied away from helping you with so many things already. Don't lose him and leave a permanent hole in your heart only he can fill."

Tears dampened Liza's cheeks. She swiped them away with the pads of her fingers. "Maybe I am afraid. Not of Jacob. Of myself. I don't want a home full of tension if Ellie's *forced* to accept me. I've always wanted a boppli, and I carry around enough disappointment. I don't want to blame myself for disappointing him too. It's not what I want for any of us."

"You're too timid and foolish about love. I've watched you turn good men away after Paul's passing. I thought you needed time to heal, or they weren't the right one for you. Jacob is a different story. You're in love with this man. You're throwing away an opportunity to have a young woman as your child who has turned her life back to God and a husband who would adore you for the rest of your days on earth. You can douse the small and big fires together."

"I'm not convinced."

"You think Abe and I don't argue? We do. Do I ever regret marrying the burly and sometimes cantankerous man? Maybe for a second or two, when he's really grumpy." She chuckled. "I love the man with all my heart and I wouldn't have wanted to miss out on the life we have together. We plow right through our problems together. It's what's made us closer through the years. I hold him when he's sad and he does the same for me. I can depend on him like I can depend on you. Have faith in God and trust Jacob at his word. Ellie will be fine."

"You sound like Jacob."

"He's a wise man." Esther elbowed her arm. "If I didn't know better, I'd think you'd been kicked in the head by your buggy horse." She hooked her arm through Liza's. "Don't make me have to drag you to the altar. I'll give you a little time to kumme to your senses, then we'll talk again."

She should be happy to have found love and excited about a future with Jacob. Her thoughts clouded her view. Was Esther right? It was ridiculous to expect that she and Jacob would never have problems. Every couple did. She sighed. She wouldn't rationalize it. Ellie had obvious objections she wouldn't ignore. In the short time she'd observed Ellie and Jacob, there was already a renewed lightheartedness about them when they were together.

Taking a deep breath, Liza headed back to the bakery. Esther's cheerful voice and hard work would be missed at the bakery. It would take a while to get used to not having her there. Hannah was overjoyed to have her new friend working with them. She'd enjoy working with both young women. Ellie had a bounce in her step, and she wore a smile most of the time. Her decision to stay in Charm seemed to agree with her. Liza didn't want anything to spoil it.

Jacob pulled the saw blade back and forth with all his might. His frustration mounted over Liza's rejection of his marriage proposal. No one had a perfect life. He scratched his head and huffed. Ellie might be an excuse Liza was using to protect herself from getting married to any man again. Liza and he had formed a deep friendship. What better way to start a marriage? He would stay away for as long as he could stand not seeing her. Maybe she would miss him and change her mind.

Hours later, he met Ellie at the barn. "Did you enjoy working at the bakery?"

"I loved it!" She handed him the reins and jumped out. "Mrs. Chupp has been offered a job she can do at home, so my services are no longer needed there. Esther's last day was today. She'll help Abe manage the financials. She said he'll be thrilled to have her home. Liza offered me Esther's full-time job and I accepted."

Jacob widened his eyes. This was excellent news. He'd be patient. Liza and Ellie would form a relationship while working together. Then Liza would have no more excuses not to marry him. Then Ellie would help encourage Liza to marry him. It might be premature and idealistic, but he didn't care. He had faith this would work out. He knew God was in this. "I'm sure you'll miss Peter. But the bakery will be fun too."

"I will miss Peter. It all worked out well for me, though. Hannah and I are having a good time working together, and it gives us time to talk. She's truly my best friend." She cocked her head and narrowed her brows. "Hannah said she thought something was wrong between you and Liza. Did you have a disagreement?"

"I asked her to marry me again. She said no." He wouldn't mince words with her. She should know the truth.

She dipped her chin to her chest and went inside the haus.

He finished feeding the mare, his eyes drifting to the small cedar box sitting on the shelf. He lifted it down and opened it. Fingering the note, he swallowed around the lump in his throat. *Dear Husband of Mine, You've blessed me richly with your love and devotion. God chose you to fill my heart and soul. It's as clear to me as a newly created pane of glass. I love you. Yours, Lydia.* He'd had a day where everything he'd touched went wrong. A sow had escaped, he'd slipped and fallen in the mud, hurting his side, a wolf had gotten half of his chickens before the noise woke him, and he'd fired off his shotgun to scare the varmint away.

She'd put the cedar box by his pillow that night. He'd found it while changing clothes and he'd kept it. He'd never forget her sweet face and melodious voice. He hadn't needed a picture of her to remember her cheerful eyes, dainty hands, and the silky tresses she brushed at night.

She left taking care of their finances to him. He'd suggested taking care of the money and bills together, but she didn't want any part of it, and she didn't question or ask anything about them. She planned and cooked their meals, planted and hoed the garden, fed the animals, and took care of their home. If they had a disagreement, it was usually over disciplining Ellie. He'd given in every time. He couldn't say no to Lydia. Maybe he should've, and then his dochder might not have gone through her rebellious phase.

Liza was different. She'd suffered a bad marriage and had emotional scars from it. A business owner, she had learned how to manage every aspect of the bakery. Abe ran her many acres of property for her, although Jacob had no doubt she could take that over should it ever be necessary. He could seek her counsel and would respect her knowledge about business decisions. This was rare in their community. Amish women were to stay at home and take care of the kinner, like Lydia had done. The community accepted Liza's role in the bakery. He knew it was because she was kind, sweet, and helpful to anyone who needed her.

He went inside and eyed the steaming boiled potatoes, stewed tomatoes, and fish on the table. "I'm impressed, Ellie."

"I took Esther home, and she insisted I take the fish from her icebox to fix for supper."

"We're blessed to have Liza's family for friends."

"I think so too."

He wouldn't say anything else about Liza during supper. Badgering Ellie about Liza would drive a wedge between them. The next few weeks could be very good or very bad.

Jacob smiled. He was pleased Ellie had accepted the job at the bakery full-time. She had commented she loved working there on Saturdays. Since returning home, she'd smiled and been more cheerful than before she'd left with Bill Phillips. The sun was shining, and he enjoyed riding alongside her to Sunday morning service at the Kanagys' home. "What a beautiful day for the first Sunday in June. The flowers are in full bloom and the pastures are thick and lush with green grass. I love this time of year."

"Me too." Ellie inhaled the warm air and pointed. "Hmmm, honeysuckle. Love the scent."

He flicked the reins. "How are you and Liza getting along at work?"

"Fine. Hannah asked me why you haven't been visiting the bakery. She said she asked Liza if anything was wrong between you. Liza told her she didn't want to talk about it, and Hannah and her mamm have agreed not to mention it again. They're waiting for Liza to tell them when she's ready."

Ellie and Hannah had formed a trust and a deep friendship. He wouldn't think Hannah would be happy about Ellie giving Liza and him trouble. "What did you tell Hannah?"

"I told her you proposed marriage and Liza declined."

"Did you tell her why?" He couldn't wait to find out what she'd given Hannah for an explanation.

"I told her I wasn't ready for you to marry anyone." She frowned and raised her shoulders. "She's frustrated with me. She said I'm selfish and foolish to cause friction between you. She said there couldn't be a better woman than Liza to marry you. Hannah said I should give you and Liza my blessing and accept Liza into our home as a friend and, maybe later, as a stepmamm." She fisted her hands in her lap. "I don't want another woman taking Mamm's place in our haus and in our lives. Maybe I need more time."

He sighed. At least Ellie had asked for more time. This was an improvement over her shutting the door on ever letting Liza into their family. "Hannah and I realize Liza would be good for our family. You should listen to her and me." He pulled into the lane and handed his reins to the eldest Kanagy son, Jeremiah.

The freckle-faced, tall, and lanky young man grinned. "I'll take care of your horse. You and Ellie are wilkom to go on in and make yourselves comfortable."

"Danki, Jeremiah." Jacob tipped his hat to the lad.

Ellie nodded to the young man and ran to meet Hannah going into the barn.

Jacob went inside the barn, spotting Ellie across the large sitting room next to Hannah. He shifted his gaze to Liza on the other side of Hannah. So beautiful, poised, and quiet.

She turned her head and smiled.

He nodded and swallowed the lump in his throat. Jerking his gaze away, he found a seat next to Abe. "How are you this fine day, friend?"

Abe slapped his leg. "I've been wondering where you've been. You haven't been over to the haus for two weeks. Esther said you're not frequenting the bakery as often."

The bishop raised his hand. "Let's pray."

Jacob wilkomed the bishop's interruption, giving him an opportunity not to answer Abe's question. He'd discuss his reasons with Abe at the after-service meal.

He glanced at Liza as he held his Ausbund and chanted the hymn. His heart sank in his chest. A sadness crept over him, as it had so often these past two weeks. He missed their times together. Had she missed him? He had prayed giving her time to dwell on her decision not to marry him and not having him in her life would bring her back to him.

The bishop's message couldn't have been more appropriate for them. He'd talked about commitment and trust in marriage. The bishop reminded them to pray to God and trust Him to help them work through their problems *together*.

The service ended two and a half hours later, and Abe motioned for him to join him outside, away from the crowd. "Jacob, is anything wrong between you and Liza? If I didn't care, I wouldn't pry. She's been quiet and sad. You can see it in her eyes. If something is wrong, tell me how I can help." He rested a hand on Jacob's shoulder.

Jacob sighed. Abe had been a faithful friend. They'd formed a close friendship, and he knew the man truly cared about Liza and him. "She refuses to plan a future with me."

Abe jerked his head back. "Why?"

"Ellie isn't in favor of me marrying again." Jacob frowned.

"How do you feel about Ellie's objection?" Abe crossed his arms against his chest.

"Who I marry is not up to Ellie. She likes Liza as a friend, not as a stepmamm. In time, I believe their relationship will grow close. Liza doesn't want to take the chance Ellie may never accept her as family."

Abe scratched his bearded chin. "Ellie has taken a long time to heal from her mamm's passing. She has closed her heart to Liza for anything more than a friend. Give them both time to get used to each other. Be patient."

"How long should I wait? I'm lost without Liza. I miss our conversations. She's my best friend."

"Please be patient in Liza reconsidering becoming your fraa. In my opinion, you're wrong to avoid her. She cares about you. Show up at the bakery, have conversations, and carry on as usual. Your visits will remind her why she loves you."

"I thought if I stayed away it would give her time to miss me."

Abe chuckled. "She'll miss you anyway when you're not with her. You love each other. I miss Esther whenever we're not together and we're married. If you ignore Liza, she may think you're attempting to get over her. Is this the message you want to send her?"

Jacob shook his head. "You're right. Danki, Abe."

"Anytime, friend. Kumme and sit with Liza, Esther, and me."

Jacob followed Abe to the table and smiled. Abe had left an empty space next to Liza on the bench. He filled his plate and sat next to her and whispered in her ear, "I've missed you."

She blushed and spoke in a low voice. "After our last conversation, I was afraid you'd stay away from me. I didn't realize how hard it would be not to talk to you."

Jacob's gaze held hers. "You have the power to change our circumstances."

Liza lowered her chin to her chest.

He'd made her uncomfortable, and Abe had said he should be patient. He shouldn't have been outspoken. "Let's talk about something else. How's Ellie doing at the bakery?"

Liza pushed her plate away. "She takes the initiative to do what needs to be done without much direction. Hannah enjoys her, and they work hard together."

"I was worried they might talk too much and get behind on baking."

"They are on time, bake more than I need, wait on customers when I get busy, and clean without complaining. I couldn't ask for two better helpers."

He rested his fork on the plate. "Is she being respectful to you?"

"She's well-behaved. You would be proud of her."

"Please don't keep her employed at the bakery because of me."

Liza wrinkled her brow. "I'd talk to you if I had an issue with her. I haven't held anything back from you so far. She's really doing an exemplary job."

He stifled his smile. She was defending Ellie. Did she realize it? Maybe Abe was right. Give the women time and they'd change their minds about becoming a family. "It's early. Let's wait a couple of weeks and, hopefully, you'll still feel the same as you do now."

"Don't be silly. She'll not disappoint me."

He had his doubts.

Chapter Ten

Liza unlocked the bakery door a week later, pulling it against the wind. Hannah and Ellie came in minutes later. Liza grimaced. "The sky is dark and the wind is kicking up. We could be in for a bad storm. This isn't how I wanted to start my week. I doubt we'll have much business today."

Ellie shivered and stared out the window. "The trees are bending and the wind is howling. I'm afraid of storms."

Hannah jumped at the clap of thunder and bright flash of lightning.

Hail pounded on the roof and windows.

The sheriff swung open the door, holding his wet hat. "You women get in the cellar. I spotted a tornado. I've got to warn one more store owner next to you. Hurry!"

Liza and the girls rushed to the back room, threw back the cotton rug, gripped the floorboard latch, and opened it. She handed Ellie a lantern. "Ellie, you go first down the stairs, and Hannah, you follow close behind." She eyed a large jar of water and handed it to Hannah. "Take this with you."

Ellie nodded and climbed down the stairs, and Hannah went next. Liza held onto the rope inside the floorboard door with her free hand and closed it gradually as she made her way down the stairs.

Hannah held up another lantern and a container of cookies. "I found this on the bench in the corner, and I brought a snack."

"Good, we may need it if our other lantern runs out of kerosene." She sat next to Hannah.

Ellie moved and snuggled close, hugging Liza's arm. "I'm scared."

"We'll be safe here." She pointed to a shelf lined with containers and jars. "We've got applesauce, canned goods, and water."

The floor rumbled above them. *Clap! Thud!*

Hannah glanced at the ceiling. "Something fell or broke. Maybe glass hitting the floor."

Ellie pressed a finger to her lips. "Listen." She waited a few moments. "Sounds like a train whistle. Daed said a tornado sometimes makes a similar sound, then the atmosphere grows quiet right before it rushes through. I'm worried about Daed!"

Liza fought to control her trembling hands. She didn't want to add to the girl's stress. She'd keep secret her worry about the man she loved. "I'm sure he's taken cover. He's probably worried about you."

"He's anxious about all of us." Hannah gave Ellie a hard stare.

Liza perked her ears. The whistle had stopped. Was the storm over? Maybe the tornado had passed. She stood.

Ellie gripped her arm harder and pulled her to the bench. "Don't open the door yet. Please stay right here with me."

Liza covered Ellie's hand. "I'm not going anywhere."

Hannah snuggled close to her other side. "The wind is howling again." She shook. "The floor is shaking above us. This is terrifying!" She took a deep breath. "Let's pray. Dear Heavenly Father, please protect us, our families, friends, and homes. Please calm this storm and my racing heart. Danki, Heavenly Father. Amen."

"Have you had to go to the cellar and wait out bad weather before, Ellie?"

"When I was eight, Daed corralled us in the cellar to shield us from a storm. Mamm removed my kapp and pins and braided my long hair and told me about a time when a tornado touched down when she was little. I was afraid and she calmed me. Daed sat quiet and listened."

Hannah peeked around Liza. "Tell us her story. We need to take our minds off the wind, jars breaking upstairs, and my fear the building will fall in on top of us."

Ellie cuddled closer to Liza. "Her daed, a short and stout man, fell asleep stretched out on the floor. He snored loudly and they laughed. They got hungry and had a jar of delicious canned peaches. She said the fruit never tasted better."

"Did they have water?" Liza swallowed the trepidation and concentrated on Ellie's words.

"Grossmammi grabbed a couple of jars she kept by the sink for emergencies." She chuckled. "Grossmammi told Mamm about this mischievous little mutt she loved named Mittens, and her stories kept them occupied the rest of the time."

Liza wrinkled her nose. "Why Mittens?"

"His fur was yellow and his paws were brown."

"I like it. What did Mittens do?" Hannah shuddered against Liza.

Clang! Bang!

"More things are breaking above us!" Ellie tightened her grip on Liza's arm.

"Tell us more about Mittens." Liza hoped she sounded more reassuring than she felt.

"Mittens chased the chickens, squirrels, and my mamm. He begged anytime she had food and she'd sneak him a piece. Grossmammi told her not to waste her cookies giving them to her pet. She wasn't allowed to take Mittens in the haus. When her parents were busy outside one day, she snuck him inside. He climbed on a chair to the table, knocked over the glasses and plates set for supper, and jumped onto the kitchen counter, removed the cloth covering on the bread, and ate it!"

Liza struggled to stifle her urge to pry Ellie's nails from digging into her skin. She didn't want to discourage her from being close. She ignored the discomfort. "What did her mamm say when she found out?"

"Mamm had to stand in the corner for an hour and write out five Bible verses before bed for seven nights." She smiled. "I fell asleep at the end of the story and she woke me up two hours later to say the storm had calmed."

Hannah leaned forward. "She was a wise mamm, and knew what to do to keep your mind occupied. Any damage?"

"I miss her so much. The windows cracked, and the roofs to our haus, outhaus, and barn were missing large portions. The horses kicked in the walls of their stalls. The livestock and chickens survived. Neighbors helped each other, and the repairs didn't take long. No one had their haus or barn flattened. Mamm said they were grateful no one was hurt."

Liza had her hand on Ellie's. The young woman had stayed close throughout telling her story. Maybe she was making progress in a positive light with Ellie. She didn't want to get her hopes up. In order to find happiness with Jacob, Ellie would have to wilkom her into her life. The floorboard door opened above them.

"Liza, Ellie, and Hannah, are you all right?"

Joy on her face, Ellie jumped to her feet. "Jah, Daed, we're fine. Liza got us talking to quiet our nerves. It worked." Ellie climbed up the stairs and accepted Jacob's hand.

Hannah followed. "Is the storm over? Did you go past Mamm and Daed's?"

"Jah, you can relax. Your parents are unharmed. Abe was in his buggy on the way here. I assured him I'd take care of all of you and he could go home. He had to repair the barn door right away. He thanked me and went to rejoin Esther. I'll stop on the way home and let him know you're fine." He helped her out of the cellar.

Liza exited and held his fingers. She met his gaze.

He stretched his neck to the other room. "Ellie and Hannah must be in the other room." He hugged her and kissed her softly on the lips. "I was so worried about all of you." His cheeks pinked and he let her go. "I know I shouldn't have kissed you. I reacted without hesitation." He released her.

Liza touched her warm cheeks. His lips on hers, and his strong arms holding her tight moments ago, had her heart racing. She had longed to stay in his arms and never move. His shirt damp, she didn't mind. She swelled with love for him. His heart beating against hers had been surreal. It had rattled her to the core. She had to gather her thoughts and hide her emotions. Ellie trusted her. They could be fleeting. She had to stay firm on her plan. Ellie's disapproval of Jacob and her having more than a friendship took precedence.

She stepped farther back from him. "Let me get you

a towel." Her mind in a fog and her voice weak, she pulled a towel off a shelf. "Here you go."

"I was helpless to get to you and the girls. The weather was too bad to travel here."

This man was in agony. It showed in his worried eyes and inability to stay still. To ease his unwarranted guilt, she said, "We're all in one piece, and we had what we needed. I'm glad you didn't kumme. I would have been sick thinking of you out in this mess. I don't know what I'd do if anything happened to you." She cupped her mouth. She'd let her guard down. Closing her eyes for a moment, she opened them and avoided making eye contact.

He brushed her cheek with the back of his fingers. "I'm going to wait for as long as it takes for you to realize we're meant for each other."

Hannah and Ellie stood at the door.

"I don't know why you'd have to wait. Why aren't we planning a wedding?" Hannah's eyes twinkled. She nudged Ellie. "Right, friend?"

"Ummm . . . Daed, we should go." Ellie chewed on her bottom lip and headed out the door.

"Ellie, we need to stay and help pick up the broken glass. Some of the jars fell off the shelves, and the furniture was knocked over. It won't take long." He moved to lift a chair.

Ellie returned.

"Hannah and I can clean this up. How is your place and the community?"

He grabbed a dustpan and broom. "The tornado uprooted trees and did roof damage to some dwellings. Otherwise, everything is in order. We'll have to check your roof here."

Ellie righted the rest of the chairs.

Hannah clasped a mop handle and a bucket. "I'm going

outside for water to clean up the floor." She left and returned moments later to finish mopping the floor. "Back to my question, Ellie. Why aren't we planning a wedding?"

Liza whirled around. "Hannah, don't ask such personal questions. It's inappropriate."

"You and Jacob love each other. Ellie is standing in your way and we tiptoe around her attitude. I don't understand why you're so opposed, Ellie."

Red-faced, Ellie hung her head and bustled outside.

"Hannah, go apologize. You shouldn't have pressed her." Liza waited until Hannah followed Ellie.

She turned to Jacob. "I'm sorry for Hannah's outburst."

"I'm glad she confronted Ellie in front of us."

"It doesn't accomplish anything. Hannah may have ruined the relationship Ellie and I were starting to build."

"God is in control. I believe He put Ellie here with you and Hannah."

Hannah rushed inside. "I'm sorry, Liza and Jacob. I don't know what got into me. I should never have forced Ellie to talk about her concern. Forgive me?"

"Did Ellie forgive you?" Liza pinched her lips.

"She did." Hannah hung her head and lifted her eyes to Liza. "Do you?"

"I forgive you." She sighed.

Jacob patted Hannah's arm. "As far as I'm concerned, there's nothing to forgive. I just told Liza I'm grateful to you for confronting Ellie in front of us. It will give her food for thought."

Hannah grinned and whispered, "I'm rooting for you, Jacob."

Liza pretended not to listen to her niece. Her family would be thrilled to attend their wedding. Hannah and she were close. Hannah's heart was in the right place. It wasn't her place to bring things to light with Ellie, putting her friend on the spot.

"Jacob, danki for your help. I'll walk you out and say farewell to Ellie." She walked to the wagon. "Ellie, I'm embarrassed Hannah prodded you about your daed and me. I don't want things to be awkward between us. I need you in the bakery. You're a good worker and friend."

Ellie gave her a weak smile. "Danki, Liza. I love working at the bakery. I don't have any intention of leaving if you'll have me."

"I'm blessed to have you working here."

Ellie met her gaze. "You're a good friend, Liza. Do you understand where I'm kumming from?"

"I do understand." Liza squeezed Ellie's hand as it rested on the rail.

Jacob cleared his throat. "Liza, I'll stop in tomorrow." She nodded.

Jacob waved to Ellie early Tuesday morning. "Enjoy your day at the bakery, Ellie."

"Danki, Daed, for harnessing the horse to the buggy for me. Have a good day."

He watched her disappear as she turned down the lane. Time had gotten away from him. It seemed Ellie had grown from a sweet, innocent child into a young woman overnight. He thought life would be easier with her taking care of herself. He'd been surprised to learn it was more complicated as she'd grown and had her own ideas. Having her home had been wonderful, and he was thankful she'd turned her life back to God. Now, if he could get her to accept Liza as part of their family, he'd be content.

He surveyed the grounds for the second time since the tornado. The tree limbs scattered across the property needed to be picked up. His fence had a few loose boards and a windowpane had cracked, and he shouldn't leave it unattended any longer. He took a deep breath and shook his head. *Time to get to work. I shouldn't be dreading these chores. It could've been worse.* He strolled inside the barn, grabbed his tool belt, and secured it around his hips. He'd start with the stalls. *The horses gave them quite a beating during the tornado. Crash!* Folded blankets, a tin can full of nails, and other metal boxes with lids fell to the dirt inside the barn. Jacob jumped. The oak shelf had given way. He cringed and lifted the board and lost his grip. *Ouch!* He shoved it off his aching and bleeding arm. He hurried to the pump, washed it off, and opened a metal box for clean bandages to cover the injury.

He finished replacing a few boards in the stalls, replaced the latches, secured the shelf on the wall, and went outside to repair the fence.

Two hours later, he finished replacing the windowpane, relieved he'd kept a spare in the barn. How had Abe faired getting his repairs done? His friend had more property to worry about than he did. He harnessed his horse to the buggy, jumped in, and went to Abe's.

Hands on his hips, Abe smiled. "A pleasure to see you, friend!"

"Thought you might need an extra pair of hands." Jacob stepped out of the wagon and tied his horse to the sturdy white hitching post.

"As a matter of fact, I do. I had a horse bolt on me. Mind taking a ride and helping me find her?"

"I'll take my horse and the wagon to leave at the edge of the woods while we search for the other horse on foot. Then we can tie the animal to the back upon our return."

"Sounds like a grand idea."

Abe climbed in beside Jacob. "Your timing was perfect." He wrinkled his nose. "Hannah said she told Ellie she didn't understand why she was opposed to Liza becoming part of your family. I understand Ellie didn't respond."

Hannah had been supportive of him being part of Liza's life from the beginning. She was well beyond her years in wisdom and maturity, and she'd been a good influence on Ellie. He was surprised she'd spoken out about her positive opinion to Ellie, but he didn't mind. "You have a smart and obedient dochder. She's been in my corner from the beginning. I really appreciate her support. Liza's got me baffled. I don't know what step to take next."

"Pray and seek God's guidance. If you and Liza are meant to be together, He'll make it happen."

"It's hard to wait. I'm so discouraged." He jerked his head up and pointed. "The mare at the pond! Is she yours?"

"Jah!" Abe smacked his leg.

Jacob guided his horse to the pond.

Abe whistled. "Kumme here, girl." He stepped off the wagon, and the horse walked slowly to him. He scratched her nose and petted her face. "You must be hungry. Let's get you home and get you fed. You gave me quite a scare."

Jacob stared at his friend. The horse had walked right to him. Amazing! The friendship they had was something to behold. Abe had a way with people and animals. He could use a good dose of the patience Abe had with this horse.

Abe tied the mare to the back and hopped in the wagon. "I'm a little hungry. I'm sure Esther won't let you leave until you have some of her warm ginger cookies. I caught a whiff of them before heading outside right before you came over."

"I never turn away sweets." Jacob grinned.

They arrived at Abe's and went to the barn to water and feed the horse.

Abe hurried to grab the bucket of feed and offered it to the animal.

Jacob fetched the water, ran back inside, and watched the horse drink.

Abe patted the horse's nose a few minutes later. "I believe we're done here. Let's go."

Jacob walked alongside him to the haus.

Esther raised her arms and smiled. "Jacob, kumme to the kitchen. You must have some of my fresh ginger cookies and milk."

Abe's eyes twinkled. "I'll take some too."

"Of course you will, dear." Esther served them refreshments and sat with them at the table. "Jacob, I'm sorry Hannah spoke out about you and Liza in front of Ellie. She shouldn't have been so bold."

"She's my little protector. I have no objection. She confronted Ellie, and it may be what Liza and Ellie needed to hear."

"My dochder thinks very highly of you and didn't mean any disrespect." She gave him a sheepish grin. "I had a hard time reprimanding her for speaking her mind. I'm praying you and Liza end up together. I'm sure Ellie will grow closer to Liza after working with my schweschder at the bakery."

Wide-eyed, Jacob slapped his knee and chuckled. "Did you quit the bakery so Liza would hire Ellie?" He grinned and pointed a finger at Esther.

She raised her shoulders and gave him an impish grin. "It wasn't the only reason. I really did want to help Abe with the financials and around here more."

"Esther, danki so much. Your family has been very gracious and supportive of me. Truly, I'm so blessed."

Abe slapped him on the arm. "You're the man for my schweschder-in-law, Jacob. This will all work itself out. You'll see."

An hour later, Jacob went to town and stopped by the bakery. It was around three, and business was usually slow then. He wouldn't stay long.

Liza whirled around and stared with her mouth wide open. "Jacob, kumme in."

Her eyes were like mirrors to her soul. She couldn't hide the deep love they revealed. His heart thumped in his chest. He had a chance.

He had to believe and have faith. "It's hard for me to stay away."

Two young women came to the counter.

He stepped back and tipped his hat. "Excuse me. I'll get out of your way."

Liza smiled. "Leah and Eva, what may I get for you?"

Eva pointed to the cranberry bread. "I'd like to buy a loaf. Was it baked this morning?"

"Jah, it's still warm." She glanced at Leah. "And for you?"

Leah held a finger to her lips. "I'm not sure. How about a loaf of cheese bread?"

"I'll wrap up your purchases." She passed them each a peach biscuit.

Eva and Leah thanked her, paid for the goodies, and sat at one of the small tables.

Leah scanned the room. "Where's Hannah?"

Liza gestured to the door. "She and Ellie went to get some sugar for me. They'll be back soon."

"I'm glad Hannah has been so accepting of Ellie," Jacob said.

Liza grinned. "They laugh and have a good time together. Your dochder has the best sense of humor. She's delightful."

Jacob stepped to Liza, and they chatted about his visit with Abe and how they'd found the mare he'd lost.

His ears perked. The two young girls whispering had
mentioned Ellie's name. He listened to them.

Liza darted a glance at him and then the girls.

Eva chuckled. "Hannah isn't too smart to keep company with Ellie. She's a wild one."

Leah wiped crumbs from her lip. "You don't think
Ellie's working here, do you?"

"Her daed probably brought her with him. He's sweet
on Liza. It's obvious the way he can't take his eyes off her.
I doubt Liza would want Ellie for a dochder. He'll have a
hard time finding any Amish woman wanting any part of
Ellie."

Red-faced, Liza walked to their table. "Girls, I can't
believe what I just heard. Ellie has returned to her Amish
life and to God. You should befriend her and show your
support."

Jacob hadn't heard Hannah or Ellie kumme in. They
stood wide-eyed, looking at Liza. Her protectiveness for
his dochder stirred him. The fire in her eyes and her hands
on her hips reminded him of a bear protecting her cub.

Eva stood, her red face covered with chagrin. "We
didn't mean any harm."

"You owe Ellie an apology." Liza crossed her arms.

"I apologize, Ellie, Hannah, and Liza. And to you, Mr.
Graber." Eva wrung her hands.

Liza moved to face Leah. "What do you have to say,
Leah?"

Leah kept her head lowered. "I'm sorry too."

Ellie gazed at Eva and Leah.

Hannah hooked her arm through Ellie's. "I'm blessed
to call Ellie my friend. You would be too if you gave her
a chance."

Eva met Ellie's gaze. "You did boast about Englisch
clothes and things forbidden to us when we first met. You

can understand why I might have doubted your change of heart in following God and Amish law."

"I'm disappointed you weren't happy I'd turned to God and Amish life again. I do agree my first impression on you would be hard to dismiss. My prayer was I would receive support from the community."

Eva shook her head. "I shouldn't make an excuse for my behavior. I'm embarrassed we talked ill of you. I regret it, Ellie. Really."

"You had every reason to doubt me after the way I behaved when we first met."

Leah gave her a regretful grin. "It's not easy to forget your conversation about the outside world. You went on and on about not covering your hair, dancing, and other things the world has to offer." She sighed. "It doesn't excuse Eva and me gossiping about you. Will you give us another chance to make it up to you?"

Ellie nodded and chuckled. "In your shoes, I might've done the same. I hold no grudges."

Liza moved between Hannah and Ellie. She circled her arms around their shoulders. "The four of you go chat a minute before you get back to work. It's slow right now and we have plenty of goods on the shelves."

The four girls went to the kitchen to talk.

Liza joined Jacob at the front of the store. "I'm relieved the girls reconciled."

"You're responsible for bringing them together. Danki." He couldn't pry his gaze from her. He'd missed the sweet sound of her voice and the way she gazed at him as if he were the handsomest man she'd ever seen, and her radiant smile sent his heart into a spin.

"You give me too much credit. Eva and Leah are decent girls. They just need a little guidance."

"I didn't hear Ellie and Hannah kumme in. I'm sure they heard every word."

"I wasn't aware of them either. It wouldn't have changed what I did or said. Ellie deserves another chance. Some of the people here will be gracious and others will judge her. Amish aren't perfect. We have our flaws like everyone else."

He whispered in her ear, "I love you for it and for so much more."

Blushing, she stared at her feet. "Jacob, be careful. The girls may be listening."

He chuckled. "They can't see us here, and they aren't paying a bit of attention to us. I'm not sure they can hear each other. They all seem to be talking at once." He chuckled.

She backed up and slid her foot on a spot of water. "Eek!" She grabbed his arm.

He winced and held her up. "Are you all right?"

She stood straight and heaved a deep breath. She patted his arm. "I'm fine. Is there a bandage under your sleeve? Did you hurt yourself?"

"A wooden shelf fell on it. I bandaged it. It's nothing."

She pointed to his sleeve. "Roll it up."

She had her mouth pinched. He might as well not argue. He had to admit he liked the attention. He pushed up his sleeve. Blood had stained the bandage.

"You need a new dressing. I'll be right back." She returned and rebandaged his arm. "There you go."

"Danki." The touch of her fingers on his skin took his breath away. Her slender fingers and smooth hands were like silk sliding across his arm. "It was worth getting hurt just to have your dainty fingers touch my arm."

She swatted the air. "Jacob, you just don't stop." She held his gaze. "I'm glad you came by."

His heart shot to the sky. This visit had turned out better than he could ever have expected. Liza had defended Ellie to Eva and Leah and she'd let him know he was still important to her. "Take care, sweet Liza."

He waved to the girls. "Ellie, I'm going home."

As he left the bakery, he glanced at the gray clouds. "I'd better get to steppin' unless I want to get drenched." Ellie loved to tease him about talking to himself. He chuckled, then hurried home, took care of his horse, and shut the barn doors.

Thunder clapped and fat drops of moisture pounded the ground. He didn't make it in time. He stomped his feet to shed the heavy wet dirt and water covering his boots. He stepped inside the small mudroom off the back porch and shrugged his feet out of his boots. He tossed his socks to the floor, next to the cream separator, went to the kitchen, and grabbed an oatmeal cookie from the covered basket centered on the table. The storm resembled the trouble he'd had with Ellie; as it would clear and the sun would shine again, so had Ellie. Like old times, she'd tease him about leaving his dirty socks lying around the haus and giggle. He had his happy and vibrant dochder back. If he could convince her to support his plan to marry Liza, he'd be the happiest man on earth.

He pictured Liza as his fraa in the kitchen, sure she would be someday soon. She and Ellie were growing their friendship more each day. On their special day, he'd stand before her and pledge his love for Liza in front of their friends and her family, take her home, and wrap his arms around her waist and plant kisses on her cheeks. He could almost hear her laugh as he stared at the window. Seconds later, lightning struck close, and the haus shook. Jacob tensed. Could he be wrong? Did God have other plans for him? He pushed the thought out of his mind.

Chapter Eleven

Liza shut the door against the wind when Jacob left. The girls joined her in the front room.

Leah went to the door. "Ellie and Hannah, Eva and I are going to my haus for supper and to work a new puzzle Daed bought me. Why don't you join us for supper later? Six o'clock? Mamm always makes extra food. She encourages me to invite friends, and I often do. Liza, why don't you kumme too? I'm sure Mamm would love to talk to you."

Ellie nodded. "I'll stop to tell Daed."

Hannah smiled. "I'll tell Mamm after work and then pick up Liza and Ellie." She glanced at Liza.

Liza nodded. "Danki, Leah."

The two girls bid them farewell and left.

Liza finished waiting on two Englischers and watched them leave. She turned to Hannah and Ellie. "You can leave after you stow the baked goods. I can sweep the floor and lock up. I'm glad you're going to Leah's."

Ellie hugged her. "Liza, I appreciate you taking up for me. You've been so generous to give me this job and defend me when people have said unkind things. Danki."

Liza blinked back tears. Ellie's arms were around her

waist. She couldn't believe it. Something she had longed for and never thought would happen. "Ellie." She leaned back to stare into her eyes. "I care about you. I want you to find happiness and contentment in Charm. We're so thankful you're a part of our lives."

Hannah wrapped her arms around them both. "Jah, I was drawn to you from the first day we met, despite our differences. You lashed out because you hurt inside. If I'd lost my mamm, I may not have reacted the same, but I can understand it. God brought you back to us and I'm so pleased."

Ellie stepped back and wiped her damp eyes. "I've not had a best friend, Hannah. You've shown me what a true best friend is supposed to do. You have accepted me with all my flaws and despite my rebellious past. It means a lot to me."

Hannah grinned. "Good, then you won't mind washing the maple syrup out of the bowls we used for the sweet potato pies."

Ellie rolled her eyes and laughed. "Maybe I'm a little less thankful at the moment to call you my best friend."

Hannah chuckled and followed her friend to the back room.

Liza watched them go. She folded her hands and held them to her chin. They were precious. She pressed a hand to her stomach. What would it have felt like to carry a child inside her? She'd been intrigued when Esther carried Hannah inside her belly. The first kick she'd felt when Esther invited her to lay a hand on her stomach. *What a thrill!* The anticipation to find out whether her schweschder would have a girl or boy had added to the fun. She loved Hannah as if she were her own child. But it wasn't the same as actually being her mamm.

An hour later, Hannah and Ellie left. Liza locked the door behind them and turned her sign. Jacob's strong jawline and handsome smile came to mind. She loved his laugh and the way his eyes twinkled when he got excited telling her about working with Abe. It warmed her heart the two men she loved had become close friends. She stepped outside and locked the door. Motorcars, buggies, and wagons filled the road.

A man held up his palm. "Watch where you're going!"

She jumped, her heart thumping in her chest. "Sorry." At the livery, she pressed coins in the owner's hand. "Danki."

He pointed. "I've got your buggy ready for you."

She nodded, crossed the dirt floor, and got in. She flicked the reins and headed home. She held her face up for a moment to the sun peeking through the clouds, glad the rain had stopped before Ellie and Hannah had left the store.

She arrived home, took care of her mare, and changed clothes. She'd had a long day. Why had she agreed to go out tonight? She twisted her mouth. Leah's mamm gossiped too much. The woman had no problem asking personal questions. She would've rather had a quiet evening on the porch after doing her chores. The moment the invitation was offered, it would've been awkward to turn it down. She didn't want Leah or Eva to think she had any ill will toward them after they'd apologized to Ellie. She rubbed the tight spot in her neck. *Too late to back out now.*

Hannah popped her head inside the door. "Liza, are you ready to go? Ellie's waiting in the buggy."

"I'm ready." She smiled and went outside and climbed in the back. "Ellie, have you talked to Peter or his mamm?"

"I haven't, and I must stop over. I miss him." She sighed. "Mrs. Chupp was kind to give me another chance. She doesn't mince words. I'm blessed she softened toward me. Hannah, would you go with me?"

Hannah clicked her tongue and batted her eyes. "Of course."

Liza observed the girls. She and Esther, her schweschder and best friend, had chatted and laughed together the same way many times.

They arrived at Leah's family's haus, and Clara Mast opened the door. "Wilkom, kumme in." She smiled at Hannah and gave Ellie a stern eye. "Ellie, Leah told me a little about you. I understand you exhibited some bad behavior before turning your life around. Don't disappoint us." She gave Ellie a patronizing pat on the back.

Ellie's face froze and stared at her feet. She didn't respond.

Hannah, wide-eyed, darted shocked eyes to Liza. She clasped Ellie's hand.

Liza bristled and opened her mouth to speak her disdain about Clara's remark.

Leah and Eva rushed into the room. "Ellie and Hannah, kumme to my room. I'll show you the soft blanket I knitted for little boppli Maryanne next door."

Hannah and Ellie followed them.

Clara gestured to Liza. "Follow me to the kitchen. I've got bacon and tomato sandwiches and vegetable soup to serve. Apricot tarts for dessert."

"Sounds delicious, Clara. Tell me what to do to assist you."

Clara, hands on hips, pointed. "Take a seat. My husband, Sam, is over at the Barkmans' place, helping with some repairs. I'll save him a plate for later."

"I hope it was all right Leah invited us for supper." Liza grimaced.

"You're always wilkom, Liza."

Liza took a deep breath. "Your remark to Ellie was condescending. I assure you, Ellie is sincere in her commitment to God and Amish law."

"Never hurts to reiterate the importance of her decision."

Liza leaned forward. She pressed her splayed fingers on the table and stared at the determined woman. She wouldn't ignore the remark. She'd had enough of Clara's negative attitude. "She doesn't need reminding. She needs support and encouragement."

"I suppose." She batted her eyes. "We're long overdue for a visit. How is everything going at the bakery?" Clara handed her a glass of water.

She swallowed a sigh of relief. The bakery would be a safe subject to discuss. "Business is steady and I'm happy to go in to work each day."

"I heard Esther quit and Ellie took her place. I'm stunned you'd hire her."

This woman irritated her to no end. The hairs on Liza's neck prickled. She took a sip of water to calm herself and her rising frustration. "I don't know why. She's learned Esther's tasks in a very short time, greets customers with a smile, follows our recipes to the letter, and doesn't complain about a thing. I'm blessed to have her at the bakery."

"Liza, what if Ellie doesn't remain true to her promise? She ran off with a young man. Who knows what she was doing with him, and you take her in as if nothing happened. I don't believe it. You should be careful. She might be robbing you blind."

The woman was bent on disparaging Ellie. She'd not listened to anything Liza had to say about the girl. Liza stood and crossed her arms. "Clara, Ellie has asked forgiveness from God for her wrongs and has turned her life back to Him. She's done nothing to warrant any suspicion on my part. I am disappointed you insist on taking a negative stance toward her."

Clara rose and fluttered her hands. "Now, don't get upset. I'm just watching out for your well-being." She set sandwiches on each plate. "Leah said Jacob Graber can't take his eyes off you. I notice he glances at you often during the church service and you spend a lot of time with him at the after-church dinners. Are you smitten with him? Is that the reason you jumped to Ellie's defense?"

Heat rushed to her cheeks. Liza sipped her water to take a moment. "I'm not comfortable with where this conversation is going. Let's change the subject."

Hand on her hip, Clara waggled a finger. "I'm not going to let you wiggle out of this. It's too important not to discuss. I don't blame you if you're not giving him a thought. I wouldn't want to raise a young girl with a questionable past. You never know what she'll do in the future. The community is still talking about her running away."

"Clara, stop talking ill of Ellie! We all make mistakes. She's moved on and so should we from this conversation. I won't stay and listen to you berate her."

"You can understand, Liza. I have a dochder to raise. I don't want her influenced by a rude and obstinate girl. I had my misgivings about Ellie being here. Leah insisted I give her a chance. I thought I could express my concerns to you and you'd sympathize with me."

"You're wrong. I love and care about Ellie. She's vibrant, funny, kind, and a good friend to Hannah. She's not perfect. None of us are without faults."

"All right, all right. I'll quit talking about Ellie. Tell me about Jacob. You didn't answer my question. Are you interested in him? He's attractive and everyone has pleasant things to say about him."

Supper, at this rate, would be painful to get through. "I'd prefer not to discuss Jacob."

"No harm in expressing how you feel about him."

"He's a kind and thoughtful man. I have nothing against him. We're friends."

The girls entered, and Leah rubbed her middle. "Is supper ready?"

"Go ahead and sit. Everything is on the table." Clara brushed her palms together.

Once everyone was at the table, Clara prayed for the food and served them soup. "Ellie, have you really decided to stay in Charm?"

Leah gasped. "Mamm, please don't ask Ellie personal questions. Of course she plans to stay."

Ellie unfolded her cloth napkin and spread it on her lap. "It's all right, Leah. I'll answer your mamm's question. First, I overheard your conversation with Liza. The door was wide open in Leah's room. I have asked forgiveness from God and those I hurt by my bad behavior. I won't change my mind. Can you find it in your heart to give me the benefit of the doubt?"

Cheeks flaming, Clara fumbled with her spoon. "Of course, dear. You can understand it will take a while to fully trust you."

Ellie nodded.

Liza beamed with pride for Ellie. She'd stamped the fire out of Clara with her humble comment.

Clara darted a glance to Liza, then to Ellie. "Maybe you'll shed some light on the subject of your daed and Liza. He beams when he talks to her." She raised her chin. "He's obviously smitten with her. What do you think?"

Liza held her breath.

Ellie sat next to her and covered Liza's hand on her lap, out of Clara's sight. "Liza is a private person. I respect her wishes and I ask you to do the same. You understand." She then slid her hand off Liza's and sipped a spoonful of soup. "Your soup is tasty."

Dumbfounded, Liza stifled her smile. Ellie had done a better job squelching this conversation with Clara than she had. Her hand still tingled where Ellie had touched it. She was hungry for any show of emotion and friendship from this girl. She mustn't do anything to jeopardize it.

Liza smiled. The young women laughed and shared funny stories. Leah and Eva treated Ellie as if they'd been friends with her for a long time. No trace of their past negative judgment about her evident.

Liza yawned and covered her mouth. "I'm afraid my eyes are growing heavy. I woke earlier than usual this morning. We should help you clean the dishes and get home before dark." She carried her glass and plate to the dry sink.

Clara rose and collected the dirty dishes. "I'm glad you came to visit. No need to bother washing dishes. Leah will help me clean up." She hooked her arm through Liza's. "We'll walk you out."

Eva came alongside Liza. "Do you mind if Hannah drops me off before taking you home? Leah picked me up today."

"I'd be happy to have you join us on the way home." Liza and the girls thanked Clara and bid her and Leah farewell. The girls chattered with Eva until they arrived at the young woman's haus.

Eva stepped out of the buggy. "Danki for dropping me off. I had a good time with all of you."

They waved back and bid her good night.

Hannah waited until Eva was inside, then headed down the lane toward Ellie's.

"Eva and Leah are interesting and sweet girls. I'm glad they forgave me for the way I acted to them in the past. I understand it's difficult to trust I have truly changed after I boasted about my outside world adventures," said Ellie.

"Leah is opinionated, but she will listen to reason and back down better than her mamm. She doesn't always have to be right. I'm not surprised she gave you a chance to show how you've changed. Her mamm is another story. Eva goes along with whatever Leah says. The girls are best friends. She's got a good sense of humor, and she can

tell the best funny stories about her barn cats and dog."
Hannah chuckled.

Ellie exaggerated a swipe of her hand across her forehead. "Mrs. Mast isn't shy. She'll ask anything. She really
pushed you to answer personal questions, Liza." Ellie
rested a hand on Liza's arm. "Danki again for taking up for
me. I'm sorry you're having to defend me to others."

Hannah grinned at Ellie. "We don't mind at all. Right,
Liza?"

"Right. And Ellie, I'm proud of how you handled yourself with Clara." Liza gave her a warm smile. Ellie didn't
bring up Clara's question about her and Jacob. Liza ignored the girls' chatter and stared out at the road ahead.
Would Ellie tell Jacob that Clara had asked about Liza's
interest in him? She'd be curious the next time they spoke
to see if he would bring the matter up. If he didn't mention it, she'd tell him. Better kumming from her than if he
heard it from someone else. She didn't want him to think
she'd discussed him with Clara. Conversations could be
misconstrued when Clara and her gossips got together.

Hannah said, "Leah and Eva have made some beautiful quilts together, and both have almost completed white
aprons. Their seams are as straight as yours, Liza."

Liza patted her shoulder. "You're too hard on yourself.
You sew beautiful pieces."

Ellie smiled back at Liza. "Hannah said you create
beautiful kapps, towels, and quilts. I love the pinwheel
quilt you have hanging on the wall at the bakery. It's exquisite."

Liza blushed. Ellie had complimented her work. They
really were making progress in their friendship. No doubt
her niece was encouraging this, and she loved Hannah
for it.

* * *

Jacob held his Bible in his lap and sipped coffee. "Ellie, sit and tell me about your visit with the girls."

She plopped on the settee across from him. "You're in from doing chores early."

"I got up earlier than usual, and I got enough done to take it easy this evening."

She took in a deep breath. "Summer is my favorite season. The days are longer, the flowers are vibrant, and the lush green grass is pretty. The heat doesn't bother me. I dislike snow and the cold. Hannah agrees with me. Another thing we have in common."

"Did you have a pleasant time with Eva and Leah?"

"They were kind and gracious hosts. Eva and Leah invited Hannah and me to join them whenever we have time. The girls get together and make aprons, blankets, and many other things. Working at the bakery doesn't allow us much extra time to do those things. I don't mind, though."

"How did you like Leah's parents?"

Ellie rolled her eyes. "Leah's daed was helping a neighbor. We didn't meet him. Leah's mamm, Clara, is quite a gossip. She asks inappropriate personal questions. I suspect she repeats what information she gathers and embellishes it to her friends. Liking her is a challenge."

Jacob closed his Bible and put it on the end table. "What kind of questions?"

"The girls and I were in Leah's bedroom. I was sitting closest to her open door and overheard Leah's mamm and Liza's conversation. The woman criticized me for leaving the community and had reservations about Leah and me being friends. Liza assured her I was genuine in my commitment to return to God and the Amish life. Then she asked Liza about her feelings for you."

His eyes wide, he jerked upright. "What did she say?"

"Clara asked her if she had a romantic interest in you.

Liza said she would rather keep the matter personal. She made it clear she didn't want to discuss you." She gave him an impish grin. "She did say you were a kind and thoughtful man."

He chuckled. "Interesting. The gossips are conversing about Liza and me. It doesn't bother me. I'd shout to the world how much I love her."

Ellie quieted.

"What are you afraid of?"

Ellie shrugged and whirled around toward her bedroom, but before she could get very far there was a knock on the front door.

Ellie approached the front door and opened it. "Peter!"

He wrapped his arms around her legs. "I miss you, Ellie. Why haven't you been to visit me?"

"Mae, please kumme in." She bent and hugged the child. "I've been working at the bakery and my job has kept me busy. I miss you too. How have you been?"

Mae held a hand to her mouth and coughed a deep, throaty cough. "I'm so sorry. I've had this cough for weeks and it's gotten worse."

Jacob went to a pitcher of water and poured her a glass. "Here you go."

"Danki."

Peter sighed. "I was sad. I begged Mamm to bring me to your haus."

Mae drank half the glass of water and passed it back to Jacob. "The water helped soothe my throat. Danki. This irritating cough kummes and goes." She raised her shoulders. "I'm sorry to intrude on you. It's getting close to dark, but this child refused to go to sleep if I didn't bring him here. He has been obsessed with you, Ellie."

"You're both wilkom to our home anytime." She smiled.

Jacob gestured to a chair. "Make yourselves comfortable. Would you like a Luden's Cough Drop?"

Mae nodded her head. "Please, anything to get rid of this misery."

He went to the kitchen and returned. He passed her a small metal box. "I've got more if you need them."

She plopped the drop in her mouth. "I appreciate it, Jacob. One should do it."

"I'm glad you came to my haus, Peter. Tell me what you've been doing." Ellie stroked his hair.

"Snuggles, my rabbit, got away, and I was afraid he'd never kumme home. I found him under the bush by the pond. He's safe now."

"I'd be sad if you lost Snuggles. I love his snow-white fur." She held him on her lap and wrapped her arm around his waist. "What else is going on with you?"

"Mr. Fisher has been kumming to our haus and having suppers with Mamm and me a lot. Mamm laughs more now." He giggled and cupped a hand to his mouth. "He asked me if it was all right for him to ask Mamm to marry him."

"Peter! You aren't to tell our personal business." Mae's cheeks pinked.

"I tell Ellie everything. She's my friend. Don't worry. She won't tell anyone, right, Ellie?"

"Right." Ellie smiled at Mae. "I'm happy for you."

Jacob grinned. "Me too."

"I'm so embarrassed." Mae hid her face in her hands, then dropped them to her lap. "He's been wonderful to us."

Jacob leaned forward in his chair, rested his elbows on his knees, and folded his hands. "You're among friends, Mae. We love and care about Peter. He's been as good for Ellie as she has been for him. If you don't mind, I think Peter needs to spill his thoughts to her." He winked. "Parents can find out some important information listening to what our kinner tell their friends about us."

"What did you tell Mr. Fisher?" Ellie gazed at Peter.

"I said I would be glad if he married Mamm. She's happier when he's with us." He gave her an impish grin and lifted his shoulders. "He took me fishing and I caught two bluegills. He said he'd take me again. It would be fun to have him live with us. He said we'd do lots of fun things together." He grew serious. "Will you take me fishing, Ellie?"

Jacob wished Ellie had the same positive attitude toward Liza as Peter did about Mr. Fisher. Mae had presented a softer side during this visit. Mr. Fisher must be bringing out the best in her. She had a radiant and happy glow.

"Of course I will. May I bring Hannah?"

"Jah, I like Hannah."

Mae coughed again. She pulled out a handkerchief tucked in her waistband and held it to her mouth. She got her cough under control and hurried to fold the cloth, wet with blood. "Ellie, you don't have to. I realize you're busy."

"I would enjoy taking Peter. We'll have a good time. Is Friday night all right with you, Mae?"

"Friday around five-thirty is fine."

"Hannah and I will have supper before we arrive."

"You're wilkom to join us for chicken and dumplings. Bring Liza with you and Hannah, if she wants to kumme."

"You don't have to ask me twice. Danki. I'll ask them."

"I'll make enough for all of you. If they don't kumme, we'll eat the leftovers the next night." Mae gripped the armrest for support and rose.

Peter hugged Ellie's neck. "I can't wait until Friday gets here."

"Ellie, I took up for you recently with some women saying unkind remarks about you concerning the time you left us. I assured them you were sincere about your change of heart, and I asked them to refrain from such talk. You have my support."

Ellie helped Peter to his feet and walked to his mamm. Tears filled her eyes. "Danki for forgiving me for letting you down and for having faith in me."

Mae circled her arms around her. "None of us are without fault, Ellie. I have had a habit of judging people and gossiping, and I'm ashamed to admit it. I've been working on changing my attitude, and Mr. Fisher has brought out the best in me. The gossips need to remember the hurtful words they're uttering are sinful. You're a dear, sweet girl who has brought life back to my son. I'll always be grateful to you."

"He's healed wounds in me too." Ellie tousled his hair.

Mae nodded to Jacob. "You were right. I did learn Mr. Fisher had approached my son about a future with us. Peter didn't mention it until now."

Jacob gave her a warm smile. "You can relax and find out what God has in store for you. Everything is falling into place. I wish you the very best and much happiness." He poked his head outside. "Maybe I should follow you home. It's getting dark."

"It's not necessary. We don't have far to go. Danki anyway. Enjoy the rest of your evening." Mae waved and walked Peter to the buggy.

Jacob waited to shut the door until they'd left. Ellie should learn a valuable lesson from Peter. He'd noticed his mamm was happier since Mr. Fisher entered their lives, and Peter, even as young as he was, recognized Mr. Fisher would be a wilkom addition to their home.

Wide-eyed, Ellie threw her head back. "Did you notice the blood Mrs. Chupp coughed up on her handkerchief?"

The blood had been hard to miss, even though Mae had hurried to keep it out of sight. Her cough was deep and concerned him. "I did notice it. I'd be lying if I didn't say I'm worried about her. Maybe Liza can ask her if she's told Dr. Harrison about it."

"I'll mention it to Liza. She would be the best one to approach Mae about it."

"I'm proud of you, Ellie. You've taken responsibility for your actions when confronted about leaving Charm and you've shown Mae and this town you have changed. Peter's innocence is refreshing. He says what's on his heart without reservation. He knows how to work you and his mamm." He smiled.

"I don't disagree. He has us both doing what he wants when he gazes at us with those big, pleading eyes."

"I'm shocked we haven't heard gossip at the bakery or in town about Mae and Mr. Fisher. Mrs. Mast didn't mention it when Liza, Hannah, and I visited her, Leah, and Eva. I didn't think she missed a thing. Mae and Mr. Fisher have done an excellent job keeping it a private matter."

Jacob tilted his head and rubbed his ear, eyeing Ellie. "I admire Peter's acceptance of Mr. Fisher. I'm certain Mae is relieved Peter and Mr. Fisher have formed a close friendship."

Ellie dipped her chin and headed for her door. "Jah, I'm happy for them. Good night, Daed."

She'd hustled out of the room, leading him to believe she'd gotten his point. He hoped she'd ponder how much easier it would be for him if she would adopt Peter's attitude to a new addition to their family. Jacob bid Ellie good night and picked up his Bible. He flipped the pages and stopped at Romans, 12:12, *"Rejoicing in hope; patient in tribulation; continuing instant in prayer."*

Jacob closed the Bible. Wide awake, he had an idea. He went to the barn, dragged out some cedar he'd been saving for a special project, and got started on a gift for Liza.

He was confident this would be a wilkom wedding gift she'd cherish for years to kumme. Even if she didn't believe they'd marry, he did. He couldn't wait to spend a lifetime with Liza. At some point they would grow old together. He cut the wood in the sizes he needed and put them aside. He'd make her present and throw a blanket over it to keep it secret. Would Liza tell him about Clara's inquiries about them? She'd shared everything with him so far. Hopefully, this wouldn't change.

Chapter Twelve

Liza studied the Englisch woman's crisp red-and-white-flowered cotton dress. Her puffed sleeves and buttons from the rounded stiff collar to waist added to the perfect design. The thick ribbon on her smart straw hat, tied in a bow, matched her ankle-length dress and added a nice touch. She had emerald green eyes and the palest flawless skin. Her smile was infectious. She breezed in like a breath of fresh air on this beautiful Wednesday morning. "Did you have anything in particular in mind to purchase?"

"No, I came in to browse." She bent and studied the glass display case. "How will I choose from all these mouthwatering offerings?" She put a forefinger to her full lips. "I'll take a rhubarb pie, a loaf of oatmeal bread, and a cherry pastry." She opened her reticule and pressed coins into Liza's hand.

Liza wrapped her purchases and handed them to her. "Danki. Please kumme again."

"You can count on it. Have a nice day." The woman swung open the door to leave as if she expected applause.

Liza chuckled. She liked her.

Ellie came in from the back. "We've been so busy, I

haven't had a chance to tell you and Hannah about Peter and his mamm's visit."

Hannah leaned her back to the wall. "How sweet he came to visit you. I'm sure he's missed you."

Liza folded her hands. "How is he?"

"He's fine. He wants me to take him fishing Friday after work. I'm going at five-thirty. I told him I'd ask Hannah to go too, and he was excited. Mae is making chicken and dumplings for supper. Will you go, Hannah?"

"Sure." Hannah opened her eyes wide. "Liza, you should go too. You love to fish."

Ellie nodded. "Jah, please do. Mae mentioned you're wilkom. She's making enough food for all of us. It's Friday. Be at the Chupps' at five-thirty."

Liza hadn't fished in a while. She'd enjoy going with the girls and Peter. "Sounds like fun. Bring your fishing poles and tackle with you to work Friday. We can leave from the bakery."

"Daed and I are worried about Peter's mamm. She has this terrible cough, and she used a handkerchief to cover her mouth. When she lowered it, the material was stained with blood."

Hannah gasped. "Her cough sounds serious."

"I noticed her cough and her having trouble getting it under control. I'll ask her if she's been to Dr. Harrison and sought his advice," Liza said. Evidence of blood suggested something more serious than her throat being irritated.

"I was hoping you would." Ellie patted flour from her apron, then rubbed Hannah's back. "We have cookies to bake."

Hannah elbowed her friend. "Let's get to work." The girls chattered as they went to the kitchen.

* * *

On Friday, Liza hurried to arrange new baked goods in the counter during the day to keep up with the steady flow of customers. Yesterday the day had dragged with the scarce number of patrons she'd had. She glanced at the door and saw Jacob stood wearing the wide smile she adored. "Jacob! You startled me. Always glad to see you."

"Good! I work at surprising you."

She blushed and poured him a cup of coffee. She gestured to a seat at the side counter. "Have a seat." She served him two slices of buttered peach bread.

He sank his teeth into the fluffy bread. "I love anything with peaches. This is delicious."

"Danki." She grinned. "Ellie told me about Mae and Peter's visit."

"Oh no! She wasn't supposed to tell about Mae and Mr. Fisher courting."

"What!" Liza cupped her open mouth.

Ellie bolted out from the kitchen. "Daed, I didn't tell Liza about Mae and Mr. Fisher."

His face red, Jacob gasped. "Me and my big mouth. I assumed Ellie told you Mr. Fisher has proposed to Mae."

"She didn't mention it." She inclined her head. "Don't worry. Your secret is safe with me."

Hannah giggled. "I won't mention it to anyone either. I'm shocked the news hasn't spread about Mae and Mr. Fisher's plans. She did a good job keeping the gossipers uninformed."

Ellie rolled her eyes. "They may know and we just haven't heard them talk about it yet."

Liza sighed. "True."

Hannah patted Liza's arm. "Jacob, Liza's going fishing with Peter, Ellie, and me. She loves to fish. They bite her line every time. We both use worms." She threw up her hands. "I don't get it."

while they entertained Peter. "We'll try! If we don't catch something, we'll bask in the sun on this beautiful afternoon. We'll go no farther than halfway around the pond. We'll not be gone too long."

Liza, the girls, and Peter bid her farewell and walked to the pond.

Ellie pointed. "Let's go where the pond is wider and deeper. The spot I'd like to dip our poles is close to the three oak trees. Fish may be hiding in the patch of weeds near them, inches away from the water's edge."

They reached Ellie's choice location and Hannah spread out a large blanket for them. "We can sit and enjoy our snacks later."

They readied their poles with bobbers and bait.

Ellie slung her pole over her shoulder and cast her line in the water. "I hope we catch some fish."

Peter threw back his pole and made an impressive cast for such a small child.

"Strong throw, Peter." Liza patted his back.

Liza and Hannah moved away and threw their lines in.

"My bobber went under. I caught something!" Liza jerked up her bent pole. The fish wiggled to free itself. "I caught a catfish."

"He's really big!" Peter ran over, pole in hand. "Someone bring the bucket. I want to keep it."

Hannah grabbed the bucket, plunged it in the pond, and brought the swishing water to Liza.

"Danki, Hannah. If we catch a couple more, Mae and Peter can have a scrumptious lunch tomorrow." Liza carefully unhooked her prize to avoid the vicious stingers and threw it in the bucket.

Peter took one more peek at the fish, then wandered to red berries surrounded by a trio of green leaves. He plucked a leaf.

"Isn't this pretty?"

Ellie ran to him and slapped it out of his hand. "Sweetheart, don't touch the poison oak."

Peter jerked his hand back. "Ouch, Ellie!"

"It will give you an itchy rash." Ellie grabbed his arm. "Let's dunk your hands in the pond. I'm sorry if I scared you."

"I'm glad you did. I don't need a nasty ol' rash." He swished his hands in the water and dried them on his pant legs.

Peter grabbed his pole, drew it back, and plunked the line into the pond. He stared at the water. Eyes wide, he pulled at his line. "I've got a big one!"

Hannah rushed to him and clutched his pole to help. They tugged hard, and a man's battered black boot filled with mud and water popped up.

They nearly collapsed with laughter at the sight.

Liza chuckled. "Strange to find a boot in the water. I hope the man who lost it didn't have to walk home without his boots. His other one might be in here somewhere."

Ellie cocked her brow. "He must've waded in the shallow end to fish and then got them stuck in the mud."

Peter shrugged. "He might've taken them off to wade in the water and his friend threw them in for a joke."

Hannah grinned. "You have an active imagination. Would you pull a joke on a friend by throwing his shoes in the pond?"

He laughed. "I might!"

Bang! Liza whipped her head toward the threatening sound. "Everyone, lay down flat on the ground. A bullet whizzed by me too close for comfort."

Ellie marched to the direction of the shot and cupped her hands to her mouth. "Hey, you need to stop firing in our direction. We're fishing and you could've injured one of us!"

Liza, on her belly, raised her head. "Ellie, get down!"

Hannah tightened her arm around Peter as they stretched out on their stomachs. "Jah, Ellie, listen to Liza."

Ellie marched in the direction of the gunfire. "We've got to let these people know we're close. They must go somewhere else to hunt."

Liza stood. "Hannah, take Peter to the haus. I'll follow Ellie."

"Peter, stand and hold my hand." Hannah winced. "Liza, be careful!" She picked up her pace and left with Peter.

Liza ran in the direction Ellie had gone and halted. Her heart pounded in her chest. Three tall, menacing men who had dirt-stained clothes, gruff faces, and angry eyes faced Ellie with shotguns slung over their shoulders. The wind sent their odiferous smell to her nose.

Liza fought to control her trembling hands. She joined Ellie. "If you would be so kind as to hunt somewhere else, we would appreciate it."

The three men formed a loose circle, boxing them in.

The shortest scallywag stepped closer and glared at them. He scrutinized Ellie. "You've got a mouth on ya. Maybe I should teach you a lesson."

Liza stepped in front of Ellie and faced the bully. "We don't want any trouble." She grasped Ellie's hand and swiveled to leave.

The burly brute grabbed her arm. "You're not goin' nowhere, missy." His evil laugh sent chills up her spine. He traced a finger down her cheek.

The third man clutched Ellie's arm. "We got us some pretty lookin' women."

Liza yanked her body, trying to wrench free of the thug's hold on her.

The huge and odorous man tightened his grip. "You best stay put or I'll throw you over my shoulder."

Terror ripped through Liza. "Please let us go. At least let her go."

Ellie kicked the man clutching her. She jerked to free herself. "Take your filthy hands off me!"

"I like a woman with fire in her." The ruffian laughed.

Bile rose in Liza's throat and her stomach rolled with fright. The ground shook beneath her feet. Liza shifted her eyes past the men.

The sheriff came around the bend. He fired a shot to the sky. "Release the women immediately!"

The three men dropped their hands.

Liza and Ellie ran next to the sheriff's stallion. Liza circled her arm around Ellie's waist.

The sheriff pointed his rifle at the bullies. "I don't recognize any of you. I've received complaints this last week from the Browns, the Mullins, and the Harshmans. They said they spotted three men trespassing on their land and found chickens missing. You're lucky those men didn't catch you. They don't take kindly to robbers. If I could prove you'd stolen from them, I'd throw you in jail."

Liza recognized the names of the Englischers. They were regular customers at the bakery.

The brute snarled and glowered at the sheriff.

"Where are you from?" Sheriff Williams glared at them.

"Massillon. We're passin' through. Going home today. Nothin' to do in this boring town anyway." The middle ruffian crossed his arms and spat on the ground.

"You best get on down the road. If I run into you again, I'll throw you in jail for harassing these women. You understand?"

The men grunted and stomped to their horses, not far away.

"Liza, take Ellie back to the Chupps' house. I want to

Ellie whipped her head to Hannah. "Do you leave your line in long enough for them to bite? You can't lift your pole out of the water to check it every minute. Daed has a habit of doing that."

They all laughed.

Hannah shot them a shy expression. "I admit it. I'd rather feed the ducks."

"Uh-oh! I forgot about the cookies! They may have been in the oven a bit too long." Ellie ran to the oven.

Hannah followed.

Jacob wiped crumbs from his lips. "Liza, Peter bubbles with excitement over Mr. Fisher courting his mamm. He and Mr. Fisher are friends, and he says his mamm laughs more when the man is around. Mae glows with happiness when she mentions his name."

Similar to the way my mouth curves in a wide smile when you walk in the room. Liza pressed fingers to her lips. She listened to his story with envy traveling from her head to her toes. "I'm thrilled for them."

"Liza, did Ellie mention Mae's horrible cough isn't any better?"

"Jah. I'll ask Mae if she's been to Dr. Harrison about it. It's gone on too long." Liza shook her head.

"You're thoughtful to care so much about others. Another reason I admire you." He drank his last sip of coffee and stood. He brushed her hand with his fingers. "Every minute of every day, I love you with all my heart, and I'm waiting on you." He left a small wrapped package on the counter. "This is for you." He hustled out the door.

She caught her breath and pressed a hand to her racing heartbeat. *I love you, too, Jacob.* "Danki." She would've shouted the words if it didn't hurt so much. He might never be her husband and she shouldn't encourage him or fool herself. Ellie had given no indication she would change her mind. She unwrapped the package and lifted out a white handkerchief with a tiny white flower embroidered in the corner.

She recognized it from the gift shop in the corner of Maybelle's Inn, where she sold several items. She held the soft material and her heart soared. She'd cherish the treasure forever.

Five in the afternoon came, and Liza and the girls went to the Chupps' haus.

Peter ran to greet them. "You're here!"

Liza jumped out and tied the reins to the crooked oak hitching post. "Who do you have in your arms?"

"This is Snuggles, my rabbit. Would you like to hold him? Be careful. He might wet on you." He held out the pet and dipped his chin to the wet spot on his shirt.

"Your friend is beautiful!" She cradled the animal in her arms. "Snuggles is so white and fluffy."

Hannah accepted the furry pet from Liza. "I love the bunny's tiny pink nose."

Ellie stroked the bunny's head. "Is your mamm inside?"

Handing the animal back to Peter, Hannah smiled. "I can understand why you love Snuggles. He's cuddly."

He waved them to the porch. "She's setting the table." He walked over to Snuggles's cage and put him inside.

Liza and the girls stepped inside the haus with him.

Peter pulled out a puzzle and sat down. "Will you play with me?"

Ellie sat and Hannah plopped down next to her. "I suppose we can work the puzzle for a few minutes until supper. We don't want to pull out any more toys and make a mess. We're going fishing later, so we don't want to waste time putting them away."

Liza went to the kitchen. "May I do something for you, Mae?"

"Wilkom! You're thoughtful to offer, but I have everything ready. May I get you something to drink?"

"Water is fine. I'm sure Hannah and Ellie will take the same."

Mae put a fist to her mouth and coughed until it was hard for her to breathe. She clutched the pitcher in her other hand. She breathed easier, then straightened. "I apologize. My coughing fits are something I can't control." She poured water into glasses for all of them. Then she set a large porcelain bowl filled with chicken and dumplings on the table. "Do you mind telling the kinner supper is ready?"

Liza bit back her urge to persuade Mae to alert Dr. Harrison about her discomfort, but Mae had changed the subject and was staring at her feet. She didn't want to talk about it. Liza wouldn't mention it. She proceeded to the girls and Peter in the sitting room. "Time to eat."

He popped up, knocking over a stack of blocks and rubbing his middle. "I'm hungry! Let's go."

The girls laughed. "We're right behind you."

Peter patted the chairs on either side of him. "Hannah, you and Ellie sit by me."

They exchanged grins and chuckled and sat.

Peter waited while Mae ladled two helpings onto his plate. "I have my fishin' pole out and everything ready."

"Ours are in the buggy. We brought our poles and tackle with us to work this morning so we could leave from the bakery."

Mae sat. "Let's bow our heads for prayer." She finished the prayer. "Hand me your plates and I'll serve you."

Liza and the girls passed their plates.

"Mae, I appreciate you cooking for us. Danki for the invitation." Liza grinned.

The girls nodded.

Mae bent and coughed, grabbed her cotton napkin, and covered her mouth. She pushed her chair back and bent to catch her breath. "This may happen often this evening. I hope it doesn't spoil your supper."

Liza had to risk Mae getting upset for her asking her to pursue treatment. She cared about the woman, and the deep cough needed attention. "Have you gone to Dr. Harrison and asked him about it?" Liza held her spoon.

She shook her head. "I haven't had time. I'll get around to it." She diverted her gaze from Liza's. "You've got good weather for fishing. The sky is clear today."

It was evident Mae didn't want to talk about her health. Liza didn't want to badger her. "I haven't fished for quite a while. It will be a treat."

"I have worms for you."

"Danki." Hannah reached for her glass.

Peter entertained them with stories about Snuggles. Liza couldn't remember when she'd laughed so long and hard. She had grown attached to Peter. He was full of compassion and wonder. She would love to have a son like him. When she hadn't been successful in having a child with Paul, she'd pushed the desire out of her mind. Peter renewed her longing to have a boppli.

Liza and the girls helped Mae clean up the kitchen and then headed outside.

Mae handed Ellie jars of water and one filled with butter cookies. "Water and a snack for later. Catch some fish."

Liza noticed Mae's pale face and slow movements. She felt guilty the woman had slaved over a stove to fix them such a wonderful meal. Maybe Mae would get some rest

Liza, on her belly, raised her head. "Ellie, get down!"

Hannah tightened her arm around Peter as they stretched out on their stomachs. "Jah, Ellie, listen to Liza."

Ellie marched in the direction of the gunfire. "We've got to let these people know we're close. They must go somewhere else to hunt."

Liza stood. "Hannah, take Peter to the haus. I'll follow Ellie."

"Peter, stand and hold my hand." Hannah winced. "Liza, be careful!" She picked up her pace and left with Peter.

Liza ran in the direction Ellie had gone and halted. Her heart pounded in her chest. Three tall, menacing men who had dirt-stained clothes, gruff faces, and angry eyes faced Ellie with shotguns slung over their shoulders. The wind sent their odiferous smell to her nose.

Liza fought to control her trembling hands. She joined Ellie. "If you would be so kind as to hunt somewhere else, we would appreciate it."

The three men formed a loose circle, boxing them in.

The shortest scallywag stepped closer and glared at them. He scrutinized Ellie. "You've got a mouth on ya. Maybe I should teach you a lesson."

Liza stepped in front of Ellie and faced the bully. "We don't want any trouble." She grasped Ellie's hand and swiveled to leave.

The burly brute grabbed her arm. "You're not goin' nowhere, missy." His evil laugh sent chills up her spine. He traced a finger down her cheek.

The third man clutched Ellie's arm. "We got us some pretty lookin' women."

Liza yanked her body, trying to wrench free of the thug's hold on her.

The huge and odorous man tightened his grip. "You best stay put or I'll throw you over my shoulder."

Terror ripped through Liza. "Please let us go. At least let her go."

Ellie kicked the man clutching her. She jerked to free herself. "Take your filthy hands off me!"

"I like a woman with fire in her." The ruffian laughed.

Bile rose in Liza's throat and her stomach rolled with fright. The ground shook beneath her feet. Liza shifted her eyes past the men.

The sheriff came around the bend. He fired a shot to the sky. "Release the women immediately!"

The three men dropped their hands.

Liza and Ellie ran next to the sheriff's stallion. Liza circled her arm around Ellie's waist.

The sheriff pointed his rifle at the bullies. "I don't recognize any of you. I've received complaints this last week from the Browns, the Mullins, and the Harshmans. They said they spotted three men trespassing on their land and found chickens missing. You're lucky those men didn't catch you. They don't take kindly to robbers. If I could prove you'd stolen from them, I'd throw you in jail."

Liza recognized the names of the Englischers. They were regular customers at the bakery.

The brute snarled and glowered at the sheriff.

"Where are you from?" Sheriff Williams glared at them.

"Massillon. We're passin' through. Going home today. Nothin' to do in this boring town anyway." The middle ruffian crossed his arms and spat on the ground.

"You best get on down the road. If I run into you again, I'll throw you in jail for harassing these women. You understand?"

The men grunted and stomped to their horses, not far away.

"Liza, take Ellie back to the Chupps' house. I want to

make sure these men leave. I'm going to follow them for a bit. I'll come back and check on you."

"Danki, Sheriff." Liza shivered, wondering if her wobbly legs would make it to the haus.

Ellie fumed. "Those men were awful." She squeezed Liza's fingers. "You stuck right beside me, Liza. I'm sorry for putting us in danger. I should've listened to you." She held out her arm. "My arm stings where that thug's nails dug into my skin. Are you all right?"

"A bit shaken." Liza lifted Ellie's sleeve. "I'm relieved he didn't draw blood. The marks should disappear in a few days."

They reached their blanket at the pond, gathered up their things, headed to the haus, and went inside.

Hannah rose. "I was worried sick. I've never been so happy to run into Sheriff Williams. Peter and I saw him as we headed to the haus. He asked where Liza and Ellie were and I told him about the gunfire and where we had fished and asked him to check on you."

Mae said, "The sheriff was making his usual widow rounds. I told him Liza, Hannah, and Ellie had taken Peter fishing somewhere by the pond and no farther than halfway around. He said he'd find you and say hello before he moved on to the next haus. I'm so glad he did, and I'm relieved he passed Hannah and found out you might be in danger."

"Liza and I were never so relieved to see him. He saved us from the mean men." Ellie pressed her elbows to her sides. "They angered me at first, then I got scared when one of them clutched my arm. I didn't listen to Liza. She warned me to lay flat. We could've moved away and avoided them."

Mae gestured for them to sit. "Ellie, you're too brave for your own good. You could've gotten shot, or those with you."

"I'm sorry. I assumed men were hunting and didn't realize we were there. I didn't suspect they'd be a bunch of thugs." She grimaced. "I regret my actions. Please forgive me, everyone."

Peter took her hand in his. "It's all right, Ellie. We love you."

Liza met Ellie's regretful eyes. "Peter's correct. You're forgiven."

Mae and Hannah nodded their agreement.

Mae stretched her neck to the window. "Sheriff Williams is back." She opened the door.

He stepped inside. "You can all relax. The scoundrels left town." He took off his hat.

"Good. Danki, Sheriff. Do you want something to drink?" Mae coughed and recovered.

"No, I should go on to the next widow's house."

Liza smiled. "Danki for your help."

"Jah, danki." Ellie stood next to Liza.

"Anytime." He put his hat on and left.

Ellie sat and patted her knee. "Peter, sit with me."

The sweet boy scooted onto her lap sideways and fixed his gaze on her. "Tell me what happened with those men."

Ellie rubbed his back. "I found three mean men with guns. I told them to hunt somewhere else, and they said some nasty things to Liza and me. The sheriff came and asked them to leave." She frowned and hugged him. "I'm sorry they cut our fishing short."

Liza listened to the young woman relate the story to Peter. She didn't shrug him off or avoid telling him what had happened. She answered his question wisely. Her loving and compassionate side had shone through since her return. Her commitment to God and to obeying Amish law had been evident this evening.

Mae tousled the boy's hair. "He had a wonderful time, despite the unfortunate interruption."

Liza shook her head. "I'm shocked we encountered these men in our community. It's a rare occasion." She sighed. "We can all put this unpleasant incident behind us, and I'm sure we can find time to go fishing again this season."

Mae held a hand to her lips and coughed. She pulled out a small white handkerchief tucked in her apron waistband, wiped a trickle of blood from her hand, and clutched the spotted cloth in her hand as if to hide it.

Liza's heart pounded against her chest. Mae's cough had generated blood again. Whatever was causing this woman to cough must be serious. She had to say something again. "Mae, I'm begging you, please see Dr. Harrison."

"I'll stop by his office eventually." She gave a little shrug.

Peter tugged on Ellie's dress. "Did I tell ya Mr. Fisher went to Pennsylvania to visit his bruder?"

Ellie smiled. "I hope he has a pleasant trip."

"What if he really likes being with his bruder? If I had a bruder, I wouldn't want to leave him." He hung his head. "I'm worried he won't kumme back."

"I'm sure he'll be knocking on your door before you know it." Ellie gently tapped his nose.

"We should let these kind people be on their way. We've kept them long enough." Mae didn't comment on Peter's remarks about Mr. Fisher and walked them out, with Peter alongside her.

Liza waved farewell and waited for Hannah and Ellie to get settled in the buggy. She waved to the Chupps and drove to Ellie's. A flash of sadness had crossed Mae's face. Did Mae have reason to suspect Mr. Fisher wouldn't be back? The woman was in a hurry to have them leave. She apparently didn't want to discuss Mr. Fisher. "Despite those scallywags, I enjoyed the time we spent with Peter."

Ellie wrinkled her nose. "Have you noticed how often Mrs. Chupp coughs? And she avoided saying anything about Mr. Fisher. I sensed she may agree with Peter. They were excited about Mr. Fisher being in their lives. I suspect something has happened between the couple."

Hannah nodded. "Jah, I agree. She seemed bothered about Peter bringing up Mr. Fisher." She grimaced. "She also tried to hide the blood going onto her hand. She hurried to wipe it off with the handkerchief. She's really sick. She hasn't been to Dr. Harrison."

"We can't do anything until she's ready to deal with the problem. Let's not jump to conclusions about Mae and Mr. Fisher." Liza sensed Mae's reluctance to discuss her illness. She couldn't force the woman to go to Dr. Harrison. She hoped Mae would relent and the doctor to examine her. She wouldn't ask Mae about Mr. Fisher. She didn't want to pry.

Liza dropped Ellie and Hannah at their homes, then went to her haus. Her heart was heavy with unease for Mae, and longing for a relationship with Jacob she could never have weighed on her shoulders. She finished her chores, warmed that morning's already made coffee, then plopped into her favorite chair.

Jacob stood on his porch overlooking the lush green grass and tall oak trees spread across his land and sipped his coffee. He was ready for church and waiting on Ellie to finish getting ready.

Ellie had told him about what had happened with the bullies Friday evening. He couldn't shake the dangerous event from his mind. He considered himself to have a level head, but his temperament would've been challenged had he been with them. Amish avoided confrontations at all costs. He would've had to have done what was necessary to protect the people he loved. He was grateful to the sheriff for his fast response in rescuing them. He pushed the thugs from his mind. After the church service, he'd talk to Liza about the incident. He was glad she was unharmed.

He'd stayed home all day yesterday, gotten his chores done, and stolen a little time to work on the wedding present he was sure he'd be giving Liza someday. It had been difficult to keep from visiting her, but he knew Saturday was her busiest day.

Sheriff Williams came down the lane.

Jacob sheltered his eyes with his hand. Why was Peter with him?

Ellie carried a mug of coffee onto the porch and joined her daed. "We've got company."

The lawman got off his horse and helped Peter down. "I've got a visitor for you both."

Peter ran to Ellie and hugged her legs.

Ellie dragged the rocking chair to her and sat. She pulled the sobbing child on her lap. "What's wrong?"

The child buried his wet face in Ellie's shoulder.

The sheriff bent over, resting his elbows on his knees while sitting in the other rocker. "I have some bad news. Mae Chupp is no longer with us. She's gone to Heaven." He nodded to Peter. "The child insisted I bring him to Ellie."

Jacob knelt and rubbed Peter's back. "Oh, Peter, I'm so sorry."

Ellie darted her eyes to the sheriff. "What's happened?"

"He won't answer my questions. He would only say I should take him to Ellie."

"Poor Peter. He must've been so frightened."

The sheriff nodded. "Mr. Beachy said Peter pounded on their door, grabbed Mr. Beachy's hand, and pulled him to his mother's body in her bedroom. Mr. Beachy came and got me, while his wife took Peter to their house." He sighed. "I picked up Dr. Harrison and the bishop and took them with me to Mae's. The good doctor suspects consumption, but he couldn't say with certainty. The bishop said it wasn't necessary to pursue the matter."

"Is Dr. Harrison still at Mae's?" Jacob sipped his coffee.

"No, he and I took Mae's body to the undertaker to prepare her remains for visitors and a funeral, and then I took both men home. The bishop headed to the Keims' for the service today. He said he'd announce Mae's passing. The bishop will round up men on Monday to get things ready at the Chupp house to receive visitors on Tuesday for the viewing and conduct the funeral service and burial on Wednesday. Mrs. Beachy volunteered to clean the house."

"I'll be glad to help, and I'm certain Liza and her family will want to assist with whatever is needed. Peter can stay with us. I'm happy to take him in permanently. He and Ellie are very close. The Amish take care of their own, as you're aware." Jacob held up his mug. "I'm sorry, Sheriff. Would you like coffee?"

"No. I've had more than I should've this morning." Sheriff Williams met his gaze. "I have something for you. I already showed it to the bishop. He was pleased with the contents." He tugged a paper out of his shirt pocket. "Mae wrote a letter dated yesterday. She requests you be his legal guardian because she has no other living relatives. She also requests her property be sold and the money be safeguarded by you for her son until the child is old enough to manage it himself."

"I'm stunned and pleased." Jacob accepted the document, read it, and passed it to Ellie.

She studied it. "I'm relieved she made this provision for Peter to stay with us."

Peter raised his head. "I can live with you and Jacob?"

"Jah, sweetheart. Our home will be yours too."

"I was scared. I didn't understand what was going to happen to me with Mamm gone."

Ellie stroked his neck. "You don't need to worry about anything. Daed and I will take good care of you." She handed the paper back to her daed. "I'm surprised she didn't mention this to you even before she wrote the letter. She had to have been contemplating it."

The sheriff sighed. "She probably thought she had more time to discuss this with your father. She must've had an inkling her illness may be serious, but no indication it would take her life this soon. I'm glad this worked out for your family and the child."

Ellie helped Peter to his feet. "I'm going to take Peter to the kitchen and give him a glass of water, then rock him more. Danki for your help, Sheriff."

"You're welcome." The sheriff reached over and tousled Peter's hair. "Take care, little one."

Peter stared at the floor and wept before Ellie walked him inside.

Jacob stared after them, then concentrated on the sheriff. "He's like a little bruder to her." Jacob brushed his palms together. "I've always wanted more kinner, and raising Peter is a gift from Mae I'll always be grateful for."

"God is good." The sheriff rubbed the stubble on his chin. "I found a letter from a Mr. Fisher on the bed. The letter said he wouldn't be back to Charm. He'd met a woman while visiting his brother in Lancaster, Pennsylvania, and he planned to stay there. He apologized to Mae and wished her and Peter good health and happiness. Did you know anything about this man?"

"Mr. Fisher asked for Peter's approval to marry his mamm. Peter was thrilled when he told us. Then we learned Mr. Fisher had gone to visit his bruder in Pennsylvania from Peter. It's sad to learn Mae received this news." Jacob shook his head.

"I'd met Mr. Fisher. He was a kind, quiet man. Hadn't been in Charm long. Came from Lancaster. Kept to himself." The sheriff shrugged and stepped off the porch and glanced over his shoulder. "Mr. Beachy is interested in buying the Chupp property for his dochder and her family. I'm sure he'll discuss it with you." The sheriff stood.

"With the Beachys living next door, it would be nice for them to have her close." He nodded to the sheriff. "Danki for all you've done."

"He's blessed to have you and your daughter." The sheriff snapped his head back to Jacob. "Did Ellie tell you about the thugs interfering with their fishing?"

Jacob, wide-eyed, smacked his head. "I forgot to say danki for rescuing them. Your timing saved them from harm."

"All in the past. No need to worry. I haven't seen any sign of them and no one has registered any complaints about them. The bullies got my message to get out of town."

"Danki again, Sheriff."

Sheriff Williams waved, mounted his stallion, and rode off.

Jacob waited until the sheriff was halfway down the lane, then went inside the haus.

Ellie swiped her tears on her sleeve and gazed at the tallest old oak tree on the property out the window while rocking Peter on her lap. "I can't believe Mae is really gone. My heart breaks for you, Peter. I remember how sad I was to no longer have Mamm with us."

Jacob nodded his head. "We have an extra bedroom just for you, Peter. We'll bring your things here and this will be your new home."

Peter's lip quivered. "I went to Mamm's room and found her on the floor. Blood dirtied her mouth and stained her dress. I shook her and she was so cold. Her eyes didn't move. I shook her harder, but she didn't make a sound."

Ellie gazed at him. "You did the right thing by going to get the Beachys. I'm proud of you."

"You are?"

"Jah. There was nothing else for you to do. You did exactly what I would've done had I been in your situation."

He hung his head. "Really? I couldn't stop shaking. I was scared." He put his face inches from hers. "Are you sure it isn't my fault she's gone to Heaven, Ellie?"

"You should never blame yourself. She was already in Heaven. Your mamm wouldn't want you to fret about her. She loved you with all her heart."

"My heart hurts. I miss her." He rested his head on Ellie's shoulder and his tears wet her dress.

She kissed his forehead and rocked him as he wept.

Jacob's eyes watered. Ellie had taken this little boy under her wing and loved him without hesitation. He ached for Peter.

A mamm was central to the household. Lydia had baked their favorite meals, given them generous hugs and kisses, and soothed their woes. She could lift their moods in seconds with her soft and gentle words of wisdom. He still hurt from the loss of the soul mate and woman who had fulfilled him in every way.

The challenges and problems of raising another child would be worth the priceless memories they'd create together. If only Liza were here to share it with them. He dreaded being the bearer of bad news to her. Her sad eyes and pain burned his soul.

Jacob rested his hand on Ellie's shoulder. "We'll stay home. I'm sure the bishop will understand our missing the service. Later, I'll go to Liza's. I'm sure she'll have questions."

He watched Ellie care for Peter most of the day. She coaxed him to eat some fried apples and scrambled eggs. She rocked him outside on the porch most of the afternoon.

Hours later, he joined them there. "Will you and Peter be all right alone for a bit?"

"Jah, we'll be fine. Daed, do you mind caring for Peter in the morning while I visit Liza at the bakery? I'd like to speak with her about him and my job at the bakery."

"I will." Jacob went to the barn, harnessed his mare, and headed to Liza's. Encouraged Ellie was meeting with Liza the next day, he smiled.

He rode to Liza's farm and found her seated on a tattered white-and-dark-blue patchwork quilt a couple of feet from the pond. She was lovely.

Liza stood and smoothed the front of her dress. "Jacob, I missed you at the service this morning. The bishop told us about Mae and her wish to have you be Peter's legal guardian. Mrs. Beachy told me what happened. How's he doing?"

"Ellie's been patient and loving with him. He adores her, she him. The child is sad, but he ate a little and is taking a nap."

"Mae's illness was serious. I should've pressed her to go to Dr. Harrison's office. I feel horrible." She covered her face with her hands.

"No one is to blame for Mae's death. Erase that notion from your mind." He gently removed one hand and then the other and held them.

"I suppose you're right." She met his gaze. "Had Mae discussed you being Peter's legal guardian with you?"

"She didn't have a chance. Her letter was dated yesterday. My guess is she suspected her illness may be serious and planned to meet with me soon. I'm sad Mae is gone, but I'm honored to abide by her wish and accept the child into our home. Ellie and I have assured him we're thrilled to have him live with us."

A sea of compassion resonated from his voice when he spoke the boy's name. His shoulders straightened as he talked about the child. He must be both overwhelmed and exhilarated to take on this responsibility. She couldn't think of anyone better to offer a home to the little one. She had no doubt Ellie would grow in maturity caring for the boy. "I'm happy you and Ellie are wilkoming Peter as part of your family."

"We're still missing you in our family."

She bowed her head. She wouldn't say another word. She would love to marry him and raise Peter together. Ellie was grown, beautiful, and smart. Amish men would kumme calling, and Liza had no doubt she'd fall in love one day. Maybe then Ellie would give her blessing for Jacob and her to marry. Maybe then she could become part of his family. Her heart was ripped in two. She felt like the outsider watching Jacob, Peter, and Ellie form this heartwarming union without her. But it was her choice. The right choice. She had to put her selfish desires to the side. "What a sense of loss for such a sweet and innocent child to endure."

"Jah. I'm sad Peter has to endure this pain."

Liza inhaled a breath. "It's difficult to watch kinner go through tragedy. They're young and innocent. We want to protect them." She widened her eyes. "Has anyone told Mr. Fisher? I don't know him or where he lives. Do you?"

"The sheriff found a letter from Mr. Fisher to Mae. The letter revealed he'd met a woman while visiting his bruder in Lancaster and was staying in Pennsylvania. He wished Mae and Peter the best. He's moved on."

"She must've been brokenhearted. His letter seemed cold and indifferent. Maybe she was better off without him." She sucked in her lips for a moment. "I apologize. I'm passing judgment on a man I've never met."

"Don't worry. I had the same thoughts." He lifted her chin to meet his gaze. "On another subject, I understand from Ellie you encountered some thugs while fishing. She told me the story and confessed she put your life in danger by not obeying your warning not to approach those men. I'm sorry, Liza."

"I'm thankful it's over. I've put it behind me."

He brushed his lips against her hand. "Ellie should've listened to you. I'm sorry she put you in danger." He sighed. "I couldn't bear it if anything ever happened to the two women I love most in this world."

"No need to give those men another thought." She took his hand in hers. "We've got Peter to consider now."

"Ellie asked me to watch Peter tomorrow. She wants to kumme to the bakery to chat with you in private about Peter."

The young girl must be overwhelmed, taking in Peter and then having to console him over his mamm's death. It was quite an undertaking. She'd been wondering how to help. Maybe Ellie would tell her how. "Give them both hugs from me."

He kissed her full on the lips. "I couldn't resist." Then he rushed to his buggy.

She waved and watched him leave, then touched her heated cheeks. She should have scolded him for the kiss. She'd made it clear they weren't planning a future together. She hadn't said a word. His kiss had sent a thrill through her. She hugged herself and longed to hold on to the sweet touch of his lips, storing it in her mind to revisit the moment often.

Poor Peter. The child must be broken, scared, and lost. She bowed her head. "Dear Heavenly Father, please wrap Your arms of love and healing around Peter. Pour out Your blessings and perform a miracle for this little one. Help him move forward and experience a joyful and fulfilling life.

"Please bless Jacob and Ellie. Guide and direct them to meet Peter's needs. Give them the wisdom and patience to help Peter heal from this tragedy. Danki for all You do for all of us already. Amen."

Liza readied her buggy and went to visit her family.

Esther invited her in. "You've been crying. What's wrong?"

Abe approached her. "Liza, tell us. What is it?"

Hannah waited, her eyes filled with worry.

Liza dabbed tears with the pads of her fingers. "Jacob came, and we talked about Mae's passing and Peter. I feel terrible for the child."

"How is Peter holding up? I was shocked at the bishop's announcement about Mae and about the letter she'd written, making Jacob Peter's legal guardian. She had no living relatives, and I can't think of anyone better than him to raise the boy. He and Ellie adore Peter."

"The sweet boy is with Ellie. Jacob said he's doing as well as can be expected."

Water pooled in Esther's eyes. "It breaks my heart this child has to suffer such a loss."

Hannah nodded. "Ellie will help Peter recover. She's been through it herself. She won't want him to go through the rebellious period to find his way like she did."

Abe took a puff of his pipe. "What can we do?"

She said, "Maybe cook food is all."

Abe waved to Liza. "I'll go on the porch and give you women privacy to talk. I'll say a prayer requesting comfort for Jacob, Ellie, and Peter."

Liza gave him a grateful smile.

Abe nodded and headed outside.

Esther pointed to the big maple rocker with its stuffed

cotton cushions. "Sit in your favorite chair, Liza." She wrung her hands. "I can't believe Mae is gone. You were worried about her cough. It must've had something to do with her death."

"We'll never be sure. We'll miss her, although she's in Heaven and happy, without any worries or discomfort. It's Peter I'm worried about. He's outlived his entire family and he's only five. It doesn't seem possible." She hugged herself and shivered. How would Peter react this week? Would he go mute again?

Chapter Thirteen

Liza arrived at the bakery at four a.m. on Monday morning. She yawned and tied her work apron around her waist. Fitful sleep and the sad days ahead were to blame. She'd miss Hannah and Ellie working with her today. She'd gotten used to them being in the bakery all day. Mrs. Beachy could use the help, and Esther and Hannah could clean faster than most women. She was sure Mrs. Beachy would be grateful to have them.

She dove into her routine and made loaves of plain and oatmeal bread, maple sugar cookies, and cherry tarts. She arranged the fresh goods on the shelves of her glass display cabinet. The clock struck eight and she flipped her sign to show she was ready for patrons.

Dr. Harrison and Sheriff Williams strolled in and sat in the same stools they did every time they frequented the bakery.

"Good morning, Liza." Dr. Harrison glanced at the kitchen's open door. "I don't hear Hannah and Ellie in the kitchen. Are you alone today?"

The sheriff opened his paper. "Ellie's probably home with Peter, but where's Hannah?"

"Hannah's helping Mrs. Beachy clean Mae's haus in

preparation for the service." Liza opened and lifted a roll of twine from the cabinet on the wall behind the counter.

"Your niece is a thoughtful and kind young woman. She's always been smiling and cheerful when I've been in the bakery. It's no surprise she'd do her part to help with Mae's services." He moved his paper. "Liza, should we be doing something to help with Mae's arrangements?"

Liza shook her head. "Our community has everything handled. The bishop stepped right in and notified the Amish to spread the word." She poured each of them a cup of coffee.

"I'll attend, with the sheriff. I'm baffled as to why she died. Several concerned friends of hers approached me about her cough. I bumped into her at the blacksmith's place and asked her about it. She gave me a polite nod and said it was nothing. I suggested she let me examine her and she declined. She did answer my questions about her symptoms. From her responses, I suspected consumption, but, under the circumstances, it was hard to determine what was truly wrong with her."

Sheriff Williams put his paper on the counter. "You shouldn't worry yourself about it. Everyone is grateful for all you do."

"Thank you." Dr. Harrison gave Sheriff Williams a smile and a curt nod.

Liza enjoyed listening to the two men. Their friendship warmed her heart. They bantered and caught up on the town gossip, the same as women. She learned the latest and most interesting news from their conversations. The newspaper had been keeping up with the Summer Olympics, and she found the different sporting events and athletes fascinating. She didn't understand how the athletes had time to train and get their chores done. It must take hours of practice for such an important event.

She was glad to have something to take her mind off Mae and Peter for a few minutes. But she couldn't concentrate and had to force her mouth to smile. She'd been so preoccupied with her sadness, she hadn't asked the men if they wanted anything to go with their coffee. "What's your selection today?"

Sheriff Williams rubbed his chin. "How about two thick slices of apple bread and butter?"

"Just coffee for me, thank you." Dr. Harrison gave the sheriff half his newspaper and read the first page. "The Summer Olympics are going strong since opening in Stockholm, Sweden, on May fifth. This will be the first time the Empire of Japan participates."

Sheriff Williams said, "Paper says women's swimming will be an event this year."

"I'm interested to learn how they do." Dr. Harrison whistled. "There are a hundred and two events taking place and twenty-eight countries will participate this year. This is the first time all five continents will be represented. I admire the time, discipline, and dedication of the men and women who are taking part in the events. I doubt I could do it even when I was young."

The sheriff moaned. "I wish I could be there to watch the events in person instead of just reading about how they are doing in the newspaper, but thinking of the athletes compete makes my bones creak, my muscles ache, and my head hurt. I have a hard time bending over to lift a pail of milk."

Dr. Harrison dipped his chin and raised his eyes. "The size of your middle may be the reason."

"It's Liza's fault." Sheriff Williams patted his stomach. "She bakes all these desserts and I can't pass them up."

She grinned and her cheeks heated. The moment of cheer lifted her sad mood.

Dr. Harrison flipped the page. "Houdini is planning another trick. He'll be in a nailed and locked box and have it wrapped in chains, then it'll be thrown overboard from a boat in the East River in New York. The magician plans to escape in less than three minutes. He'll take out a boat and allow the press on board to take pictures."

Sheriff Williams reared back. "When?"

"Sometime in July. He does some strange and dangerous things. I don't understand why." Dr. Harrison shook his head.

"I don't get it. Why would you risk your life for some silly magic trick, and why would people care to gather around and watch him?" The sheriff cocked his head to his friend.

Liza trembled. Why indeed? This thinking was foreign to the Amish way of life. A waste of precious time and a foolish way to spend the day. She would never consent to being locked away in a box and thrown in a river. The man must be out of his mind.

The men finished reading the paper and told her if the Amish community needed anything in preparation for Mae's funeral to let them know.

"Danki to you both. Men and women are working today at the Chupps' to prepare the haus and grounds for the viewing and funeral. It was kind of you to offer." She gave them a warm smile and bid them a good day.

A few minutes later, Ellie breezed through the door. "Liza, I'm sorry I left you to manage the bakery alone."

"Don't apologize. You're an angel for taking care of Peter. It can't be easy under the circumstances."

Ellie slumped on the stool earlier occupied by the sheriff. "He's pitiful. He cries and cries. I feel so helpless around him. I left him with Daed while I came here. He was working a puzzle with him when I left. He's so quiet."

"It will be hard to watch him mourn his mamm's death," Liza said. "I'm going to close the bakery the day of the funeral and burial. The women will bring food for after the burial, then it will all be over. I'm so glad the bishop agreed not to draw this out for days. Is Peter talking to you? I'm worried he'll withdraw again."

"I don't foresee him going back into his shell. He's asking questions and telling me what's in his heart." She gave Liza a sheepish smile. "Would you mind accompanying me and Peter to Mae's viewing tomorrow? I'm going to take him before everyone arrives and bring him right back home." She winced. "I know it's a lot to ask. You'd have to close the bakery for two days instead of one."

Liza gave Ellie's hand a gentle squeeze. "I'd be happy to. Would you like me to return to your haus with the two of you afterward?"

"Would you?"

"Of course." Liza wanted to shout with joy. Ellie had chosen to turn to her during this difficult time. What a blessing! She loved Ellie, and the young woman had given her the best gift. For a moment, she felt like a mamm.

Ellie rounded the counter and hugged Liza. "Danki. You never let me down."

"I'm not perfect, Ellie. I'm sure, although unintentionally, I'll disappoint you. I promise to try my best not to."

"The number of times I've disappointed you and Daed would equal the large pile of firewood he has stacked outside the haus. I doubt you'd catch up in your lifetime." She chuckled, then grew serious. "Liza, I can't danki enough for all you've done for me, and here I'm asking you to do more."

Liza hugged her close. "Don't ever hesitate to ask me for anything. I love you, Ellie."

Ellie met Liza's gaze. "I love you too, Liza. I really do."

They both dabbed their damp eyes with the pads of their thumbs.

Ellie took a deep breath and exhaled. "You made oatmeal cookies this morning. The aroma has filled this place. They smell delicious."

Liza wrapped up half a dozen cookies. "Take these with you. Peter will like them too." She wiped her hands on a towel. "What time should I be at your haus in the morning?"

"Around seven?"

"Seven is fine. Give Peter a hug for me."

"I will, and I'll tell Daed our plan. He wants to stay all day and help the Beachys with whatever they need as mourners kumme and go."

"Your daed always puts others before himself." It was one of his most admirable traits.

He would've been the perfect husband for her, but she couldn't marry him so long as Ellie objected to their union. Her heart plummeted in her chest. The man had a gentle soul, yet he had the strength to shoulder the agony he'd experienced with Lydia's passing, raising Ellie during her rebellious period, her running away, and his not knowing if she was dead or alive.

Since Ellie had matured and warmed to her, Liza had hoped the girl would want her to marry Jacob. She sensed Ellie liked her as a friend, but nothing more. She shouldn't allow herself to fantasize about being a mamm to Ellie and Peter one day. She yearned to step into their everyday lives alongside Jacob and become a part of their routine. To love them with her whole being. To hurt when they hurt, share in their joys, and protect them as best she could.

She pressed a hand to the sad ache in her throat and

swallowed. She had to accept her position. Close enough for Ellie's friendship. Not family.

Liza arrived at Jacob's haus on Tuesday morning to find Ellie and Peter gaunt and quiet. She hugged them both. "We can take my buggy."

Ellie released her hand from Peter's. "I need to speak to Liza before we leave. Would you check on Snuggles?"

Peter nodded and dragged his feet outside.

Ellie patted the spot next to her on the settee. "Let's not take Peter to the funeral or burial tomorrow. Daed had the same idea. We talked about it before he left this morning. I would rather he have private time with Mae, then we should bring him home.

"When I attended Mamm's services, I longed to be alone. I believed she'd gone to Heaven, but I couldn't get the burial portion of the service out of my mind. The lowering of the coffin into the deep, dark hole rattled my soul. Even though I knew she wasn't in there, it was so final. I'm afraid Peter may experience the same."

"Have you told Peter your plan?"

She nodded. "He was relieved. Are you still kumming back to the haus with us after we take him to have his time with Mae?"

Liza nodded and wiped a tear from Ellie's cheek. "I wouldn't want to be anywhere else." It would be difficult to watch Peter suffer through these next few days.

No doubt Mae's passing had dredged up memories of similar days for Ellie, when her mamm passed. The young woman's raw pain ripped Liza's heart in two. Ellie had blossomed into a happy and healthy young woman with purpose to plow ahead with her faith, work hard at her job at the bakery, and make new friends. She'd begun to heal, and then her world had kumme crashing down with Peter's agony over Mae's death. For Ellie to watch someone she loved go through the same tragedy must be even worse. "I'm sorry you're having to observe Peter's anguish. You know firsthand what he's going through."

Ellie pressed her elbows to her sides. "It's heart-wrenching to watch someone you love suffer and know the depth of the hurt. But the worst part is being aware of the time it will take to heal. It took me until recently to tame the raging, painful ache over Mamm and store it in a special place in my heart. I can now recall memories during my quiet time and smile instead of cry."

Liza reached for her and held her tight. She stroked her back. "We'll get through this together. Both of you can rely on me anytime. And you and Peter will have each other and your daed."

Peter, head bent and taking reluctant steps, came inside. He leaned against Liza. "Will you stand on the other side of me and hold my hand when I go to visit my mamm? I'm scared."

Liza pulled him onto her lap. "Peter, I'll do anything you need. You just ask."

Ellie exchanged an endearing look with Liza.

A spark of joy rose in Liza's chest despite her sorrow for Mae. She warmed inside. Her patience with Ellie had won out. Their special times together had been precious and she looked forward to creating more memories with her. Jacob's dochder's expression spoke volumes about the bridge they'd built since the first day they'd met. They'd kumme a long way.

Peter clasped their hands and the three of them went to the buggy. He sat squeezed between them and remained quiet on the ride to his former home.

Liza stole a glance at Ellie. She had an arm wrapped

around Peter's shoulders and her eyes stared straight ahead. Scattered gray clouds decorated the blue sky and the sun peeked through them for a moment. She prayed, "Dear Heavenly Father, wrap Your arms around Ellie and Peter. We don't understand why You chose to take Mae home, but we trust and believe You do what is best for us. Give Peter and Ellie the strength to get through this day. We love You. Amen."

Ellie's lips trembled. "Amen."

Peter wiped his runny nose with his sleeve. "Amen from me too." He rested his head against Ellie's side for the duration of the ride.

Jacob greeted them when they arrived and reached for the reins. "No one's inside at the moment. The Beachys and others in the community should be here shortly to pay their respects." He reached for Peter and held the child in his arms "I know this is hard on you, Peter. Please understand, we're all here for you." He put the child's feet on the ground.

Ellie got out of the buggy and squeezed her daed's arm, then rubbed Peter's back. "He's been a very good boy through all this. Are you ready to go inside the haus?"

Peter stuck out his bottom lip. "I don't know if I want to go in. I'm afraid."

Liza jumped down, and Peter ran to her and grasped her hand. She thought her fingers would break if he gripped them any harder. The child could squeeze her hand until it bled for all she cared.

Jacob knelt before the frightened little boy. "Your mamm is dressed in dark blue and her eyes are closed as if she's sleeping. Remember, she's already with God in Heaven."

Peter whispered, "I know. I just want her to kumme back." He fell against Jacob and wept.

Jacob's eyes pooled with tears.

He lifted Peter in his arms, and the child's arms wrapped around the compassionate man's neck. "I love you, Peter."

Peter raised his head. "I love you too, Jacob."

Liza turned her head. She choked back the sob struggling to escape. She loved each one of them with all her heart.

Jacob met the child's gaze. "God is with you, Peter."

Peter pointed to his heart. "Jah, He is." He stuck out his chest. "I think I can go in now."

"Would you prefer I go with you?" Jacob put a hand on his shoulder.

Peter shook his head. "Liza and Ellie can take me." He pointed to five men getting out of a wagon. "Those men are waving at you. They might need you."

Jacob grimaced. "They can wait if you need me."

"I'll be all right going with Liza and Ellie." Peter took a step toward the haus.

The two women nodded to Jacob and accompanied Peter to his mamm.

Liza studied Mae. The thin woman, dressed in dark blue, lay in the plain pine casket on the long oak dining room table.

Peter raised his eyes to Ellie. "Can I stand on a chair to look at her?"

Ellie pulled over a chair and lifted him up to stand on it. She held her arm around his waist.

Peter crawled onto the table and knelt staring into the coffin. Tears dripped onto his cheeks. He reached out to touch her folded hands and jerked his fingers back. "They're cold. Oh, I wish she could hear me. I love you, Mamm. Why did you leave me?" He covered his face and his small shoulders heaved as he sobbed.

Liza draped her arm across his back. She blinked back blinding tears. "Peter, your mamm didn't leave you on purpose. She didn't know she was going to Heaven. She loved you and would never have left you if it had been up to her. God knew she was sick, and He didn't want her to suffer. He gave her a new body and gave you a new family to take good care of you."

Ellie wept beside him.

"I want to hear her tell me a story before bed. She cut up my chicken in the smallest pieces and made them easy for me to swallow. She woke me up with a kiss on my cheek every morning. I don't ever want to forget her special mamm smell and the sound of her voice." He buried his face in the side of her neck and cried.

Ellie sobbed harder.

Liza reached her other arm out to her. Ellie moved and nestled on Liza's other side and pressed into her. She held her arms across the kinners' backs and immersed herself in the warmth of their bodies and absorbed their deep sadness, which spilled out in an abundance of tears and pain. The ache within her swelled and the desire to take this sorrow from them squeezed her heart until she thought it would burst. She blinked back tears to no avail. They insisted on running down her cheeks.

Peter leaned in and kissed his mamm's cheek. Without a sound, he moved from Liza's arm as he climbed off the chair to the floor and ran outside.

Liza and Ellie hurried after him.

He came to an abrupt halt, shielded his eyes, and stared at the sky. "Mamm, I'm sorry I yelled at you. Liza said you didn't leave me on purpose. Watch out for me. I'll be with you one day in Heaven. For now, Ellie and Jacob are going to let me live with them." He heaved a big sigh and stared at his feet, then lifted his eyes to the sky again. "Oh, and Snuggles is kumming with me." He ignored the flood of tears running down his face. "I love you, Mamm. Farewell for now."

Peter took Liza and Ellie's hands in his again. "If she's already in Heaven, then I had to talk to her outside, where she could hear me. The bishop talked about Heaven not long ago."

Liza clutched his little fingers. "You're right." She was surprised he'd listened so closely to the bishop's messages. The child had understood much more of the information the bishop delivered from the Bible than she'd have guessed.

Ellie removed a handkerchief from inside the waist of her skirt and blew her nose. "Are you ready to head home? Do you want anything from the haus other than what Daed brought over earlier?"

Peter dropped their hands and ran inside.

"Should we follow him?" Ellie took a step toward the haus.

"Wait. Let him go. If he takes long, we'll go in." Liza stretched her neck to peer through the window. He wasn't in sight.

He rejoined them in moments. He held up a brush and Mae's Bible. "I want to keep these to remember her."

"Why did you choose the brush?"

"She brushed her hair every night, and I could hear her sing. It was the only time she sang. I loved listening to her."

Liza had never heard Mae sing. She kept quiet during the hymns on Sundays when they had church. It brought joy to her heart.

"Please take me home, Ellie." He pleaded with Liza, "And please kumme with us."

She nodded.

Jacob approached them. He tousled Peter's hair. "Are you all right?"

"I'm sad and my stomach hurts. Please make it go away." He leaned against Jacob and sobbed.

Jacob carried him to the buggy. "You go home and get some rest. It may take a while, but you'll feel better. I promise."

"I also promise in time it will get better. I know that to be true." Ellie kissed her daed's cheek, then clasped her hand in Liza's.

Liza's breath caught in her throat. The young woman had sought comfort from her and her gesture sent a river of gratitude to God for another moment of bliss on such a dark and sorrowful day.

Jacob waved and bid farewell to them.

Peter fell asleep in Ellie's lap on the way home. Ellie and Liza kept quiet so as not to disturb him.

They arrived, and Liza woke him to walk him inside. She took him to his room, removed his shoes, and tucked him in bed. He fell back to sleep.

She found Ellie in the kitchen, pouring tea into cups. "He's exhausted. I don't think he could've withstood speaking to people today."

Ellie sat down and placed a filled teacup in front of Liza. "I would struggle to make decent conversation today, let alone expecting Peter to respond to them." She sipped her tea. "I still can't believe Mae is gone. I didn't know what to expect from Peter. He handled it better than I anticipated." She tilted her head. "Do you mind missing the service? I would really appreciate it if you would stay with us instead." Ellie reached over and covered Liza's hand for a moment.

"We'll fix some ham spread sandwiches for tomorrow and bake oatmeal and butter cookies. Peter can help, and it will help occupy his mind. I'll deliver the food to Mae's haus in the morning and then rejoin you and Peter here."

"Liza, danki. I appreciate it."

"Let's cook some ham and beans and corn bread for supper. When Peter wakes, we'll get him involved."

Liza and Ellie chatted about the bakery, and Ellie told her stories about her and Jacob building a sled and then taking it to the hill behind their haus year after year until she got older.

"Daed had more fun than I did. I'm certain of it." She chuckled. "It felt wonderful to feel happy for a while. Danki, Liza."

Liza could get used to cooking with Ellie and having these talks. She would've loved having a dochder like Ellie and a son like Peter. She felt needed and loved by both these kinner. What was God's plan for them and for her?

Jacob met Liza's buggy Wednesday morning at the Chupps'. "You're a ray of sunshine on this sad day." He tied her buggy to the big oak tree and lifted the pot from the back. "I'll carry your dish to the food table for you."

"Danki. You must be exhausted between working here and your place."

Jacob rolled his shoulders back. "My muscles ache from the heavy lifting of benches and tables, but I'm doing all right. I appreciate you closing the bakery and staying with Ellie and Peter. This will be a reminder for Ellie of her mamm's funeral, and it's all so fresh for little Peter."

"I consider it a privilege. They are both dear to me."

"As I am. Right?" He gave her his best pleading eyes.

Liza stifled her chuckle. "Jah, you're dear to me too."

And much more. "I'm going to scoot out of here before the crowd arrives. I want to get to Ellie and Peter."

"Go ahead. Maybe I'll see you later, after the viewing."

She held his gaze for a long moment. "I hope so."

Jacob helped her into the buggy and watched her expertly direct the mare to the main road.

The bishop gave him a gentle slap on the back. "I believe Peter's getting a good home with you and Ellie, Jacob."

"Danki, Bishop."

"I'm glad you moved to Charm, Jacob."

"I appreciate your friendship, Bishop. We couldn't have chosen a better place to move to."

The bishop smiled and clutched his Bible to his chest. "I should get inside and receive the guests. Pardon me."

"I'll kumme with you." Jacob followed him.

The bishop got pulled aside by Ezra Yoder. Jacob went to the plain pine box. The coffin seemed out of place on the long oak dining room table. Mae's face wasn't remarkable. Skin on bones, she appeared older than her age of thirty-five, with deep wrinkles in her too small forehead and under her closed eyelids. It'd been shocking that she died at such a young age. Mae's passing reminded him that he shouldn't take each day of life on earth for granted.

Didn't Liza realize they were wasting time? They didn't know what lay before them. He stared at Mae, and his mind drifted to Lydia, who lay in a similar casket at her viewing.

The sorrowful wound left by the death of his fraa tore open and a raging fire shot through his body. He grabbed his middle and bent over. That day came rushing back to him. He'd walked in a fog. Friends' voices had sounded muddled, and he'd fought to concentrate enough to hold

Ellie's hand. His chest tightened. Lydia's memory would forever abide in the corner of his heart. He breathed deep and let it out slowly, then took long strides out of the haus. The solitude of the open fields and the birds singing soothed the ragged edges of his emotions. He prayed for peace of mind and stayed all day to help with the guests' horses. The crowd thinned, and after the last buggy was claimed, he rode home exhausted and pensive.

He found Ellie curled up in a chair with her eyes closed. She popped her head up and put a finger to her lips. "Liza left and Peter's asleep. He may not wake until morning."

He sat in his favorite chair. "I'm relieved he's able to sleep."

She got up and hugged him. "Danki, Daed, for taking Peter in to live with us. I realize it's not easy taking in a small child. I'll do my part."

"I know you will. I'm happy to have him with us. I'm as attached to him as you are."

She sat back down. "Liza isn't going to the funeral or burial. She's closing the bakery and kumming to stay with Peter and me. She's so good with him, and he loves being with her."

"How did Peter do today?"

Ellie made a steeple of her fingers under her chin. "He's not eating much, and he cries when we haven't got him occupied doing games or puzzles. I can't stand to have him sad. I remember the awful day of Mamm's services. I didn't want to do anything." She cocked her head. "After the funeral and burial are over, I have something I need to talk to you about."

"Why not now?"

"I'd rather wait."

His heart plummeted. He never knew what to expect with her. She seemed happy with being home, and now adding Peter to their family. What could she possibly want to talk to him about? He'd be on pins and needles until he found out. Should he push her to tell him? *Not a good idea. Better to honor her request.*

Liza handed her food contribution to Mrs. Beachy on Wednesday for the funeral meal and hurried to Ellie and Peter at their haus. She opened the door. "Is it all right if I kumme in?"

Peter carried a blanket and hugged her legs. "I'm glad you're here, Liza. Ellie said we're going to make all kinds of good food today, and I get to help."

She sat on the maple rocker with the knitted pillow and lifted him to her lap. He rested his head against her shoulder.

"She's right. Do you like mixing the cookie dough and getting flour in your hair?"

"In my hair?" He combed his hair with his fingers.

"Getting messy is half the fun."

"You're silly, Liza." He grinned briefly, then grew quiet.

Liza stroked his back. She and Ellie could occupy him, but it wouldn't wash away the thoughts of his mamm on this sad day.

Ellie had her cooking apron on. "There you are, Peter. I couldn't find you. Liza, I didn't hear you kumme in. May I offer you something to eat or drink?"

She shook her head. "Danki, but I had a little breakfast before I left home. I dropped off our dish."

"I appreciate it. Do you mind sitting with Peter?"

Liza nodded and held him. She sang a hymn and he kept his head still against her shoulder.

He surprised her. "Liza, will Mamm be upset if I don't go to the funeral?"

"She won't be upset one bit. She'll understand."

He wept against her. "I miss her so much. My tummy hurts all the time. When will it get better?"

"It will go away someday. I don't have an answer as to how long it will take. It's different for everyone. Let's ask God to help you get through this day."

Peter folded his little hands. "You pray, Liza."

"Dear Heavenly Father, Peter and I ask You to mend his broken heart. Wrap Your arms of love and grace around him. Shelter him from the pain of losing his mamm. Give him the strength to get through this. Heavenly Father, please bless him, Jacob, and Ellie. Amen."

Peter whispered, "And bless Liza too. Amen." He lifted his brows. "You'll let me kumme to your haus and you'll still visit me here, won't you?"

"Jah, Peter. I plan to visit you often, and you are wilkom at my haus or the bakery anytime."

He snuggled against her as she rocked and sang another hymn. Two songs later, Peter fell asleep and Liza stared lovingly at the peaceful boy.

Ellie tiptoed in. She made a bed out of blankets on the floor. "Can you lower him to the blankets?"

"I think so." She got him to the makeshift bed and stood.

Ellie pointed to the kitchen.

Liza followed her. "If you'd like to rest, I'll watch in case he wakes. You must be tired if he woke you several times last night."

"I'm wide awake. I don't know why." She reached for a bowl for baking. "I've been contemplating working at the bakery. I'll miss you, Hannah, and the work. Peter will go to school in September. It would leave you short of help the rest of the summer. What do you think?"

"Esther offered to watch him if you want to keep your

job at the bakery. She would keep Peter busy, and she'd love having him. Abe would too. You'd have to drop him off and pick him up each day."

Ellie clasped her hands and held them under her chin. "Esther is a sweetheart for offering. The arrangement would work out perfectly." She pinched her nose, then sneezed. "Excuse me!" She pulled a handkerchief from her waistband and wiped her nose. "I hope Daed doesn't disagree. My head is starting to ache at the thought of it."

Liza put her hands on Ellie's arms. "I've got good news. Your daed was there when Esther offered. He plans to talk to you about her suggestion. I don't think he'll mind I spilled the beans to you first."

"Oh, Liza, danki. It puts my mind at ease. I didn't want Peter to think I was abandoning him. He'll love going to Esther's. I'm so relieved to have this problem solved."

Jacob sat on the bench next to Abe and sang the hymns the bishop directed them to sing out of the Ausbund. His body felt numb. This day was too familiar. His hands folded tight in his lap, he just wanted this over. It had been the right decision for Peter to remain at home and for Ellie to be with him. The overwhelming crowd filled the haus, porch, and yard. The warm weather sent beads of sweat across his brow. Women fanned themselves.

The bishop put his Ausbund aside. He opened his Bible. "John 3:16, *For God so loved the world that He gave His only begotten Son, that whosoever believeth in Him should not perish but have everlasting life.*" He scanned the sea of black hats and kapps. "Mae believed this verse with all her heart. She is in her new home in Heaven, with no more pain or suffering. We will miss her, but she's happy and full of joy right now."

The bishop finished his message about two and a half hours later and ended the service with a dismissal prayer.

He went with Abe's family to the burial, and even though Mae's meager shell of a body was in the casket, he shed tears as her coffin was lowered in the dark hole that would soon be covered with dirt. This part always unnerved him. He had to remember it didn't matter. She was with God. He stayed and helped the men fill the large hole, and then he placed the modest wooden marker with her name and the date of her death on the grave. Mr. Beachy had made the marker, along with the coffin. Mae had had a short life, but she'd had a family who loved her, and she'd left him and Ellie a precious gift. Her son, Peter. He vowed to give him a good life.

The majority of the crowd shook his hand and offered their blessing for taking Peter into his home. They were kind and offered to help with whatever he might need. He thanked them and blinked back tears. Their sincerity gripped his heart. They went to their wagons, took out containers, and insisted he take the remaining food home.

He hauled enough food home to feed all of Charm. He couldn't wait to have supper with his new family. After this day, albeit a mixture of sadness and of joy for Mae, he was ready to move forward. Maybe Liza would still be there. Smiling, he urged his mare to a gallop.

He found Liza, Ellie, and Peter with flour in their hair and on their faces, arms, and hands.

He laughed. "What have you been up to?"

Peter chuckled. "We threw flour on one another. Liza said we could make a mess. We had fun."

Jacob grinned. "Did you leave enough to make cookies?"

"Oh, jah. We made butter, oatmeal, and molasses cookies."

Ellie washed her hands. "We've baked all day. I need to heat leftover beans and ham for supper."

Waving his hand, Jacob said, "Don't bother. The women sent home a load of food for supper. I'll bring it in."

Liza rinsed her hands. "I'll kumme outside with you to help carry dishes."

"I'd love the company." He ushered her outside. On impulse, he kissed her cheek. "I've been wanting to kiss you all day."

"Jacob Graber! The children could've caught us. They might be peeking out the window."

"I don't care, Liza. I'd shout to the world that I love you. You're the stubborn one." He hurried inside before she could protest again.

Jacob set the containers on the counter. He walked Peter to the basin of clean water. "Wash your hands and kumme with me to check on the animals."

Peter rinsed his hands. "May I have a towel, please?"

Jacob couldn't believe how well Peter was doing. He'd heard him get up last night and wake Ellie. He'd heard them talking and Peter's whimpering. Ellie and Liza must've done a miraculous job keeping him occupied. He held Peter's hand as they crossed the yard to the barn.

He lifted Peter to pet the mare's nose. "Want to feed her an apple?"

Peter nodded. He held the apple on his open palm to the horse's lips. The mare grabbed it with her teeth.

"She tickled me." He jerked his hand back and rubbed it against his pant leg. He grew silent, picked up a piece of straw, and ran his fingers the length of it. "Will you tell me about the funeral?"

Jacob dragged over an old weathered maple chair and sat. He patted his legs. "Kumme sit on my lap." He wrapped an arm around the boy's waist. "The bishop talked about how beautiful Heaven is and the joy we'll experience beholding God and His Son, Jesus Christ. We sang songs, and he told everyone you were living with Ellie and me. They were happy and shook my hand. They wish you the very best and want you to know they're thinking of you."

Peter let tears fall on his cheeks. He made no attempt to wipe them. He buried his face in Jacob's shoulder and wet his shirt with his crying. Jacob held him until he fell asleep. The child brought back memories of all the times he was helpless to take away Ellie's hurt when she suffered over her mamm's passing. He took him inside to bed and covered him.

Liza found him in the hallway. "Is he all right?"

"He asked me to tell him about the service. I elaborated on the joy of Heaven. He's a smart lad. It helped, but it did nothing to diminish his anguish over losing his mamm."

She swept her hand against his. "We had a good day. He mentioned Mae now and then, but he managed to laugh and enjoy baking with Ellie and me. I have no doubt this is where he belongs. Mae would be thrilled to know you took him in. I'm sure of it."

He gazed deep into her eyes. "Your support and encouragement through all my trials since I met you have given me the added strength I've needed to cope."

Ellie called out to them, "Supper is ready."

Liza hurried to the kitchen and put a finger to her lips. "Peter is asleep."

Ellie covered her mouth. "I'll be quieter. I'm glad he's at peace. I'll feed him when he wakes. I probably let him eat too many cookies. He won't want supper."

Liza squeezed her shoulder. "It won't hurt him. Anything to make him happy today."

"Jah, it was worth it to see him giggle." Hands on hips,

she pointed to the floor dusted with flour. "After I've cleaned this mess, I'm not sure I'll have the same opinion."

"I'll help you clean it up. It won't take long."

"I won't turn you down. I'd be up all night doing it myself." She chuckled.

Jacob watched them. It was as if Liza was already his fraa and a part of this family, the way Ellie and Liza were acting.

"Daed, Liza told me about Esther's offer to watch Peter. I'd like to accept."

"You should." He'd never thought his dochder would be excited to work for Liza after the way she treated her the day they'd first met. The two women had plowed through some difficult circumstances and become closer. He loved that Liza was a good influence on Ellie; his dochder listened to her.

"Take the rest of the week off and observe Peter. If you're comfortable with how he's doing, kumme back to work Monday. I'm sure Esther doesn't mind which day you choose to drop him off at her haus."

"He's sad today, but he's doing better than I would've anticipated. I believe a week will be plenty of time for us to establish a good routine to assist his adjustment to his new life." She stood and twirled. "I believe we'll have an exciting year." She kissed Liza's cheek, rushed to the door, and left.

Liza stood. What did Ellie mean by her statement? She'd had a mischievous grin on her face, as if she was hiding something. She couldn't imagine what Ellie was talking about.

A week and a half later, on Saturday early evening, Jacob wondered if Ellie would ever have the conversation with him she'd mentioned after Mae's funeral. He'd anticipated each day she might say something about it, but she didn't. If she didn't speak of it today, he'd finally ask her. Part of him didn't want to ask. His neck stiffened. Was it bad news?

He waited for her to arrive home. She was picking up Peter from Esther's. The child had loved being with Esther. She had him working with her in the garden and kitchen, and she found time to play games with him.

She was like the aunt he'd never had. The young boy had adjusted to his schedule and had kumme out of his slump. He mentioned his mamm, but he was chipper more often than he was sad.

Ellie and Peter strolled into the kitchen. "Daed, Peter and Esther made us supper." She held up a dish.

"We made beef and noodles." He patted his middle. "I'll put the utensils on the table."

"Where's my hug, young man?" Jacob opened his arms.

Peter giggled and wrapped his thin arms around Jacob's neck. "What did you do today?"

"Our ornery sow escaped when I went in to feed the rest of the sows and pigs. She tests my patience."

Peter and Ellie laughed.

Ellie poured the dish of beef and noodles in a large iron pot. She lit the cook stove and sat to wait for the fire to heat the food. "Peter, you can play until supper. Stay close to the haus."

"I'll swing on the tree swing Jacob made me."

"When you're tired of swinging, kumme back inside."

He leaned on Ellie. "I will."

She watched him scamper off. "I've been waiting for the right time to talk to you about something important. I wanted to wait until after Mae was put to rest to give us all time to mourn and get over the shock. I'm sure we'll need more time, but we're doing better than I expected. I don't need to put this off any longer."

Jacob's heart thumped in his chest. He pressed his back hard against the chair. His nerves jittered. Ellie had surprised and challenged him a lot in the last few years. At last, he'd grown accustomed to her positive attitude and stellar behavior. He'd enjoyed their closeness again. They'd included Peter into their routine and their future appeared bright. He didn't want anything to ruin it.

Ellie tilted her head and grinned. "Daed, relax."

He sighed. His expression must've given his anxiousness away.

She covered his hand with hers, drew in a deep breath, and looked him in the eye. "I love Liza and I want you to ask her to marry you and be a part of our family."

Jacob's eyes filled with tears. He rested his hand on top of hers. "Ellie, you've given me the best gift. I can't wait to tell Liza. What changed your mind?"

"I've been selfish and immature. I put myself first and disregarded yours and Liza's happiness. Liza has shown me over and over again how much she loves me. Her patience has never wavered, even when I put her in danger the day we went fishing. She hasn't judged me, even when I left and gave her every reason to. I want her to live with us as part of our family."

Peter skipped into the kitchen. "Who will be part of our family?"

"Liza." Ellie grinned.

Peter bounced on his toes and clapped his hands. "Yippee! Let's go get her now and bring her here."

"She and I have to get married first." Jacob laughed.

"Can you marry her tomorrow?" Peter wrinkled his nose.

"Today is June twenty-ninth. We'll need a month to plan at least." Ellie paused. She tapped her foot.

Jacob held out a palm. "Ellie, when you tap your foot, you've got something on your mind. What is it?"

"I'm concerned that this is everyone's busiest season. Not the right time for a wedding." She frowned. "Like you, Peter and I don't want to wait for months." She laughed. "You do have to ask Liza first. We're assuming she wants to marry you and take on all of us."

Peter shook his head and gave her an exasperated grin. "She'll say jah. She gives him googly eyes all the time. Like Mamm did with Mr. Fisher until he wrote Mamm and said he wasn't kumming back. He hurt my heart." He pressed a hand to his chest.

"You don't need to worry about him. You have us!" Jacob scooped him in his arms and twirled in a circle.

"Jah! Let's go tell Liza to marry us right now!"

Jacob set him on the floor.

"Let's have supper first, and you and I aren't going. Liza and Daed need their privacy." Ellie stirred the mixture in the iron pot.

"Daed wants us to go. Don't you?" Peter's puppy-dog eyes met his.

Jacob's eyes watered. Peter had called him Daed. His heart swelled with joy. He'd wondered if Peter would call him Daed one day, but he hadn't expected it this soon. He beheld Ellie.

Tears stained her cheeks.

"Jah, you and Ellie should be with me. We'll ask her together."

Peter gave him a shy grin. "Is it all right for me to call you daed?"

Jacob reached for him. "I'm happy you called me daed. May I call you son?"

Peter nodded and wrapped his arms around Jacob's neck. "Ellie, then you're my schweschder and I'm your bruder."

"Jah, I am." She bit her quivering lip. "You're smart for such a little boy."

He beamed and held up his chin. "Danki."

Jacob blinked back tears. Peter had inserted himself into their lives and claimed him and Ellie and soon Liza, if she agreed, as his family. He and Ellie had worked hard to prove to Peter their love and acceptance of him. He breathed in a sigh of relief. Their efforts had paid off.

Jacob prayed for the food. "Dear Heavenly Father, danki for this food You have provided for the nourishment of our bodies. You've blessed us with Peter and cleared the path for us to have a possible future with Liza. Prepare Liza's heart to accept us as her family. I pour out my gratitude to You, Heavenly Father. We love You. Amen."

Jacob listened to Ellie telling Peter what had to happen to prepare for the wedding. He rehearsed in his mind what he would say to Liza. He'd waited for this day and been sure it would arrive. Joy bubbled inside him. The excitement building from head to toe took away his appetite. He pushed his plate aside. "Are you two finished yet?"

"You're about to leap out of this haus!" Ellie rose and pushed back her chair. "I'll clear the dishes and leave them to soak. I'll wash and dry them when we return."

Peter waved them outside. "If we can go now, I'll help dry when we kumme home. Let's go!"

Jacob followed behind Ellie and Peter to the buggy, readied it, and they left. When they arrived, he herded his kinner to the door and knocked.

Peter rapped again on the door. "No one's home."

"We'll go to her family's haus. She may have had supper with them." Jacob returned to his buggy and waited impatiently for Ellie and Peter to get in. He drove them to the Lapps'.

Esther answered the door with Abe and Hannah behind her. "What a wonderful surprise! I'm happy you're all here. Would you like something to eat or drink?"

"We finished supper right before kumming to your haus. Nothing for me, danki." Ellie grinned and nudged Jacob. She went to Hannah and winked.

Hannah raised her eyebrows. "What are you up to?"

"You'll see!" Ellie grinned.

Liza entered the room, wide-eyed. "I'm happy to see all of you. What brings you here?"

Peter blurted out, "We want to marry you. Will you marry us, Liza?"

Liza's hands flew to her mouth, her eyes watery with tears.

The Lapps, Jacob, and Ellie gasped.

Ellie smiled and shook her head. "Peter, Daed is supposed to ask her."

"He was too slow." Peter shrugged and stared at Liza with anticipation.

Ellie grinned. "Peter's right. He was too slow. Will you marry our daed?"

Jacob knelt before her. "What do you say?"

"Jah! Jah! Jah! I love all of you!"

Jacob picked her up and twirled her around. "I couldn't be happier." He ran outside, still holding her. "We're getting married!"

"Put me down, you silly, wonderful man!" Liza gasped for breath, she was laughing so hard.

Jacob went back inside the haus and put her on her feet.

Abe, Esther, Hannah, Ellie, and Peter bent over, laughing and clapping their hands.

Ellie placed her hands on Liza's shoulders. "I'm sorry, Liza. I've tested you many times since we met. I'm ashamed of how I've stood in the way of your and Daed's happiness."

"You and I have had more fun these last few weeks. I

enjoy our talks, your hugs, and considered you a dochder before this day, Ellie." She pulled Peter to her. "I love you, Peter, like a son. You're a sweetheart." She glanced at Ellie, then Peter. "But I'm not attempting to take the place of either of your mamms."

"I understand, but our mamms are gone and you're with us. We love you and want you to join our family. I promise to help you and to respect you." Ellie exchanged an endearing gaze with Liza.

"I don't worry about you, Ellie. You've proven your maturity. I sense we'll enjoy a wonderful future together."

"Let's plan the wedding. I'm ready to get married." Jacob danced a jig.

Hannah hugged Ellie. "You'll never regret giving your blessing for them to marry. Liza's the best!"

"I couldn't agree with you more. She loved me when I wasn't easy to love."

Liza squeezed Ellie's arm. "You've been patient with me and loved me too. I appreciate you, dear friend."

Peter hugged both girls.

Hannah knelt and held his small shoulders. "When Liza marries Jacob, my mamm and daed and I will officially be part of your family."

"I've never had a big family before. I like it!" Peter's eyes sparkled and he danced on his toes. Peter grabbed Liza's hands and dragged her to the kitchen.

Everyone followed.

Abe slapped Jacob's back. "Your patience won out and God has answered our prayers. I couldn't ask for a better bruder-in-law!"

Esther's cheeks dimpled. "I'm so excited! I couldn't be happier for you both."

Jacob flattened his palm against his chest. God had answered his prayer and given him more than he'd ever hoped or dreamed possible. He'd given him Liza, Peter, Ellie, and now the Lapps. He agreed with Peter. It would be wonderful to have a big family! He couldn't wait to set the date of the wedding with the bishop tomorrow. There was so much to plan!

Chapter Fourteen

Jacob inhaled the fresh scent of hyacinth and enjoyed the warmth of the sun on his face on the way to the bishop's haus. He'd been anxious on Sunday to ask the bishop to schedule a wedding date, but he knew it wouldn't be appropriate. The man had spoken a powerful message on God having a plan for those who loved Him. The bishop reminded the congregation to have patience, pray, and obey God's scriptures. The words had hit home. God had surprised him with Liza and Peter.

He arrived, stepped to the bishop's door, and knocked.

The jolly man's cheeks dimpled. "You're here early and you have a big grin on your face. I take it you have good news. Join me inside the haus."

Jacob nodded and stepped into the sitting room. "I hope I'm not too early."

"I get up at five. You're fine. What's on your mind?"

"I've asked Liza to marry me and I want to schedule a date for the wedding."

The bishop grabbed his calendar. "I'd be happy to pencil a date on my schedule for such a lovely couple. How about November fifth?"

"Oh no! I don't want to wait. Would you consider August twenty-ninth?"

The bishop chuckled. "You aren't giving the women much time to make Liza a dress or gifts. Will Liza be comfortable with August twenty-ninth?"

He should've asked her for possible dates. Was it selfish of him to rush the wedding? He'd take his chances Liza would be happy with the date he'd chosen. "If she isn't, I'll ask you for another day."

The bishop chuckled. "August twenty-ninth is on my calendar. Congratulations!" He slapped Jacob's back. "I'm thrilled for you both."

Jacob and the bishop chatted about Peter and his adjustment to his new life with him and Ellie. "I should let you get back to whatever you were doing. I'm anxious to tell Liza the news."

His heart racing, he bid the bishop farewell and drove to the bakery.

Liza, Ellie, and Hannah were talking.

"Good morning!"

Liza tilted her head and smiled. "You're chipper! What are you up to, Jacob?"

Ellie said, "Good morning. You should've been with us when I dropped Peter off at Esther's today. He couldn't wait! He kissed my cheek and jumped out of the buggy like it was on fire. She opened the door and he ran right into her arms. And here I was worried he wouldn't want to leave me!" She laughed.

Hannah handed Jacob a mug of coffee. "Mamm dragged my old puzzles and games out. She baked sugar cookies and couldn't wait for him to kumme to our haus. They'll have fun." Hannah crept up to him and chuckled. "When will you speak to the bishop?"

"I already have. That's the reason I'm here."

Liza beamed. "What did he say?"

"On August twenty-ninth, you'll be Mrs. Jacob Graber."

Hannah and Ellie threw up their hands. "We have a lot to do in a short time!"

Ellie rested a hand on Liza's. "May I make your dress and kapp?"

"Let's do it together." Hannah smiled.

"I'd love it!" Liza circled her arms around them.

"Mamm will coordinate the food with the women in the community. The women will spread the wedding date around like wildfire." Ellie giggled and held a hand to her middle.

"Where will we live?" Liza tapped a finger on her lips.

"Do you want to live in your haus?"

"I do. Do you mind selling yours?"

"Absolutely not." Jacob kissed her nose. "Home is where you are."

Ellie bounced on her toes. "Liza's haus is much larger than ours. We'll have more room for all of us. Her rooms are more spacious and will allow us to have a sewing room and a playroom for Peter. He loves her haus. He'll be thrilled."

Hannah clapped her hands. "Yay! You'll be closer to me!"

Ellie and Hannah scampered back to the kitchen. "We'll be in the back if you need us."

Liza and Jacob discussed selling his haus and wedding plans. She bid him farewell and wiped off the countertop. Her heart sang with joy. God had given her a husband and kinner. She would have the chatter, feet padding against the floor, food sizzling in the skillet for more than her, and her empty rooms would ring with laughter and life.

* * *

Liza couldn't believe her wedding day had finally arrived. She stood dressed in the dark blue dress Hannah and Ellie had stitched for her, staring into Jacob's deep brown eyes and vowed to love, honor, and submit herself to this wonderful man for the rest of her life. She was on bated breath for the bishop to announce her new name.

The bishop stepped back. "I now pronounce Liza and Jacob Graber married!"

Jacob clasped and held up her hand. They returned to their seats, and the bishop prayed for the meal they were about to receive. Her heart raced in her chest. She let happy tears stain her cheeks and drip onto her new dress.

Friends and family pulled them apart and poured out their good wishes. Liza thanked them and weaved through the crowd.

She found Jacob. "I love you, husband. Oh, it is wonderful to call you husband."

"I have longed for this day. I've rehearsed it in my mind many times. You're everything and more I would want in a fraa, Liza. I promise to love, protect, and honor you all the days of my life. There's nothing you can't discuss with me. Your happiness is important to me. Understand?"

"I do." The day she married Paul, she hadn't been in love with him. She'd been nervous and anxious with hope of falling in love with him, and the next day, she'd found her dreams shattered. She had no doubt she'd never fall in love with him.

The two wedding days were drastically different. Today, she was in love, confident, enthusiastic, and over-joyed to marry Jacob. To have a lifetime with him. To make him the happiest husband she possibly could.

Liza scanned the yard filled with tables and benches. An array of food filled dishes crowding the table and gifts were piled high on blankets. Her thick, lush green grass was peppered with friends clustered in groups. Laughter, conversations, and kinner playing buzzed around her. The weeks to prepare for this day with the help of her family and friends had been fun, and their thoughtfulness, kindness, and willingness to pitch in and do what was needed had warmed her heart. The vows they'd exchanged earlier seemed like a blur with all the people crowded around them at their wedding meal.

She loved being Mrs. Jacob Graber already. An hour later, she'd only had time to finish a portion of her selections. She and Jacob hadn't said two words to each other as they thanked their guests. She didn't mind. She had a lifetime to have all the conversations she wanted with him. He'd flashed her loving smiles all day.

Esther guided her and Jacob to two chairs. "Time to open your gifts."

Friends gathered around and oohed and aahed as they opened each thoughtful handcrafted present. Liza thanked their friends and family for bath and kitchen towels, kitchen utensils, quilt racks, pot holders, work aprons, saws, hammers, and other gifts. Her heart warmed at Jacob's genuine expressions of gratitude for their gifts.

Her friends' thoughtfulness touched her heart. She handed the last present to Jacob to open. He unwrapped an iron pot from Ezra and Annabelle. "This is perfect. Danki!"

The crowd thinned an hour later, and Liza watched Jacob talking to Ezra, then she smiled at Peter playing ball with other kinner. He nodded, then held his arms open wide to catch the ball.

Abe, Esther, and Hannah dragged Liza to Jacob, then to their wagon. Hannah climbed in the back and peeled off the blanket on top of a pile of gifts.

Liza gasped. She reached in and ran her hand along the new potato box, breadbox, and set of bundled handmade kitchen towels. "I had wanted new ones of each of these! Danki!" She hugged them.

Hannah said, "I made the towels. You can never have enough of them!"

Liza studied one of them. "Hannah, you did a magnificent job! I'll use these on special occasions."

"You saved me time, Abe. I would've had to make these boxes if you didn't. And you did a much better job! They're exquisite." Jacob elbowed Abe's arm.

Esther hooked her arm through Abe's. "We did it together. I'm surprised Peter kept the pieces a secret. He hammered in a nail or two with Abe's assistance."

"I'm glad you like them," Abe said. "We're thrilled our families have joined together. I've longed for this day, friend." Abe rested a hand on Jacob's shoulder. "You're a perfect addition to our family."

Liza waited while Abe and the men carried their gifts to the haus. She'd attempted to rid the table of dishes and return them to their respective baskets, but her friends wouldn't let her. She quirked her brow. Ellie had pinked cheeks and laughed throughout the meal with Joel Wenger. Ellie hadn't mentioned him to her. Liza hadn't learned much about the family. They'd moved to Charm from Lancaster, Pennsylvania.

Peter ran and hugged her legs. "I'm going to help Esther carry her dishes to the buggy."

"You're a thoughtful boy, Peter. Esther will appreciate your help."

He grinned and scampered off.

Ellie pulled her aside. She passed her a present wrapped in sackcloth and tied in a bow with twine. "I hope you like it."

"I'm sure I will." She unwrapped the gift and tugged the letter inside the pocket on the wedding quilt. *Dear Liza, When we met, my heart had been shattered to pieces*

*by my mamm's death. I couldn't fit the pieces together
again. You showed me how with your unwavering love,
even when I pushed you away. I grew to love and respect
you. Our friendship has blossomed, and I'm excited about
the memories we're going to create together as a family.
I love you, and Liza, I need you in my life. Ellie.*

Liza held the letter and draped the quilt over her arm.
She blinked and tears wet her cheeks. "Ellie, I'll treasure
this gift forever. I'll read this note in the years to kumme
and enjoy the heartwarming message again and again. I
love you, Ellie." She kissed a tear on Ellie's cheek.

Ellie hugged her tight, her body trembling. "I never
thought I'd be this happy again. Danki, Liza. It's because
of you." She glanced at Joel across the yard. "Joel
Wenger came up to me and formally introduced himself.
We had a pleasant conversation. He's got the bluest eyes
and he's wonderfully tall. He seems nice." She blushed
and paused.

Liza didn't want to spoil her day or Ellie's. "Why
wouldn't he? With your beautiful skin, sky-blue eyes, and
compassion, any man would be blessed to get your attention. I'm not surprised Joel would seek you out."

"Really?"

"Jah, really." Liza gave her a bright smile.

Jacob joined them. "The last of our friends are leaving.
Who wants to sit on the porch with me for a few minutes?
I need a little rest."

Ellie shook her head. "Peter and I are going to spend
the night at Hannah's. I packed us an overnight bag."

Peter scampered to them. "Is it time to go to Hannah's
yet?"

Jacob picked him up and tickled him. "You anxious to
leave me?"

Giggling, Peter squirmed away and ran to Hannah. "I'll
be gone for one day and night." He held up his forefinger.

Jacob set his feet to the ground. "You have fun."

Liza bid her family farewell, then twirled in a circle. "Mrs. Graber. I'll have to get used to my new name!"

"I'll have to get used to my new haus!" He laughed. "I have more room in your haus, now ours, than I ever had at mine. I like it much better. I'm glad the Yoders' son is buying my property. He's a gentle soul, and his fraa and kinner are soft-spoken and the kindest people."

"It's a good haus for them. They've outgrown their place with the addition of the boppli. She's young to have four kinner."

He winked and his lips curved in a smile. "I have a gift for you." He clasped her hand and walked with her to the barn. He covered her eyes with his hand and guided her to the gift. He dropped his hand and peeled back the tattered cloth cover.

"Jacob, I've never had a hope chest. It's perfect." She bent and opened it. "I love the scent of cedar. I'll put Ellie's quilt in it."

"She told me about the quilt and I read her letter. She keeps amazing me." He circled his arm around her waist. "I'm glad you like the chest. I worked on it a little each night."

"I have a gift for you." She'd stayed up late at night and worked on it every spare minute. A keepsake pocket quilt for Jacob to warm him by the fire on cool nights when winter came. He carried the cedar chest and they went inside the haus. She lifted the wrapped package off the chair in the corner and handed it to him.

Jacob opened his present. "A pinwheel quilt! It's beautiful! Danki. There's a pocket on it." He patted it. "Did you write me a note?" He didn't wait for her to answer. He pulled the paper out and unfolded it. *Dear Jacob, my loving husband, you've restored my faith in marriage, made me laugh more times than I can count, and provided me with two kinner I love and adore. God has bestowed His blessings on us, and I'm overflowing with gratitude that He gave me you. I love you with all my heart. Liza.*

He set the gift and letter on top of the cedar chest, wrapped his strong arms around her waist, and kissed her hard on the lips. "I'm going to save your note. I'll read it every year on our anniversary to remember this day." He held her hand and led her outside. "God provided sunshine, a clear blue sky, and a slight breeze to take the bite out of the heat. Our wedding day couldn't have gone better."

Jacob had swept into her life and erased the pain she'd experienced with Paul. He was more than a husband. He was her best friend and soul mate. Someone to pour out her most vulnerable, intimate, and creative thoughts to without worry of judgment.

Liza held out her arms, twirled in a circle, and admired the beautiful blue sky. "I want to memorize this entire day and never forget a minute of it. The day I married the love of my life and inherited sweet Peter and beautiful Ellie!"

Liza's Molasses Cookies

1½ cups butter (or vegetable oil)
1 cup sugar
2 eggs
½ cup molasses
4 tsp. baking soda
½ tsp. ginger
½ tsp. salt
2½ tsp. cinnamon
4 cups flour

Mix all ingredients together in a bowl, store in refrigerator for two and a half hours or overnight. Roll the cookie dough in balls, then in sugar. Bake at 325 degrees for ten minutes. Bake two minutes longer for crisper cookies.

Pennsylvania Dutch/German
Glossary

boppli	baby
bruder	brother
daed	dad, father
dochder	daughter
Englischer	non-Amish male or female
fraa	wife
grossmammi	grandmother
haus	house
jah	yes
kapp	covering for Amish woman's hair
kinner	children
kumme	come
mamm	mother, mom
schweschder	sister
wilkom	welcome